Goodnight, Mr. Knight

Goodnight, Mr. Knight

Allan Davis

IGUANA

Copyright © 2022 Allan Davis
Published by Iguana Books
720 Bathurst Street, Suite 410
Toronto, ON M5S 2R4

Publisher: Meghan Behse
Editors: Toby Keymer, Cheryl Hawley, Paula Chiarcos
Front cover design and cemetery image: Ruth Dwight, designplayground.ca

ISBN 978-1-77180-594-0 (paperback)
ISBN 978-1-77180-593-3 (epub)

This is an original print edition of *Goodnight, Mr. Knight.*

Goodnight, Mr. Knight is the fourth novel in the Discards Series. In each book, an early twenties main character finds her way out of a dysfunctional situation: abuse, abandonment, addiction, isolation. The list will never end, so neither will this series.

Other books in the Discards Series

Discards

From Muddy Water

Beyond the Headlights

Chapter 1

OWEN

I was found lying face up in the Open Hatch drop-off container at North Bay General, my twin sister face down on top of me. I remember what I thought was the swish-swishing of the hospital doors as the nurse took us to Neonatal. Of course, I was only a few hours old, too young to remember anything. But, if the swish-swishing was coming from my baby sister's tiny mouth pressed against my tiny ear as she drew her last tiny breath, I would remember. We were twins so that would have been a different kind of remembering. Although just the other day, the day after my eighteenth birthday, in fact, standing in the cemetery with Martha, my foster sister, and Peter, my foster father, watching the smoke slanting from the crematorium chimney into the spires of St. Mary's church, I could hear that same swish-swish in what I thought the wings of a white pigeon landing on the crematorium roof.

After one month in the neonatal unit, I was placed by Catholic Family and Children's Services for the Diocese of Nipissing with Audrey and Robert Reynolds. They lived in a ranch-style house in the North Bay suburbs. Audrey was a fat forty-something; Robert was a thin elementary school teacher. Audrey took me to mass twice a week, and every Sunday afternoon to Tim Hortons for chocolate donuts. The donuts were for her, not for me. She fed me Cheerios from a plastic bag that she kept in her purse.

I was five years old when Audrey enrolled me in Saturday Play Time at the North Bay Library, which she pronounced "libary." While the other kids played silly games, I sat at one of the big round tables and taught myself to read. I got curious about the four deaf ladies who arrived every Saturday morning at ten o'clock and sat at a table in the corner. They looked like the Channel 12 Breaking News women that Audrey watched every evening at six o'clock, except these ladies talked with their hands. As I watched the dance of their fingers, I felt my brain organizing the wiggles into patterns. I found a book on American Sign Language and pretty soon I could read what they were saying. So, like an electronic CIA bug under their table, with the sound piped remotely into my ear without the ladies knowing, I could tap into their secret conversations.

I learned how they removed hair from their legs. I thought you just shaved it off and flushed the stubbles down the sewer. That's what Audrey did. But no, they used wax. The following week I learned about blind dating sites. I thought I read that wrong. They weren't blind; they were deaf. But no, because the next week, they talked about going to bed on the first blind date. They each said no, that was wrong. Then they talked about all the times they went to bed on the first blind date. Well, of course, now I know they were talking about a different kind of going to bed.

After playtime at the library, me and Audrey had a Big Mac and fries and cherry pie for lunch. Audrey talked about going on a diet. That's all she could think about — that and eating.

"Inside me is a thin woman yelling to get out, Owen."

To shut up the thin woman, Audrey filled her mouth with more Tim Hortons, like on TV when you shove a rag into the mouth of the guy you put into the trunk while you drive to the two-rut road through the bush to the secluded spot where you take him for a boat ride.

One day, she said, "I think I've found a solution to my weight problem, Owen. I have to get rid of all this tempting junk food."

So she laid the chocolate bars she'd just bought on the table. She took her time unwrapping each one, like she was opening presents at her birthday party. She broke each one in half and placed the pieces on a plate. Then she opened her mouth for each half, chewed on it, and swallowed each one by one until they were gone, not there to tempt her. Problem solved. Except that afterward she seemed disappointed with herself, as though she felt like a failure. Perhaps it was because Robert had given her a diet book the day before.

I remember this because, for my eighteenth birthday, my foster sister, Martha, gave me a personal care kit with a brush and a comb and nail clippers. I felt like a failure for all those years using Martha to help me catch bugs, never once realizing that, for her, my personal appearance was probably an embarrassment.

Robert didn't take me to McDonald's or Tim Hortons or to anywhere. He was too busy in his basement lab, processing and packaging his Economy Articulated Cat Skeletons mounted on attractive wooden bases. The cats came from the Humane Society for free, so the only cost in making them into skeletons was acid to eat away the fur and the flesh, and the wooden base they stood on. He sold them to the Ontario school boards, $59.99 plus tax.

Robert was in his basement lab, scraping scabbed blood off a cat skeleton. I asked, "How do you kill the cats?"

He said, "The Humane Society injects them with sodium pentobarbital."

So I looked it up. As well as killing cats, it could be used as a truth serum to tell when people were lying. I asked Robert, "Can you get me some so I can tell when people are lying?"

He was busy separating cat skulls from the backbones for his sideline business, Skulls Unlimited. He hesitated. "Why would you want to know that?"

"Audrey thinks you've been lying to her about that woman who works at the Humane Society who gets you the cats. I thought you might like me to check it out."

He went back to scraping with his wooden-handled hooker-picker thing. "The pentobarbital has to be injected, and even if you got a needle, you can't buy the drug without a licence."

The neighbours complained about the dead cat smell, and the city shut his dead cat business down. After that he sold Ant Viewer Observatory Cylinders on the internet. Raising and packaging ants didn't cause any smell.

Audrey's goal and plan for me was private gifted school, but Robert said no, so I started grade one in the same elementary school Robert taught at. After about a week, Mrs. McCarthy said to him, "Your little guy Owen is the smartest kid I ever taught."

"Who?"

"Owen."

"My Owen?" He looked at me.

Mrs. McCarthy said, "He needs to be in a gifted program. If he's a foster child, he should be moved to that Montcrest School in Toronto."

"And pay twenty-seven thousand dollars a year?"

"Well it was Bishop Humphries who mentioned Montcrest. Maybe he can get the money from the church. After all, he's the major dumbo for Nipissing Foster Care."

"What's Bishop Humphries got to do with Owen?"

"Nothing, other than Owen's intelligence is being wasted up here."

When Robert asked me, I said I didn't want to go. I liked it where I was.

So Robert bought me a junior scientist microscope kit and showed me the experiments in viscosity and liquids and laws of motion he was doing with his grade eight kids. These experiments led to DNA research in colour and tail shapes in guppies. I had three tanks of different types: spotted, rainbow, fantail, forktail. I had two separate breeding tanks, which made five altogether in my bedroom. Pretty soon me and Robert were selling weird-coloured guppies on the internet.

Chapter 2

OWEN

In my bedroom, still papered blue with little red puppies from when I moved in seven years earlier, hung a picture of the pope who had a glass eye. When I was five, the pictures I looked at were the puppies. As I got bigger, the picture I looked at was of the pope. The wooden picture frame looked like a door, and the pope's narrow nose and one glass eye looked like a keyhole slanted sideways, sort of like a Salvador Dali painting in those art books at the library. While I was putting on my PJs, the glass eye stared at me, and the good eye, which seemed to be on the other side of a door, watched me through the keyhole. In the middle of the night, my bedroom filled with shadows, that glinting glass eye winked at me like the cyclops in those Greek myths. First thing in the morning, there they both were, the one eye watching and the other eye winking as I got out of my PJs and into my school stuff. At night, the same thing, except backward.

One evening, as I was climbing into my PJs, Robert came into my bedroom. He sat on my bed and put his arm around my shoulders, something he never did.

He said, "Come with me into the backyard."

We sat in the grass by an anthill next to the wild daisies growing along the fence. We watched one little black ant that had come out from under one green leaf. It crossed from petal to petal to the edge of the flower, climbed down the stem to disappear under another green leaf. Out from under the leaf and up the branch again it came, stopping halfway to look around, little head wagging back and forth, before climbing to the top.

"Ants are always busy," he said. "Each one has a job to do. Each one has a goal and a direction. A small part in the big plan. Learn a lesson from the ant, Owen."

At the top, it wagged its head left to right to left, looking around before starting down the stem and up another to look around from the top of the second daisy stem. Down again and up the third, the fourth, the fifth, until it had climbed each one of the five, each time looking about at the top, following its goal and plan.

"You're a smart boy, Owen. I'm sorry I didn't realize earlier just how smart you are. But there are two things about you that are very apparent to me now. You have a goal and you have a plan. You don't know yet what it will be, but I know it's in your destiny. It's in your DNA. I'm sorry I won't be the one to help you get where you're going."

He left. Audrey came out and put her arms around me, something she always did. "I'm sorry, Owen. You're a good boy, but I can't take you with me."

The next morning Audrey and Robert drove off in separate cars. The CFCS moved me and my science stuff to a placement with a lady named Bobbie in Kenora. I liked Bobbie because every evening at tuck-in she read me ten pages of *Alice in Wonderland*. But Bobbie went down the rabbit hole when her husband, Reggie, left her. After that, she stayed all day in her bedroom as though she was hiding from someone, which she was — the drug dealers she owed money. Or waiting for someone, which she was — the dealers she didn't owe money. When the Catholic Family and Children's Services came for a visit and found Bobbie covered with scabs and nodding off, I was moved with all my science stuff to Shelly and Joe Radley's in North Bay, a Catholic foster-care placement with four other kids: Martha, Luke, William, and Timothy, who had fetal alcohol syndrome. Martha, who was eight, the same age as me, stayed only two days. Then she was moved to an all-girls short-term place with the Sisters of Sorrows to wait to be placed with a family. I remember Martha because, when Timothy stole the BlackBerry Robert gave me, Martha, who was big and strong for her age, beat him up and got it back for me.

Chapter 3

OWEN

"Don't call me Dad," said my new foster father, "and don't call me Mr. Radley. Call me Big Joe."

There was a story going around among other foster kids about why Big Joe was called Joe the Hammer. He had run an Indigenous foster-care place farther north, in Moosonee. If his foster kids misbehaved, Big Joe took the kid and his favourite toy out the back door and into his converted-to-workshop garage.

I wasn't sure what I had done wrong the day Big Joe took me out to the converted-to-workshop garage he'd built behind the North Bay house after he had moved down from his Moosonee house. I'd only been at this placement for about a week, so I didn't know the rules. But here is what happened: First Big Joe removed his aviator sunglasses. Next he removed his baseball hat. Next he removed his ring of keys from his belt loop. Next he tidied away his saws and chisels to clear space on his workbench. Finally, to get a good swing, Big Joe removed his plaid shirt. Then, chest hair curling around the edges of his tank-top undershirt, he held my Air Hogs Thunder Trax in front of my face for one last look before he put it on his workbench. Then Big Joe opened his toolbox and picked up his hammer. He tap-tapped it three times in his palm before raising it up, almost touching the overhead rafters. Then down it came, smashing with a crash to smithereens my Air Hogs Remote Control Thunder Trax. That was how me and every other kid at Big Joe's got his name tattooed on our brains, and that's how Big Joe got the nickname Joe the Hammer.

Big Joe's plaid shirt had ten buttons and ten buttonholes which, because of his big belly, he never did up over his t-shirt. The fly of his work pants had six buttons and six buttonholes. These he did up. Most people had zippers, but he wore homemade pants he brought down from Moosonee where he worked with the Indigenous foster kids.

Big Joe taught me to undo my Sunday shirt buttons starting at the top. When I first started unbuttoning, I unbuttoned beginning at the bottom, because I was little and the buttons were easy to reach. Big Joe was taller, so his top buttons were closer for him to reach.

Big Joe said, "You're eight years old. It's time you learned to do it properly. You start at the top, not at the bottom."

He undid his button at the top and then the next and the next until there were six, and then, when he opened his shirt, I saw Big Joe's hairy belly button winking at me like the glass eye of the pope.

Every Sunday, we went to St. John's Church, where everyone called him Mr. Radley. He went around extending his hand, washed and scrubbed and wiped clean. Lovely weather, did you see the game, how's your mother, and so on, in a soft, soothing manner. Me and Mr. Radley always came home early from the Sunday service while Shelly and the other kids stayed for Meet and Greet Coffee Hour.

Big Joe didn't want my good Sunday suit pants dropped on the floor because they would lose their crease. He made me hold them up while he straightened the crease before I hung them on the hanger. I never knew why I couldn't take off my pants and hold them by the waistband and shake down the crease and fold them over my bedroom chair the way Shelly let me do it.

But Big Joe was the boss.

After I took off my Sunday clothes, I put on my t-shirt and jeans and sneakers and then I looked like every other day through the week. After Big Joe took off his Sunday clothes, he put on his work pants and his plaid shirt over his grey-white undershirt, and then his aviator sunglasses over his grey-blue eyes, and then his baseball hat over his brown brush-cut hair, and then he looked like every day through the week.

One day — not one day, it was an exact day, the Belmont Stakes 2010 — Big Joe sat me in his special chair with wheels on it in front of his computer. He pulled up a chair from the kitchen for himself.

He said, "I need you to help me with a statistical analysis program called Thoro-Graph. First, I check out the horses. I pick the one I want and I make a bet online. But I usually pick the wrong one."

I studied the graphs and the charts for the six horses running that afternoon: distance, time, workouts, breeding, and claiming. I read page after page of DNA statistics for each horse, It wasn't much more complicated than following Big Joe's button pattern or learning sign language and way more interesting than reading the fingers of deaf ladies, and mind-blowing when I realized, while studying racehorse genetics, the possibility that twin DNA telepathy was the reason I remembered the swish-swish of the last few breaths of my dying sister. Every horse was a brother, a sister, or a son or daughter of their grandfather who was a cousin of their mother who was also their aunt.

He handed me the pre-race odds for each entry. First I assigned my own number to entry number 1, which, according to the graph-determined number would come in last, and according to the odds would come in fourth, but according to me would come in fifth. Then the same for the number 2 entry, which, according to the graph should come second, and according to the odds would be fifth, but according to me would come in last; and next the number 3 entry, which would come in fourth; and next the number 4 entry, which should be third; and next the number 5 entry, which should be second; and next number 6 entry, which would come in first. Win. Place. Show.

I thought the reason Big Joe did this every Sunday after church was in the Bible, where it says about racing that the first shall be last and the last shall be first. When I had finished, Big Joe placed his pick online, and twenty minutes later we sat back to watch the race. I wasn't too sure how it worked out because I wasn't paying attention — like, boring, out the gate and turn left around the circle and in three minutes the race is over and so are most of the horses, as they go down the claimer ladder to the dog-food plant.

But from then on, after each online race, Big Joe got up off his kitchen chair and lay down sleepy eyed on his bed to think about the money he'd won. I went back to my room and lay down sleepy eyed, not so much from getting the numbers right, not so much from knowing that as long as I did a good job predicting winners Big Joe might not take me out to his workshop and smash my toys with his hammer, but from realizing that, if I could figure out how genetics and cells worked, I could, through twin telepathy, connect with my dead sister. Why not? If Shelly with a dry wafer and a sip of wine could connect through telepathy with a guy she didn't even know who'd died hanging toes down from a cross two thousand years ago, I could connect through telepathy with my sister who died toes down eight years ago in a plastic container. Why not? I just had to find a substitute for the wine and the cracker.

Shelly's Sunday Communion, eating Jesus on a cracker, guaranteed her forgiveness for what she'd done every day last week and guaranteed her forgiveness for doing the same thing the coming week. But it didn't give her forgiveness from me for making me eat her Shelly Healthy Morning Breakfast.

"I know you don't like my Shelly Healthy Morning Breakfast, but every growing boy needs a Shelly Healthy Morning Breakfast."

A cracker would have been better. That stuff looked like frog eggs with added seeds and tiny worms. I couldn't find those worms with my fingers to fish them out of my mouth, and I didn't want to swallow them, so they stayed stuck to the roof of my mouth and the inside of my cheeks and got mixed up with spit and turned to yellow glue that stuck on my teeth so that I stayed in the washroom brushing my teeth and scrubbing my lips until the white foam of my toothbrush turned pink with blood.

"What happened to your lips?" asked my teacher, Mr. Gordon, one Monday morning. "What have you been doing this weekend?"

What have I been doing this weekend? No candles lit, no hymns sung, no prayers prayed in that after-church Sunday horse-race ritual with Big Joe. We did all that Jesus ritual stuff at church, plus the other hoodwinkeries, like reciting gibberish and then eating Christ on the cracker. That cracker tasted pretty awful but at least it didn't have worms on it.

"I'm allergic to the cracker."

After the horse races, I went grocery shopping with Big Joe. One day as I stood at the checkout, I noticed a magazine called *National Enquirer*. The front page article was about a millionaire who got his start in 1966, when he was driving a Heavenly Dreams ice cream truck. While he sold Heavenly Dreams ice cream to the kids, he sold Heavenly Dreams pills to the parents.

From then on, first thing in the morning, as soon as Shelly left for work, Big Joe would fasten on his aviator sunglasses and pull his baseball hat low over his eyes so God looking down could not recognize him and could not see what he was doing in that workshop. As Big Joe unpacked the little bags of white stuff that looked like powder, he liked to open one and stick in a finger and lick off the stuff he called special baking sugar. First one bag and then a few bags later, another bag, the second tasting better than the first, said Big Joe. This was true because after the second bag, Big Joe's lips curled back in a grin so wide God would have seen him for sure, except Big Joe's teeth were far from sparkling white from eating all that baking sugar.

I thought that maybe God, like the pope, looked at Big Joe through a glass eye when he should have been looking with his good eye. No disrespect to God intended. Here's what happened. Big Joe's house was a hundred years old and had the old-fashioned doors with skeleton keyholes, like the one I saw in the pope's picture at Audrey and Robert's. Here's what I did. Three other kids at Big Joe's house, three other bedroom doors, three other keyholes. Peeking through each as I passed, I could watch Big Joe with Timothy, keyhole one; with William, keyhole two; and Luke, keyhole three. Big Joe skipped me because I could pick his winners.

My school counsellor said, "Mr. Gordon told me your IQ is off the charts. You're very good at math and facts and details. That means you're very smart. You should be in a school with a gifted program."

I didn't feel smart or gifted. I felt like the pope looking through his keyhole, trying to figure stuff out with a glass eye.

***

The other day — not the other day, the day Martha was a week late with my eighteenth birthday present, the present that for this special day was a personal care kit, that day — me and Martha were sitting on the cemetery chapel steps watching the smoke coming out of the crematorium chimney. "When I was little, like eight, I used to wonder how could Big Joe's voice have been hard and mean at home and soft and soothing at church? How could he wear a smirk at home and a smile at church? How could he have stubbly brown cheeks at home and clean white cheeks at church? In other words, how could he be Big Joe the Hammer through the week and Mr. Radley on Sunday?"

Martha said, "Big Joe was two people in one: him and Mr. Radley. You're two people in one: you and your sister."

Chapter 4

OWEN

My grade four teacher, Mr. Gordon, asked, "Why does Timothy call you Winkie?"

I was afraid to say anything about the keyholes.

"Why do you spend so much time in the bathroom, washing your lips and brushing your teeth, Owen?"

I'd already said I was allergic to the cracker.

Mr. Gordon set up another appointment for me with the school counsellor.

The counsellor wrote with his pencil that I was nine years old, and the date was September 10, 2011.

The counsellor said, "You're living with Shelly and Joe Radley. How many others are there?"

"Three boys."

"It says here a girl called Martha was placed there."

"She was there for two days. Now she lives at that Sisters of Sorrows place."

"So if there's no girls at Joe Radley's, why do you look through keyholes?"

I could picture the words tumbling out of Timothy's weasel head and landing, already written, on the counsellor's notepad: Owen is a pervert. He looks at us through the keyholes.

"I want to know what the pope's eye sees."

"Pope's eye?" The counsellor checked his notepad.

"I had this picture on my wall. It looked like the pope's cyclops glass eye was watching me."

"Glass eyes can't see, Owen."

"I know, but sometimes it winked at me. Like one of those lizards, you know, with different winks, one eye looking one way and the other eye looking the other way. It must be hard to figure out what you're seeing with your eyes looking and winking in two different directions. I asked Big Joe if he could get me one of those lizards to see if—"

"The glass eye can't see, Owen."

"But he's the pope. He sees and knows almost everything. But how can he see and know anything if he's looking from two different directions at the same time?"

"From one direction he can't see, Owen."

"If he had one eye that looked from this way and the other eye that looked from the other way and both eyes could see, would he be able to see himself looking at himself?"

"Your interest in the pope's eye — is that why Timothy calls you Winkie?"

"I guess so."

"Or does he call you that for looking through keyholes?"

"Just sometimes."

"Okey dokey. But why do you spend so much time in the bathroom, washing your lips and brushing your teeth? And don't say you're allergic to the cracker."

I hesitated before I told him. I needed to explain it in a way that made sense. "Because of the porridge that covers my lips with sticky cream-of-wheat stuff that Shelly buys at the health food store in plastic tubs. The pope's cyclops eye won't stop winking at me until I've cleaned all the sticky stuff off my teeth. First thing in the morning I start brushing, and I have to brush all day because it's so sticky and slimy."

"Winking like a cyclops eye? And how is this connected to brushing?"

"I can't stop brushing until the eye stops winking, telling me sort of when I can stop."

"Which eye, the glass eye or the watching eye?"

"The winking one."

"Like the cyclops?"

"I think so." I was getting confused.

The counsellor nodded. "Okey dokey, Owen."

I thought the counsellor liked to say okey dokey because he thought this made him like a friend. He didn't know that no kid said okey dokey. The counsellor was old, wearing black-rimmed glasses from back in 1950, when all kids had real parents.

"Are you feeling guilty, Owen?"

"I have to brush thirty-two times. But my brain plays tricks on me and mixes up my count, like losing my place when I'm reading."

"Why thirty-two, Owen?"

"Because that's how many teeth I have. My mouth is kind of crowded so the slime sticks to my teeth, so I have to brush each one. I stand in front of the mirror and brush one at a time, but with the toothbrush in my mouth, I can't see each separate tooth to know if I've brushed it, so usually I have to brush lots of times. I start after breakfast, and if I don't finish before leaving for school I start again at school in the boys' washroom."

"Okey dokey, Owen. It says here you won't go to the dentist. Why is that?"

"I don't want the dentist to see the slimy stuff on my teeth."

"All right, Owen. You brush your teeth thirty-two times. How do you feel after you've done that?"

"I feel better."

"Not guilty."

"I guess so."

The counsellor nodded and wrote it down. As far as he was concerned, it was all making sense. I should have left out the toothbrushing part and explained the real reason: that looking through a keyhole was like looking through a microscope, about how looking at the same thing from this end was different from what you saw by looking through the other end. When I looked one-eyed through my Junior Scientist microscope at frog eggs, I saw a complete universe of mysteries at the other end. For example, in one drop of frog sperm before the cells began to split, before the DNA began to twist, in this cream-of-wheat porridge, tiny spermatozoa honed with a will to their mission, flexed their flagellum and swam in circles like newborn guppies in a bowl, trying to find their way through the glass and upstream to wherever they were destined to go. Where they were destined to go was not into my mouth.

Another story that went around: If you said you were being abused, the social worker would come knocking on the front door and say, "We've found your mother and she wants you back," and next thing, you got put on an airplane and sent to a treatment centre for pharma therapy, never to be seen again.

Here is what happened. Shelly took me and William and Timothy and Luke to the zoo. After looking at the lizards, we visited the marmoset monkeys with their cages built like front porches on a six-sided house called the Monkey Mansion. When the monkeys, hand in hand, weren't doing what Shelly said not to look at, they stared with wide, wondering eyes big as saucers at the mothers and the fathers hand in hand with their children with wide wondering eyes big as saucers staring back.

The next day Timothy learned in Mr. Gordon's health class about 911 and inappropriate touching. So he dialed the number. But when the lady asked his name, instead of saying Timothy, and telling her what Big Joe was doing, Timothy said, "Big Joe won't take me to McDonald's."

On the next call to 911, Timothy said the same thing, but this time gave the lady his name. The third time he phoned, the lady said, "Is that you again, Timothy, phoning 911 to complain about not going to McDonald's?"

So Timothy said, "Big Joe is doing inappropriate touching."

So the lady said, "Shame on you, Timothy. No more phoning 911 with your silly stories."

That's when Timothy told Mr. Gordon, who told Okey Dokey, who put two and two together and phoned 911.

Baseball hat pulled low over his brush-cut head, blank television-screen aviator sunglasses reflecting questioning faces back to asking eyes, Mr. Joe the Hammer Radley was led to the waiting cruiser. The next day a man in a blue business suit rang our doorbell and showed Shelly his social worker card. He had an accent, Irish, I think. He told Shelly that when wee Timothy was just a wee baby his mother had been forced to give up her flesh and blood. Poor wee child, she had loved him dearly. But now, having reformed herself, she was overjoyed at the possibility of getting wee Timothy back.

Not true. Even an Irish mother would have a hard time loving Timothy's narrow head with weasel eyes and thin nose and buckteeth with no chin from fetal alcohol syndrome. Timothy, who couldn't read or write but talked all the time because he had FAS and couldn't learn how to keep quiet no matter how many times Joe the Hammer smashed his toys, poor wee Timothy, hand in hand with the social worker, took a short walk to the car that would take him to a long ride on the airplane.

Shelly came into my room and sat on the edge of my bed. I closed my eyes and reached up to put my arms around the warmth of her neck. It was damp beneath the butterfly scarf she always wore, and her face was wet from her tears.

"It's not your fault," she said.

"Can I keep your picture?"

Shelly stared at the photo I kept on my dresser. "Of course you can."

"Can I have the scarf?"

"Of course you can."

"What's going to happen to me?"

"I don't know, Owen." And she started to cry.

I don't know what happened to William and Luke. I didn't care. All I cared about was I didn't want to be told my mother wanted me back and then be taken to the airport and sent to some pharmacological treatment centre to get therapy for my condition.

***

The CFCS sent me with all my science stuff to a new place, this one on Erskine Avenue in Toronto. Eric, my new social worker, delivered me.

The house had five bedrooms, a living room, dining room, and kitchen, with a TV room in the basement next to the furnace room. Outside, there was a white picket fence and a wide lawn and a wide veranda across the front of the white house with black shutters on each window, except the living room, which faced the tree-lined street dead-ending at the fence surrounding a two-acre L-shaped cemetery, the foot of the L at the fence, the leg of the L behind the house. At the back of the cemetery, inside an iron fence, was a chapel with a belfry, and beyond that stood a grey cement building with a brick chimney with smoke slanting out and disappearing beyond the spires of a Catholic church.

"You'll be in a regular school for the time being, but Bishop Humphries is raising the money to move you into a gifted program as soon as you're ready."

Eric said this three times.

Three times I said, "I don't want to go."

My new foster parent, Peter, had a scar on his hand from a car accident in his yellow taxi. He was young but looked old because he was bald.

"Owen, this is my wife, Sarah."

Oh boy. Sarah looked younger than Shelly, maybe twenty-five. She had blonde hair worn curly to her shoulders and had blue stuff on her eyes.

"Owen is nine," Eric told them. "He's clever with science and with numbers. For example, what is 963 times 965?"

"929,295," I answered.

"And he remembers everything he reads and is smart enough to understand this very big and heavy book on genetics and cell division. He has his own microscopes. He brought his complete lab from his last placement, I hope you don't mind, and will set it up in his room. He tells me he wants to start a blog on the internet, where he writes up his experiments in genetics. Dr. Owen, he wants to call himself. But he has other interests. Yesterday he was reading *Alice in Wonderland* for the third time."

"My favourite story," exclaimed Sarah, hugging me. Sarah felt warm and smelled like springtime, and I felt like the Cheshire Cat's smile.

The next day or maybe it was the day after, the front doorbell rang. I couldn't believe it. There with her social worker stood Martha. She looked the same, stocky with long brown hair. She didn't look too happy to see me. There was no like, remember me? I've been wondering how you're doing. I was sorry we couldn't, you know, hang out.

She said, "OhmyGod. You again."

Chapter 5

MARTHA

Me and Peter were sitting in the backyard on his green bench next to the apple tree watching Owen unwrap his late eighteenth birthday present, a personal repair kit. I was remembering my foster mother, Gretta, the one before I moved to Sarah and Peter's, asking in her Russian accent, "What do you tink of foster care, Marta?"

Shrug, sniffle, nothing.

"What did you tink of your last placement, Marta?"

Shrug, sniffle, nothing.

"What do you tink of this placement with me, Marta?"

What did I tink of my placement with you, Gretta? Well, let me tink. Sniffle, sniffle. If I had photographs starting from when I was a baby, albums like ordinary kids, I could connect all the pictures from all the placements into a completed puzzle, like an umbilical cord going backward to the day my mother wrapped me in the towel she stole from the Holiday Inn she delivered me in, and then, instead of taking me home and looking after me, left me on the floor of the North Bay Walmart washroom. But I don't have any photographs, so I don't know what to tink, Gretta.

I was remembering my first Sunday at Sarah and Peter's church, St. Mary's, across the cemetery. Father Small's sermon started with grass and flowers, which led him into shepherds minding the grazing sheep. This bent my mind into the direction of shepherds not abandoning their lambs and putting them into foster care. It's only people who do that. The mother tells herself that her baby would be better off with someone else raising it, like you, Gretta. That way, she doesn't have to be a mother. She can just be a person who had a baby. She can get up off her hospital bed and walk away, back to her life as a person before the baby. Not even a mother sheep would do that, Gretta.

I was remembering Gretta saying more than once, like every day, "Foster care is better now than in the old days, Marta, when a birth certificate was stamped illegitimate and you got sent on the orphan trains to work on a farm out west. Or you got sent to a rich family in the city to work as a servant."

Instead of reading me a bedtime story, Gretta walked that stupid dog. Walkie walkies, Marta. To keep up with the stupid dog, she walked so fast and so far ahead I couldn't keep up with her. I called, but she didn't hear.

So I made up my own bedtime story. One day while we were walkie walkies, I stopped her and faced her and said, "You treat that stupid dog better than me. You don't care about me, and you don't read me a bedtime story. I'm leaving and I'm going to find a different family to look after me."

After a while, this story changed itself around. I didn't mean it to. It changed on its own. It said, I'm going looking for my mother and I'm going to find her and I'm going to live with her. Every night I told myself this bedtime story, and even though it wasn't true, reciting it made me feel better. It made me feel like I was going forward, which is what the reciting of stories does. It changes how things are now.

All these years later, sitting on the bench with Peter and Owen, his scrunched-up birthday present wrapper lying in the grass at his feet — I wished that I had back-then pictures I could show them of me wrapped up in my blankie with my fist in my mouth. I wished that I had a back-then album so they could see what I looked like as a toddler playing This Little Piggie. My other foster families had photographs, but they were for income tax purposes, to prove I was an illegitimate baby who'd become a legitimate write-off.

The day I gave Owen his personal repair kit, he took it inside and left the paper in the grass. I stayed sitting on the green bench with Peter, who was watching the smoke coming out of the crematorium chimney. He asked me, "Now that you'll soon be leaving foster care,

Martha, tell me —being sent from place to place at two years old, five years old, nine years old — how did that make you feel?"

All those years with Peter, he had never once asked me how anything made me feel.

"Does it make you angry thinking about it?"

No one had ever asked me that before. But I had spent my entire life, well, my entire life, like, age zero to eighteen, being angry, and I had spent my entire life rehearsing the answer in case someone bothered to ask it.

So I gave him my rehearsed answer. "Of course I have anger. The foster system is full of anger. The kid is angry at the mother for being given away. The kid is angry at the system for not telling who her parents are. Foster parents are angry because the kid they have is a replacement for the kid they wanted. The foster father is angry at the foster mother for not being able to have kids. The foster mother is angry at the kid for not turning out the way they wanted. Every foster kid is a kid with anger."

Peter said, "My mother had different-coloured threads in her sewing kit and different-sized needles and a silver needle-pusher thing for the end of my finger. She mended cast-off rummage sale clothing for foster kids like you."

"It doesn't matter, Peter. She can throw all that stuff away. People don't donate their cast-off rummage-sale clothes anymore. Now people donate their cast-off rummage sale children to be mended and seamed and stitched together, not by fingers with threads and needles but by the sewing kit of the CFCS that trades kids back and forth like those grade four boys in Kenora traded hockey cards. That's how you got me, Peter. They sat around the table with their Starbucks and their hockey cards and said, 'This kid goes from this pretend mother to that pretend mother. This kid goes from this pretend mother to that pretend mother. This kid's a runner so send him to Teddy Freddy in Sudbury. He's got bars on his windows.'"

Peter did what he always did when he needed to think up an answer. He stretched out his arms and laid them across the back of the bench. "Perhaps you should look at it from a different perspective. It was the stitching together of what should have been with what was: a real mother with substitute mother, the real father with substitute father."

OhmyGodprayforme. "In your dreams, Peter, like the pictures of pretend young couples on the CFCS website with a credit card box to check, not for sending clothes but for sending money. So here I am, grown up and ready to leave foster care, so now you're supposed to say something wise or something sympathetic so I can stop being angry."

Peter took my hand. "None of us get to choose our parents and none of us get to choose who we will be. Our only choice is to do our best with what we got. So here I am and here you are and here we are together, Martha, right at this minute, trying to do the best with what we got."

Yeah right, Peter.

***

After his car accident, Peter had stopped playing sports, but around the time Owen and I moved in, I was nine, I think, he coached a boys' over-twelve fastball team that was losing every game because it didn't have a good pitcher.

"I bet you've got a good strong arm, Martha. Let's see what it will do for us."

That was a nicer way of saying, you're built good and sturdy, so why not put that sturdy arm to work.

He put the ball into my hand. "Hold your fingers like this and throw me one."

I pitched the way he showed me.

"Think Superman, stretch forward both arms as though you're going to fly. Then lean back on your left and kick forward on your right and drive the right arm like a punch."

Before long I had an arm so wicked he lobbied to put me on his twelve-and-older team as pitcher, even though I was a girl.

And you know what, Gretta, I think often about that day, like a destiny thing, how the pitch of the baseball back then at nine years old took away all those years of anger, nine years later, at eighteen.

Chapter 6

OWEN

Sarah said words like "ah-right" and "awesome." She served Pop-Tarts for breakfast and made peanut butter-and-jelly white-bread sandwiches for lunch. She let the house get messy and forgot to do the laundry and let me and Martha spend as much time as we wanted watching the sixty-inch flatscreen in the basement TV room next to the furnace room.

Both basement rooms had narrow rectangular windows, level with the flower gardens that were looked after by Peter. From the window facing the street, looking up, I could watch Sarah in her tight miniskirt wiggling sort of bouncy down the front walk to the gate, heading off to the corner store for groceries.

Me and Martha were on the living-room couch reading. I had been helping her with her grade four math. After we had finished, Martha picked up where she left off in my copy of *Alice in Wonderland*, every five seconds asking me what something meant. I saw Sarah open the door to the basement. She switched on the light at the top of the stairs. At the bottom of the stairs, she turned it off.

I waited for Sarah to return.

I explained another page of *Alice*. Time passed. I stood at the kitchen window watching Peter working in the flower garden at the back of the property. From St. Mary's church, Father Small's miniature bulldog, Petunia, wandered into the yard for an ear scratch from Peter. Petunia should have been tied up at the back door of the church, but Father Small didn't bother about it. Petunia poked around the flowers. Peter didn't bother about it. After a while she cut across the cemetery, back to St. Mary's.

I went back to my seat to explain another page to Martha. Sarah had not returned. I got up and pushed back my glasses, which, because of my stooped posture, insisted on sliding to the end of my nose. I crept to the door. I reached out and turned the knob. The stairway was dark. I couldn't see beyond the second step, but I didn't want to switch on the light. Down the rabbit hole I went, groping along the wall to the bottom. At the end of the hall, beyond the furnace room, from under the TV-room door, I saw a sliver of light. Quiet as a dormouse, my shoulders curled around my thin chest, I crept through the shadows along the wall, although I knew that even in this dim light anyone one could see me if anyone wanted to look. I could hear moanings and gruntings. I crouched on my hands and knees with my head near the floor. Eric and Sarah were on the floor next to the television, which someone had forgotten to turn off. Eric's fingers, which were in Sarah's curly blonde hair, wriggled down from neck to buttons to zipper, and then came the other stuff I wasn't supposed to know about.

Some weeks passed. Then one day, Peter, who by this time, with the help of Sarah, had turned Martha and me into the family none of us had ever had, announced with tears in his eyes, "Sarah will be leaving."

For the next few days, Sarah and Peter sulked and moped around the house, heads hung like those sackcloth brothers from the *Dead Sea Scrolls* movie me and Martha watched three times. For the next few nights, Sarah and Peter cried in their beds. For the next three days and nights, Martha sulked and moped and cried in her bed.

As usual I didn't feel much of anything. Well there was one other thing I felt sorry about. I would not be able to watch Sarah walk bouncy anymore. It didn't matter, I guess, because she was pregnant, so soon she'd be walking as trudgey as Martha.

Chapter 7

OWEN

We were sitting on the bench next to the apple tree. Peter had this habit of rubbing his fingertips back and forth over the scar on the back of his hand he got driving his cab late at night on a return run from the airport. "No passengers, thank God. I got hit by an eighteen-wheeler."

Peter rubbed the tips of his fingers along the scar. "Sister Charlotte from the Sisters of Sorrows foster care up north has arthritis and needs a lighter workload in a warmer climate. Bishop Humphries, who's in charge of the foster program for Nipissing, suggested that for the time being Sister Charlotte could help out here."

Peter was rubbing the scar like a blind person trying to read Braille, unsure about what he was reading, as though he was not sure this was a good idea. "Do you remember Sister Charlotte, Martha?"

Martha shook her head. "I saw her one time, I think. The day that bishop guy sent me and Owen here. So what's with the arthritis?"

Peter wiggled his fingers. "Makes your joints sore so you can't do things like sewing or opening jars, and she has to climb the stairs with her right leg first. But her doctor says with some stronger medication in a warmer climate, she'll be better."

Peter was rubbing the scar, like rubbing a smudge of dirt off his hand. "Sister Charlotte is a nun and will run a tight ship. You'll learn solid Christian values. I've been taking time off work to keep things going, but I need to get back to earning money."

Peter showed me the picture Sister Charlotte had sent from when she joined the Sisters of Sorrows and another one of her from when she worked with some group-home kids up north. In the first she had a nice smile, I think because she liked being married to Jesus, that's why nuns don't get married to real men, and in the second she had a fake smile with a mean scowl, I guess from the pain of her arthritis.

So when she limped through the front door of our house, I shouldn't have been surprised. But I was. Her face was lined, her skin grey, and her hair dead and stringy, as though she belonged in a coffin. She didn't wear a nun's white head cover; her plain blue dress with black socks and flat black shoes was the nun uniform for the Sisters of Sorrows.

The first thing she said, before even being introduced, was "What a relief. These stronger pills are a miracle. I'll be back in shape in no time."

Sister Charlotte took the pills daily, lubricating her frozen 7:00 a.m. joints into spring-loaded 8:00 a.m. housework. "The children" — that's what she called us, me and Martha — "need to start the day with good food, namely old-fashioned oatmeal."

Not as bad as Shelly's — but almost. Sister Charlotte boiled it for twenty minutes while Martha made brown-bread tuna sandwiches for our lunch. For supper, Sister Charlotte prepared a meatloaf that tasted like she'd added soap, probably to wash from our mouths the bad words we brought home from school. We complained about the no Pop-Tarts rule, so instead of sweets, she baked angel food cakes every Saturday.

"Angel food cake won't turn out if you're thinking bad thoughts," warned Sister Charlotte. "That's how I'll know about the bad thoughts you're learning now that you're both getting older."

"What bad thoughts?" I asked.

"What they teach you in grade six sex ed. The bad thoughts in your mind get into the batter for the cake. That's why it's called angel food."

So, if the cake turned out good, we weren't thinking bad thoughts. Or maybe it was the other way 'round, depending on your definition of good and bad.

She did the laundry every Saturday and ironed the clean tablecloth every Monday. She took down the picture of Tom Cruise on a motorcycle hanging opposite her bed and hung her favourite picture of crucified Jesus hanging toes down from his cross; Mary, his mother, at his feet on one side; Mary Magdalene, the prostitute, on the other. Next to Jesus, she hung the Blessed Virgin Mary riding on a donkey with a white pigeon with black legs on her shoulder. Next to that hung the pope on the stage of a televised anti-abortion barn-and-tent revival in Louisiana, parking lot overflowing with bused-in anti-abortionists carrying signs and shouting slogans that promised more foster children for CFCS.

She restricted television-watching because, according to the pope, TV was the cause of the rot of America. She insisted on double-dosing her pills on Sunday so she could play the organ for the ten o'clock St. Mary's Sinner Sanctum service, even though, despite the pills, her fingers were so stiff she hit lots of wrong notes. Added to that, the pills dried her stomach into burps loud enough to hear in the parking lot.

On the go, dawn to dusk, the devil makes work for idle hands, never dressed in any other way but a plain blue dress; her Sisters of Sorrows nun button, blue with white lettering, pinned proudly to the left-hand pocket of her blue blouse; hair like dead twitch grass flat down after the snow had melted and held in place with furrowed bobby pins. "OhmyGod," said Martha.

After Sister Charlotte moved in, Peter never went anywhere with us together, never talked much. I think in Peter's memories, Sarah curled her hair into long and swinging and wiggled herself into tight jeans for walking bouncy, and in these memories she and Peter snuck out the back door and went to the bars. But Peter never said what his memories were, and I never asked. But I think that's where he was spending his time, in his memories while driving his taxi, leaving Sister Charlotte in charge. Well no. Sister Charlotte had *taken* charge. So there was nothing much for me and Martha to do other than indoor rainy-day chores with Sister Charlotte, even if the day was sunny.

Sister Charlotte assigned Martha the job of dishes because she wouldn't break anything, and me the job of garbage because I would break everything. Sister Charlotte instructed us to stack the pots with their handles all facing in the correct direction and the forks and the spoons pointing in the correct direction. The plates and saucers were round, so they couldn't point in any correct direction, but they had to be stacked correctly. Twenty of everything. Twenty cups and twenty knives and twenty forks. But not twenty pots. Four pots and four fry pans and two silver tea sets with matching sugar bowls and creamers.

"OhmyGod," said Martha.

Boots lined up at the door, and Bible in the correct spot in each bedroom, and beds made the correct way, and hair combed the correct number of times. At first I couldn't figure out why something was correct one day but the same thing incorrect the next day. After about a week with Sister Charlotte, I figured out that to make sure she was always in charge and we never had idle hands, she turned some things that were correct today into incorrect tomorrow so she would never run out of things to correct.

Chapter 8

SISTER CHARLOTTE

When Owen's glasses slid off his nose, they snagged in his shoelaces, where he stepped on them with both clumsy feet when he tried to pick them up. Clothes hanging off his thin frame, he climbed into the front seat of my car, one leg curled underneath him. From school to home, the back seat full of the books he had borrowed from the library, none of them looking like anything a ten-year-old would read. His head, cocked this way and that, seemed to be like a satellite surveillance system in an ambulatory computer, filing information as we drove along: his ears recording the hum of my tires on the asphalt and the whirr of the traffic; his eyes scanning the tall buildings and tabulating the sequencing of the red, yellow, and green traffic lights. And at the same time, like an ordinary ten-year-old, he was scowling at the shoppers along the storefronts and staring at the dog walkers on the sidewalk.

This observation was consistent with the information in his file, which put him somewhere on the high-functioning autistic spectrum. I was familiar enough with the system to know labels don't mean much, especially after working with the Indigenous boys in the North. But it seemed Owen was exceptionally smart, which was why Bishop Humphries had rescued him from the northern foster-care system before he ended up in the Treatment Centre.

At the meeting we had about Owen, Bishop Humphries said that any school Owen went to he would be teased and picked on. Bishop Humphries called it "difficulty navigating the schoolyard." Then Bishop Humphries remembered a girl called Martha, also needing a placement. He said the woman Gretta had six younger foster kids that had been bullied at school, that is, until Martha stepped in. He recommended Martha and Owen be placed together, Martha the protector of Owen the gifted, although one look at Owen would raise the question, gifted to do what? He looked like that painting of odd shapes and colours that everyone said was the work of a genius but it turned out his dog did it. For that reason I knew Bishop Humphries's protector idea was silly. Stupid, for that matter. Suspicious, in fact. In the school yard Owen would be fair game and there would be nothing Martha could do about it.

I asked Owen; he seemed surprised. "Picked on? When have I been picked on?"

"Bishop Humphries mentioned something like that. But I'm sure he was thinking of someone else."

Well, whatever. According to her file, Martha had gone from one foster family to another and would benefit from a permanent placement and would certainly be help around the house.

As I turned along Yonge Street and passed the iron gate of the cemetery, Owen rearranged himself, one leg stretched out and one pulled under his chin, his running shoe flat on the seat. His attention seemed to be directed at the smoke coming from the crematorium chimney, not just watching it, but studying it, looking for something in it.

I turned along Erskine Avenue, a lovely dead-ender lined with tall trees, their leaves beginning to fall, covering the front lawn of Peter's old house and blowing against his white picket fence. Very lovely.

As I parked I glanced at the apple tree in the centre of the grassy backyard, with a flower garden along the stone fence at the rear, and beyond that the cemetery we had passed earlier. In the middle of the cemetery, on a hill, stood a brick chapel with an iron fence and a tall belfry, and to the right, like the backdrop picture for the flock of pigeons that lived on the roof and in the steeples of St. Mary's church, stood the chimney of the crematorium that Owen had been studying. From a distance, the picture belonged on the front cover of a Victorian gothic novel. Take away the cemetery and leave the apple tree and the flower garden, and the picture was almost identical to my childhood home, in particular the pigeons in the church spires. It was like a postcard from when I was ten years old, wearing my knee socks and knee-length skirt, skipping through the grass under the apple tree.

Owen got out and disappeared into the Tiny Tots playground across the street. I opened the car door and started up the walk. This was the end of my first month here with Peter, but I still rang the bell and waited under the shadow of the veranda roof until, realizing I had a key, I let myself in.

I walked along the hallway, past the wooden staircase, and into a kitchen smelling of the Mr. Clean that Martha had used on the counter. She was a sturdy girl, unlike me at her age. I was a beauty. I sang solos at St. Mary's Christmas concerts. Not this St. Mary's. The other one. But now my voice, which had been as soft as the cooing of those pigeons living in the spires of St. Mary's, not this St. Mary's, although there were pigeons in this St. Mary's too — did I mention that? What was I thinking? Oh yes, my voice had turned as raspy as the cawing of crows I heard last evening. When I looked out the kitchen window, I saw them in the poplars next to the crematorium chimney. The black crows set against the grey smoke that seemed to be going on ahead of me gave me the shivers.

I set my car keys on the table, removed my glasses, and wiped them with a Kleenex. I folded it and returned it to the pocket of my Sisters of Sorrows dress. I removed a bobby pin from my hair, brown like my mother's but longer and frizzed at the ends. I flattened it down and replaced the pin.

As I walked along the upper hallway, I heard through one shut bedroom door the dull rattle of drawers opening and closing, hangers rasping. That was Martha's room. It looked so much like my room when I was her age that it could have been mine, painted the way I remembered mine: beige with a bare wooden floor and a narrow metal bed between a brown dresser and desk; austere, neat, tidy.

"Children don't need material things," Bishop Humphries had said to me. "They need spiritual values. That is your mission to Martha and Owen, Sister Charlotte. If I had my way, I would have all foster children keep a journal where they collect all the proverbs and parables and teachings that would speak loud as resounding trumpets in their hearts, if only we forced them to do the readings."

I reminded him, "But not the way Father Eagleman was doing with those Indigenous boys."

"Certainly not, Sister. He was a black belt in judo. Not that way. I would have the children write all those salient truths in their journals, like making their own Bible, like the Book of Owen, the Book of Martha, and this would become the cornerstone of their soul."

In the top drawer of her dresser, Martha kept her Bible and prayer book, as I did mine when I was her age. Tucked into her Bible was the list of rules I made up for them the day after I arrived: bedtime, chore time, and so on. In each of their closets hung the church clothes I got for them two days after I arrived: a blue blouse and blue plaid skirt for Martha; and for Owen, a blue blazer, grey trousers, and a white shirt with a blue tie.

Well. How time flies. Time for the next pill.

Chapter 9

OWEN

Dressed in a long red robe, Sister Charlotte, who had taken over from the last organist who'd died, sat before the organ that stood in one corner at the front of St. Mary's Sinner Sanctum, like a piano with gold stovepipes side by side. Down the aisles of Sinner Sanctum to the pews, me and Martha went. Partway along, I tripped over my feet and sprawled on the floor. What Martha should have done was kneel beside me, her blue eyes warm on my face and her hand soft on my arm. Are you all right? Can you get up?

First of all, Martha's eyes were brown. Second of all, she didn't have blonde hair. And third, she didn't kneel. She kicked me in the thigh and hissed, "Don't act stupid. Stand up and sit down."

We filed into the pews, Martha first.

We waited.

First sounded three long notes followed by several short chords in a series. Then, after a silence, as though the silent pipes were waiting for consent from the rooftop pigeons cooing and flapping outside, the hollow moanings of a hymn began, climbing the bare walls and disappearing through the high-arced ceiling to drift among the waiting flock gathered in the three tall crosses.

Seated next to me, Martha was looking around, scowling, wondering what was wrong with the organ. The overhead light was bouncing off each of her unblinking eyes, which I saw were black not brown, as they looked from one view to another, the one ear asking the other ear, what's going on with the organ?

I leaned close. "The arthritis makes her fingers twitch, like a stutter, and she double plunks."

I saw one light over Sister Charlotte's head had a blue haze. At first it was dim enough I didn't notice it. But bit by bit it got stronger. Martha said, "Sister Charlotte had that light put there. She told me when she was my age she sang a passion solo, 'You'll Know the Angel When She Comes,' using a light like that. She said she never heard that song before, the words just came to her. In her little blue outfit, she sat on a stool and held the palms of her hands in her lap, open like a dish, and as that blue faded into a halo, she would get up from her stool and sing, 'You'll Know the Angel When She Comes.'"

I pictured a ten-year-old Sister Charlotte singing the words under the halo. I pictured the blue fade to white. I pictured the white open and take Sister Charlotte from the stool and, before my very eyes, I watched this white halo turn Sister Charlotte from old and rusted to young and oiled.

My imagination could repair Sister Charlotte's body, but my ears could not do the same for her organ playing. It was terrible.

Father Small, dressed in black robes, a Bible under his arm, entered from a door at the back next to a stained-glass window. He walked past the altar and approached the pulpit and climbed up on a little platform, like a wide wooden box, to make him look taller. He set down his Bible, put on his wire-rimmed glasses, and opened a hymn book.

The music stopped.

"Hymn number 673," said Father Small, his voice so loud for such a small man that Martha jumped.

I noticed in a mirror hanging above Sister Charlotte's head that she was watching the congregation, waiting for everyone to find the page. When we were ready, she began to play. The congregation, a mix of old and young, parents and kids, followed along through the first stanza and into the last. The hymn over and everyone seated, Martha got up, her turn to read the scriptures, Sister Charlotte's idea. Martha stepped to the front and began to read from her Bible in a small voice, unusual for her because she was big and pushy. Father Small, sitting in his highbacked chair beside the pulpit, scowled at Martha through his wire-rimmed glasses, for she was making a lot of mistakes because, instead of practising her reading in her room, she had been feeding the pigeons in the church parking lot.

I was wondering — since earlier in the service Father Small had prayed for the organist who died — I was wondering if the funeral services were the same as Sunday service. First you sit down in the pews. Next you do the Bible reading, next the hymns, next the prayers. Stand up, sit down, finished. The only difference would be, while the congregation went out the front door, out the back door and into the holey would goest the organist in the coffin.

From his little platform, his glasses glinting over the congregation, Father Small began his sermon. I had heard this story lots of times at Big Joe's church. But now it made more sense because I had decided that Jesus, like Sister Charlotte, had OCD. For Jesus, everything had to be in threes. He had three wise men come to his birthday; he had them bring three presents; he spent three days on the cross with three nails driven into him, two into the hands and one into the feet. He spent three days in the cave before rising from totally stone dead, rolling away a boulder the size of three tractor wheels, and letting himself out to walk for three days the stony ground.

The OCD part was right. But I had some questions. For example, how did Jesus move that boulder? With a pry? Did someone put it into the cave in advance? Maybe Jesus had a boyfriend in there strong enough to roll it away. And what about driving in those two spikes? The small bones of the hand would not be strong enough to hold the weight of a body. For Jesus to hang from the cross for three days, the spikes would have to go through the wrist.

Father Small's black robes rustled in the silence. He stepped down from the box and came forward to recite the benediction. His arms outstretched, the wide folds of his robes fanned out like wings, he looked like a pigeon in flight. He dropped his arms, clasped his hands, and bowed his head. Everyone in the Sinner Sanctum silently waited, heads fallen forward, eyes closed. He gave one last glance over the congregation, said, "Amen," and headed for the exit.

The organ again. I could not understand why Father Small would put up with an organ that sounded like those cats that yowled every night in the cemetery. Perfect for me, though. It gave me a good bounce out of my pew and out the door and into the street and along to the cemetery to look for frogs' eggs for the Junior Scientist Contest. If I won it, I'd for sure go into high school in a special gifted class, not because I wanted to be gifted but because I wouldn't have Martha following me around in the hallway telling me to do up my fly and tie my shoes.

Chapter 10

MARTHA

Petunia liked to sit in the grassy spot next to the apple tree, her bulldog face filled with sadness and frowns like a foster baby, then so happy to see us after waiting hours for Owen and me to come home from school and dress her in booties and snuggly and blankie and push her in the baby carriage Peter had brought home in his taxi from the secondhand store. Up and down the cemetery lanes we strolled, like mother and father, Owen being the father. What choice did I have?

Peter had brought a high chair home in his taxi. We dressed Petunia in a sweater and bib and fed her leftover Sister Charlotte Special Meatloaf with added doggy bits to wash the bad barks from her mouth. Peter brought home a little desk, so we dressed her up in a skirt and sweater and packed her a snack, which she ate at recess in the backyard. Peter got her a beret and said, "Petunia looks like that French artist Levina Teerlinc. Maybe we can teach her to draw."

Peter got some powdered paint, which we mixed with water and put on her front paws to smear onto pieces of cardboard. The results looked like something from the Group of Seven, said Peter, so we hung them in the backyard shed and had a "showing."

Nobody came. Didn't matter. After all the fun I got from doing it, and then looking back into my memories, I could do it all again.

Owen caught crawly bugs in the graveyard grass and kept them in beakers in his bedroom where they died instead of changing into flying bugs to start all over again. He said it was a revenge fantasy from lying in the Open Hatch with his dead sister. The Open Hatch was full of flying maggots waiting their turn to chew their way through his sister and into him, he said.

From the gate of the graveyard fence, me and Owen noticed the two men dressed like undertakers in black suits step out of a black car and come up the front walk. By the time we got there, Peter had answered the door, invited them in, and offered them coffee. The big one with pockets under his eyes said, "This will take only a minute. We thought your children might be able to help us, living as they do by the cemetery. Your children play there, we've seen them, no one has complained, they're well-behaved kids. But we've been looking for a particular grave."

He turned to Owen. "I understand, Owen, that you catch bugs and such. A naturalist, poking about in the grass."

Owen didn't understand. "Are you social workers?"

"We're with the OPP. I'm Paul."

Paul turned to me. "You're Martha. How's Bella doing?"

"Who?"

Peter stepped in. "We don't know anything about any Bella."

"Martha's mother. You must have records."

Peter hesitated. He rubbed his fingertips back and forth over the scar on the back of his hand. He glanced from Paul to me before saying, "Sometimes the CFCS will conveniently not have records, to protect the children."

The other detective, who'd been writing in a little notebook, said, "Sometimes the CFCS will conveniently not have records, to protect the parents of the children. We're trying to find Martha's mother, Bella, who worked with Father Eagleman in the Nipissing CFCS. We thought the children might have found Bella's father's gravestone. We think he's buried somewhere in this cemetery. It could be Bella might visit him from time to time and the children might have noticed."

Peter said, "Then check with the church. There should be death certificates, a cemetery registry, something."

"Sometimes the Catholic Church records go conveniently missing," Paul said, "usually to hide the paternity of the children."

"I know nothing of Martha's father or mother, nor does Martha. We have no idea where Bella's father is buried. But I do know a lot of children were moved out of Nipissing because of some scandal with Father Eagleman. So perhaps you could explain to us what this about?"

Paul said, "It's been all over the news, so I guess I can tell you. Father Eagleman claimed many of the Indigenous boys had wheat allergies —serious enough to kill them — so he asked if the wafers could be made with barley. But Bishop Humphries said no because ... something about the wheat being needed for the actual physical transformation into the flesh and blood of Christ. So Eagleman was being charged with the wrongful death of those Indigenous boys because Bishop Humphries insisted they be given wheat wafers." He shrugged. "That's the story, but that's not how those boys died. Those boys OD'd on drugs allegedly given to them by Father Eagleman, otherwise known as 'The Eagle.'"

Peter nodded. "One scandal after another."

Paul glanced at his watch. "We have a few minutes. I noticed as I was coming up the walk that you have a lovely garden. Could you give us a tour?"

They followed Peter single file across the kitchen and into the backyard.

I went up to my room and lay on my bed. What do you tink about that, Marta? They're looking for your mother.

What I tink, Gretta, is if my mother ever entered that cemetery, I would know it.

Well, Marta, you have never seen your mother, so how would you know her?

Shrug, sniffle, don't know.

But I did know. Right from when I was little, I knew. Like about five years old, I knew if I saw my mother in the store or at the bus stop, I would recognize her. The reason I knew all this was I read that a baby in the womb can smell her mother and can know her feelings and her movements and recognize her voice. And especially her heartbeat. A baby lives nine months with that heartbeat and nine months with the sound of her mother's voice. A baby knows her mother even before she's born. For months after being born, the baby is still attached in its emotions to the mother. Then the mother disappears, and the baby's emotions ask, Where did she go? Why did she leave me? Who is this different person who sounds different and smells different and speaks different?

And then comes the big question, What's going to happen to me?

And then comes the bigger question, Why did she leave me on the washroom floor in Walmart?

I thought that one day my mother would telephone. I thought that one day I would come home from school and open the door and, instead of my foster mother, there would be my real mother, and there would be her face lighting up in a smile so happy to see me. Every birthday I looked through the mail for a card from my mother. Every Christmas I looked under the tree for a present from my mother. None of these things ever happened. I told myself it was because my first foster parents, Al and Fran, had changed my name so my mother couldn't find me. Or that maybe my mother had come to the house and asked if she could stay and look after me but was told there was no room for mothers.

I wanted to tell my mother all about me. I would say, I'm small and delicate with fine hair and pale skin and perfect legs and everything I do is graceful, something as simple as sitting in a chair, I do it gracefully. I wanted to say, I'm one of those grade seven girls that all the boys ask to go to the dance.

Then I would feel guilty and tell the truth. I walk kind of clunky and sit down on a chair with a plunk and don't care about my legs, thin or otherwise. If anyone asks what I look like, which one is Martha, the answer is the sturdy one, her hair cut square to just above her shoulders and held to one side with one of those plastic things. Add to that a plain blouse and a plain skirt and plain shoes, so those filthy grade eight boys in the hallways don't get any ideas about asking her to the dance.

After the police left, Owen had that sort of dizzy look he gets, like waiting for a sneeze. This look told me he was planning something, like let's find Martha's mother. I could see him thinking that. I could see him sneaking into the cemetery chapel, sitting in the back pew, waiting till dark had fallen to turn on his BlackBerry and record the voices of the dead who walked the lanes at midnight. I could see him asking the dead, like in a TV interview, Have you seen Martha's mother?

Sure enough, the next morning, he said, "Guess who I recorded last night. I went into the chapel and turned on my BlackBerry, and pretty soon this is what I got."

And you know what, when he played the recording, I couldn't believe my ears. At first I thought it was those cats yowling in the background, but no, it was a baby crying. But the chapel was nowhere near any houses, and there weren't any babies in the cemetery in the middle of the night, and well, I had this thing about foster babies. In fact, I was as obsessed with foster babies as Owen was with bugs and experiments.

Owen was fiddling with his BlackBerry. He said, "Listen to this."

I heard what sounded like soft footfalls of the dead on the floorboards in the belfry — and then louder, as though their shoes were getting bigger as they paced, or maybe they'd switched to bigger boots.

I couldn't believe it. I have this thing about being plugged into the dead, since I spent so much time wondering if my mother was dead, like Owen was plugged into the dead from lying underneath his dead sister.

I asked him, "Who is it?"

"Your mother."

"Wearing boots?"

"If you want to talk to the dead, there are steps you have to take before you can make contact. Number one: Wait in your bedroom until midnight, watching the big hand of the clock on the wall tick its way to the twelve. Number two: As the gongs begin to sound — one, two, three — you have to creep, creep out of your bedroom and down the hall and across the yard and over the stone fence. Number three: You have to climb through the chapel window and wait for the soft, slow tread, one step at a time, on the stairs. Number four: You have to wait for the heavier foot beats on the floorboards above. Number five: You have to wait on your knees while the dead person kneels at the altar to say prayers before going back up the stairs to the belfry. Then, still on your knees, you ask your questions."

OhmyGodputmeoutofmisery. Captain Midnight almost had me. "Owen, you don't have a clock on your wall, and we have no clock anywhere in the house that sounds like twelve gongs at midnight. Besides, my mother would not wear boots — your mother, maybe —

and besides, dead people don't have knees, not ones that bend anyway, so how can they kneel?"

Owen was like a mosquito. Listening to him made me itchy, even though he hadn't bitten me yet, I got the itch and decided to hang with him, out of sight under the poplars behind the chapel, while he did his creeping and peeking. When no dead person appeared, we jimmied the chapel window and climbed inside to look for one. We sat side by side in the last pew, not a word, not a whisper, until we both fell asleep.

Chapter 11

SISTER CHARLOTTE

Dear Jesus. I lie alone on my bed in my room, propped up on my pillow, staring at you, hanging there on my wall, the two of us drifting together. I listen to the sound of the water running through the pipes at the flush of the toilet, but I don't hear water running into the sink for a handwash, so I know it's Owen. I hear soft footsteps in the hallway, and I know it's Martha. I hear clumping down the stairs, and I know it's Owen. If I got up, I would see them crossing the yard and going up the street to the Bluejay for ice cream. After ice cream, they will go to Tiny Tots Daycare parking lot, so Martha can practise her baseball.

No friends, other than themselves, not unusual according to the SixSteps foster care manual. These kids need to find their comfort zone, and having found it, that is where they stay until they're ready to leave. I never had any friends, and I found no comfort zone until I entered the Sisters.

Peter, not the kids, is the problem. Peter arrives home at midnight, goes to work at noon, and stays gone for twelve-hour shifts, still grieving his Sarah. I understand. I had an old uncle. He had a small pig farm. When his wife left him, Uncle Merv stopped looking after his pigs. He hid a case of beer in the oven to drink if he ran out of home-brewed liquor he bought from Bull Beasley. God rest his soul. He choked to death on his own vomit.

Sometimes, dear Jesus, and you'll like this, if a fare in his cab does not have enough money, Peter will give his address to the person and say, Pay me when you can. There will be a knock on our door, and there will be a stranger who will say, Give this to Peter. Peter said there never was a time when the money was not repaid, although I know he doesn't keep track, and maybe he doesn't remember the ones who didn't pay, although he mentioned one time that a lot of people owe him favours. Peter says he's a graduate of the Academy of Monkeys. On his dresser, he has a bronze of Hear no evil, See no evil, Speak no evil, so even if they don't pay right away, he doesn't care.

Dear Jesus, I hope you don't disapprove. Bishop Humphries told Eric that his affair with Sarah won't be reported providing Eric never shows his face on the property again. So now Bishop Humphries writes up the CFCS reports for the main office. The reason he gives is he has a special interest in Owen because he gets picked on by the schoolyard bullies. But when I asked Martha, she says no one bothers him. He's like the school mascot because he wins all those science contests. So I think there's something fishy going on because of the problem with The Eagle and the Indigenous boys in group homes in the Diocese of Moosonee. The media is calling it The Eagle and the Boys from Snowy River. Definitely something fishy going on, my father would say. Like what did Adam say when he woke up with one rib missing? There's something fishy going on.

Did I already say that about Bishop Humphries's involvement with both Owen and Martha? First he pulled the strings to get Martha placed here with Owen, something fishy about that. Now he pulls the strings to keep an Eric replacement away from Owen and Martha. Maybe it's nothing more than Bishop Humphries trying to save Owen from the foster care revolving door system that Martha was in. A child as peculiar as Owen would be bounced around from placement to placement, school to school, until he ended up in the Treatment Centre. That must be the answer.

But there's something fishy going on. The fishiest part is that I was chosen as foster mother for both children. I know, I know, dear Jesus, it's not my job to question God's intentions, but I was planning to go on long-term disability, which this placement certainly isn't.

And back to Peter. When he's home he dreams up fun things to do with the kids, like go to the Bluejay for ice cream or order in a pizza and watch movies. But that leaves me to pay the bills and add up the accounts and do the groceries and supervise the housework and carry onward Christian soldiers. All this I would gladly do, dear Jesus, but not with arthritis. That day a few days ago, as I said these very words, you were hanging from your cross, head tilted in thought, considering my predicament, the Virgin Mary hanging next to you, the one with the dove on her shoulder that reminds me of the white homing pigeons my father raised when we lived down the road from Uncle Merv. That was before my father bought the house in North Bay, almost identical to this one, when … where was I? Oh yes, I prayed to the Virgin and to you, dear Jesus, because Dr. Rebeneck, noticing my Sisters button, asked, Are you a creation of God, or is God a creation of you? He's an atheist and likes to push my buttons.

I am a creation of God, I said.

Reductio ad absurdum, said the doctor.

I need stronger pills, Doctor.

Is the pain a creation of God, or is it a creation of you, Sister Charlotte? The dose you're now taking of oxycodone along with Rheumatrex would fell a horse. Oxycodone, over time, will scramble your brain. I'm surprised it hasn't disconnected a few wires already. I'm going to write you a prescription for Suboxone so you can get off it.

That day I limped out of the doctor's office and hobbled to the subway. A week later, I heard a knock on the door. That is how prayer works. I had doubted God's directions for me here with Owen and Martha, and I prayed to you, dear Jesus, hanging there as you are, not saying much, and to you, Holy Mary with the dove on your shoulder, looking like you were taking my predicament as no more serious than a blister on my foot. Yes, that's what I thought. But in fact, you had both been worrying over my concerns that there was something fishy going on, and if I'd paid more attention, I would have seen that concern on your faces, for there at the door stood a slight man with piercing blue eyes and thinning brown hair, dressed in a white suit with a white shirt and a black tie and black shoes who said, My name is Mr. Knight. Bishop Humphries told me your doctor would not prescribe narcotics strong enough to handle the pain, and without the pills you can't look after your two foster children.

Mr. Knight handed me a bottle of — not pills but what looked like little wooden buttons. He said, Stronger than oxycodone, Sister Charlotte. And they won't break down the pathways to your brain like oxy does, and they can't be traced in your bloodstream, if ever you're tested by CFCS.

I must have looked a little stunned for he said, Let me step in, Sister, so I can explain.

I didn't let him step in. Peter was driving his taxi, and Martha was at school, and Owen was off in the clouds somewhere, so I was alone.

I said, Who is paying for these, whatever they are?

There's no charge for you, Sister Charlotte. Bishop Humphries will pay.

This smelled more than fishy. I said, He's a bishop. He has no money.

This little man in this ridiculous outfit was starting to annoy me. My father would say, There is no such thing as a free lunch. This man, Mr. Knight, is after something.

If you won't tell me where the money is from, I don't want these, whatever they are. What are they?

May I come in and sit down, Sister?

I wanted nothing to do with this strange white creature and was about to send him away when, I don't know, maybe something about that white suit made me lead Mr. Knight into the living room. I pointed to the chair.

Mr. Knight folded one white leg over one white knee. He adjusted his black tie and wiped a spot of dust off one black shoe. He said, I sat for months with my wife, a devoted Catholic, who was dying from a terminal illness. The doctor told her there were no medications available that would both control the pain and at the same time allow her to function. Near the end the doctor refused her strong enough medication to relieve her pain and let her die in comfort. This was up in the North. Medical services were limited. Having no choice, I changed from her quiet unassuming husband to her knight in white armour, injecting her with a cactus-bud narcotic that I bought off the street. The cactus buds gave her pain-free function until the RCMP cut off the supply. My wife died a cruel death.

After my wife died, I took a pilgrimage to the source of this drug, a community in remote Central Africa known as the Terminals. To get to this community, I travelled by raft, propelled by what looked like a makeshift tablecloth, up a river into the jungle. The Terminals lived in little houses with dirt floors. They spent their remaining days in functional pain-free bliss, smoking the cactus buds that contained this illegal ingredient. They lived on goat stew flavoured with medicinal herbs and cooked in a pot over the open fire.

With a bag full of cactus buds, I went into the desert to meditate. I wandered barefoot for forty days, no maps, guidebooks, or passport; intestines filled with parasites from eating goat stew; sometimes standing for hours one-legged on my balance point; flies crawling across my eyes wide open in blank meditation; collapsing finally in the dirt, falling into a deep sleep, a stone for a pillow, the stars for a roof.

And then, upon awakening, I had an epiphany, and the rapture broke upon me, and I received direct instructions explaining the reason for my earthly mission. I didn't join the Terminals. I didn't gather with them to eat goat stew and smoke buds around a plain wooden table covered with a linen cloth embroidered with the cactus-bud symbol. I came home to minister to the Terminals in my own country the cactus buds that would give them time to complete, in peace and comfort, what needs to be completed here in their sojourn on earth. But this does not go on forever. The body gives out eventually, but at least they're not comatose with a pee bag and diapers in a hospital purgatory. So, when their time is up, they receive a final visit from me. They say, 'Goodnight, Mr. Knight,' and I put them to sleep. For a price, of course.

He handed me the pills. Paid for by the Catholic Church. Both Owen and Martha are Vat Babies, Sister Charlotte, children fathered by the clergy and hidden in the CFCS. The father of both Owen and Martha is Bishop Humphries. Of course, for the sake of the both the children and the church, this information must be kept secret.

Chapter 12

OWEN

Like an Elvis sighting, slipping in without a sound, it seemed, without even a door opening, revealing himself suddenly, appearing bones and marrow dressed in white, in stepped a slim man with thinning hair and a thin black tie and shiny black shoes. There he was, sitting in the living room with Sister Charlotte, handing her a package.

I think often about Mr. Knight's arrival that morning. It was late spring. I was in grade seven. I remember at the time wondering if Mr. Knight was an actual sighting or a spirit sighting, and whether it was an actual Mr. Knight talking to an actual Sister Charlotte or an imagined Sister Charlotte talking to an imagined Mr. Knight. Like the difference for me when I'm looking through a microscope, first from this end seeing the picture in this dimension and then from the other end seeing the same picture in another dimension, and then there, in a lightbulb moment in between dimensions, in that moment of discovery, I'll hear in the swish-swish of the neonatal doors soft whispers from my upside-down sister. But not in words.

Sister Charlotte and Mr. Knight were in the living room and I was in the kitchen, so I didn't hear any words. But I didn't need words to know there was something upside down about Mr. Knight all dressed in white with a black tie and black shoes.

As the clacks in Morse code follow one after another to some predetermined destination, the visits from Mr. Knight would follow one after another to some predetermined end. First I would hear the swish-swish of the neonatal doors and then, out of nowhere, Mr. Knight would appear in Sister Charlotte's living room. After each sighting, Sister Charlotte would sit staring at her open Bible, as though she already knew that Mr. Knight, not Jesus, would soon be turning her pages.

***

Sunday afternoon, Peter not driving his taxi, we gathered in the television room to watch a movie. Martha sat down, and I sat down. Peter pressed the remote, and there on the movie channel was the repeat of the *Dead Sea Scrolls* movie we'd already seen. Peter flipped channels to find something else.

I noticed Martha had stopped watching the TV and was leaning forward, her head turned to one side, her shoulders upside down almost, as she stared out the little window at the rectangular faraway patch of blue sky above the crematorium chimney. I tilted my head so that I could look out the little window at the upside-down sky to see if I could see what Martha saw. Usually, it didn't matter if the sky was right side up or upside down, it always looked the same, and the chimney always looked the same. But not the smoke coming out of the chimney. To me each person seemed to make a different smoke. These different smokes made me curious about what was up there above the church spires, where the smoked dead hung out, warming themselves on a chilly day while they waited for the upwind thermals to fly them into the stratosphere. I thought, I'll ask Peter. Maybe we can set up a telescope on the veranda roof and I can make connections with my sister.

The thing is, when one twin dies, the other feels only half there. Half is gone. But the gone half is still there, like a shadow. I think it must have taken a long time before someone found me and my sister because I kept getting signals, you know, from the smoke above The Chimney. I don't know what chimney, maybe all the chimneys together, a Supreme Chimney, its Supreme Smoke filling me with feelings of dead and alive going backward and forward from one to the other, me and my sister, like banana and yogurt in a blender with a reverse gear, together then separate then together, back and forth.

The thing is, I had all those feelings every time I saw Mr. Knight. But since they weren't normal feelings, like feeling sorry for Sister Charlotte, her white face, her limping around, sometimes sitting at the kitchen table sucking her thumb to ease her pain at the tail end of a pill, I could not explain those feelings to anyone, not that anyone would care. Maybe that's why the feelings wouldn't go away. They hung around like drones hovering in the wavelength patterns of the different smokes coming out of one chimney.

A cloudy, misty day in early October, I short-cutted home from school through the tombstones and the statues and climbed the black iron fence around the chapel. Peeking in the window, I could see the steep staircase leading to the tall belfry. I jimmied the window and climbed in and sat in one of the pews and waited. Pretty soon, sure enough, I heard the soft footsteps at the door. I turned. There before me stood Martha. She looked exactly the same as the last time I looked at Martha, except she was taller and thinner now, dressed in tight blue jeans and tight blue t-shirt, looking older than the last time I looked at her, which was an hour ago. When she reached up to swat a mosquito on one cheek, I saw that she was wearing blue eye shadow like Shelly wore, and I saw that her thumb had a blue nail, like Big Joe sometimes got from hitting it with a hammer. But then I noticed all her nails were blue, like Big Joe had hit all his nails with a hammer.

She sat beside me. "Eye shadow. So what? Nail polish. So what?"

"You're only thirteen years old."

"So I take it off before I go home."

"That blue makes me think of my sister floating around in the blue sky above the chimney, watching over me."

"She's watching you at the back of the cemetery near the pond when you piddle pictures into the puddles after a rain. She said to tell you it's okay to catch bugs in a cemetery but not okay to pee in a cemetery."

I don't know. The things I do, catching bugs to let them die in jars and peeing into puddles. But at least I don't paint my fingernails and eyes blue.

Chapter 13

MARTHA

For my grade nine religious assignment, I watched a special broadcast from the Catholic Gospel Centre in Scarborough. Sister Charlotte and Owen joined me. The pope's voice, dubbed into eleven languages, talked about children falling on stony ground in blighted Africa. The television screen showed the fallen children with eyes filled with stony-ground loneliness staring out at the mothers and fathers seated in leather-chaired living rooms, eating snacks prepared in kitchens full of groceries. So what do you tink about that, Marta, all those starving children?

Shrug, sniffle, I guess I have to tink up something.

"Nothing so moves me to grief as the shame of a starving child," said Sister Charlotte. Then her eyes grew cloudy and she stared at her hands resting in her lap.

I asked, "What's the matter, Sister?"

"Those starving children, Martha."

"You want my opinion, Sister Charlotte? There's no sign of God over there in Africa, is my opinion."

Owen said, "Starving children are sprouting up like weeds in the stony ground all over the place, even on the other side of the moon, not just in Africa."

"Africa is not on the dark side of the moon, dimwit. Africa is over there where the sun shines twenty-four hours a day, so yeah, on a nice spring morning, all the mothers of those starving children need to do is go out the back door and pick a banana. Or if there are no bananas, hop on the bus and get a job at the Holiday Inn. That's my opinion."

Owen said, "It doesn't matter how much food you send, they'll need more. No one wants children anymore, but they keep on coming, and I hope they don't send more here or send me there. That's my opinion."

"Were you a starving child in Africa, Sister? Is that why you feel sorry for the starving children?"

"No, Martha. I was a very lucky child. At sixteen, two years older than you, Martha, I was barely five feet tall and still looked like a little girl in a storybook. By sixteen, my voice had developed like two voices side by side, a little girl voice and an adult voice. I sang songs about Jesus even before I knew what the words meant. Sometimes I didn't understand the words that came to me, and everyone thought I was singing about the Descent of the Dove, but I didn't know what that meant. They dressed me up in white, pure as a virgin, but I didn't know what that meant. Imagine me in a little white dress and blue knee socks on the stage they built especially for me at St. Michael's in downtown North Bay."

Even after listening fifty times to how Sister Charlotte used to be, I could not imagine how she could have changed to how she was. Sarah, yes. She would have been a little girl like Sister described. If Sarah told me such a story, I would have felt warm at the thought of me when I got older and lost some weight being like her. While Sarah had made me feel warm, Sister Charlotte made me feel a cold chill, like the fan blowing in the bathroom when I got out of the shower.

Owen got some stuff off the internet and wrote me up a paper on foreign aid to Africa. At the bottom of the page, the teacher wrote, "Brilliant." Then in brackets, "Did you get help from Owen?"

The next day was Halloween. Peter decided we should dress up as the Dead Sea people in that movie, with me wearing a print dress and bonnet.

I said, "Duh, Peter, I think we're too old for trick or treating."

But when Peter got out the baby clothes and carriage from a long time ago and dressed Petunia up as a Dead Sea monk baby, and showed me all the odd stuff from the secondhand store he'd got, shawls and long dresses and bonnets, I said, "Well, okay, maybe."

Each house had pumpkins carved into toothy jack-o-lanterns, some with candles scorching smoke in our faces as we waited our turn with the ghosts and goblins carrying enormous shopping bags. Peter lifted the carriage up on the porch so the neighbours could peek in at baby lying on her back, smiling as handsome as Toad of Toad Hall from *The Wind in the Willows*, her short legs kicking and stumpy tail thumping at all the attention.

"Don't give her any candy," I said.

I had the most fun ever. And I was thirteen years old.

Chapter 14

OWEN

My head was home to a wonderland of curiosities to find answers for, either by looking through microscopes, peeking through keyholes, or reading ladies' fingers. Sorting garbage was not my choice, but Sister Charlotte had given me the job.

So when I found an empty Betty Crocker Angel Food cake box, I checked out the ingredients to try and find out what might be in the angel food batter that, when mixed with the pills Mr. Knight was feeding Sister Charlotte, would cause her jawbones to click and pop and clack while she was eating a fresh-baked slice. I had added up the clacks in each bite to see if I could get a Morse code pattern, like reading fingers and discovering those ladies went to bed on their first date. I knew Sister Charlotte didn't go to bed with Mr. Knight on their first date or on any other date, but I did learn by reading those clacks that Sister Charlotte might end up in bed with Mr. Knight eventually. This had to be true because it was impossible to imagine.

Deciphering her thoughts by unscrambling clack patterns seemed like a cleaner way of getting information than sorting through the garbage and separating bits and pieces of paper from the ketchup blobs and tuna fish cans and eggs shells. But that is what happened. Martha was cleaning up the angel food dessert dishes and I was looking through the garbage for the angel food box, when I found two ripped-up letters, one from Bella to Sister Charlotte and the other from Timothy to me.

Timothy, who still lived in North Bay, wanted to know if in two years, when we turned sixteen, since we were foster brothers, would I help him kill Big Joe, who lived down in Toronto now, and he,

Timothy, had his address. I wrote back, "Okay, let me know." Like, to humour him. Timothy had FAS, so his brain was totally scrambled back when he lived with Big Joe and was probably worse by now.

The letter from Bella, including a return address, wondered if she could meet her daughter, Martha. What I felt in the swish-swishing of those two letters, reading the one from wee Timothy in my left hand and the one from Martha's mother in the right, was as clear as a road sign for dangerous curves ahead.

In foster care language, Be careful when your mother shows up wanting to be a real mother. In foster care language, Be careful when a foster brother shows up wanting to be a real brother.

I took the subway and the streetcar to Bella's basement apartment on Gwynne Ave. Creeping along the alley between the two houses and looking in the basement windows, I found Bella sitting at the kitchen table in her dressing gown, her face a little puffy, like my foster mother Bobbie's had been, the rest of her twice as fat as Bobbie. She was eating a slice of toast. I wanted to tap on the window and say, "You know what, Mom? I had toast with your daughter just an hour ago. It looks like the same toast."

And it was; on the counter I saw Weston's Brown Bread. A different toaster, though. I wanted to say, It looks like you've gained a little weight, Mom. Looks like your eyes have a bit of a droop, Mom. Looks like your hair needs a bit of a wash, Mom. Looks like your chin has a bit of a sag, Mom.

Mother of Martha finished her toast, but instead of taking the plate to the sink and rinsing it and putting it in the dishwasher, as daughter Martha would do, she left it on the table, which was already covered with dirty plates and glasses and empty beer bottles. She opened a bottle of whisky and poured some into her coffee cup. I left her sitting there in the middle of a kitchen, drinking her whisky, staring off, like she was waiting for Mr. Knight.

As I was walking along, heading for the subway, looking back, I thought I saw a black limousine pulling up, and Mr. Knight stepping out, dressed in his white suit and white shirt and black tie and shiny black shoes. I guessed he probably had white socks and white underwear and a white watchband trimmed with black and, who knows, white mitts trimmed in black to wear on a white winter day. But I was a block away and my glasses were tilted sideways on my nose, so who knows what I saw.

Martha would shrug, sniffle. Right, Owen, you see all kinds of stupid stuff, like you're a bottomless pit of stupid stuff, so tell me what my mother really looked like. Swish-swish, don't think so.

Chapter 15

SISTER CHARLOTTE

Dressed in his white suit with matching white shirt and black tie, Mr. Knight greeted me at the door of his tenth-floor apartment two blocks from the subway. He wouldn't deliver his buds to my door anymore because, in his words, "Owen is a curious little fellow. Too curious."

I followed him into a small but tidy living room. He offered me tea. We sat across from one another, me on the chesterfield and Mr. Knight in the matching chair.

"Life, in itself, is very simple, Sister, a theory that every child in kindergarten knows and understands. Number one: Everything that happens is supposed to happen. Otherwise, it would not have happened. Number two: If there's a happen there must be a Happener, namely the mover that is in charge of the laws of movement, the cause-and-effect process underlying *happen*. This, of course, is a rudimentary form of design theory because, no matter what way you put it, either there's design or there's chaos. And if there's design, there must be a designer, what we would now call *intelligent cause*."

"Mr. Knight, I'm here for my pills."

"John's Gospel, Sister Charlotte. In the beginning was The Word. But in the original Greek it's written as 'In the beginning was Logos.'"

"My Logos is reminding me I have a taxi waiting."

"Are you not interested in the rest of my explanation, Sister Charlotte?"

"Of course. As long as it doesn't take you ten hours to get to it. Have you no friends that you need me to talk to?"

"Something we need to discuss, Sister. The one who is paying me for your pills is Bishop Humphries. He wants to thank you for the care you're giving Martha and Owen. He wants to thank you for your years of service with those Indigenous boys in the north."

I should not have let Mr. Knight get started. It would take him two days to get to what he wanted to say, and I needed a pill now, this minute.

"Bishop Humphries would like you to pay a visit to Martha's mother, Bella."

My knees were throbbing and I was anxious to get home. "I barely knew Bella — and that was years ago. Tears ago. Those poor Indigenous boys. If you're going to tell me what this is about, get on with it."

"I don't have any particulars but it's about the upcoming trial of Father Eagleman. When I get more details, I can fill you in. But a word from the wise: The past is unpredictable. Do you agree, Sister Charlotte?"

"I have a taxi waiting, Mr. Knight."

***

I got up and went to my bathroom for a glass of water. One bud every four hours, the directions say. But time does not take into account the weather, and it's a cold, damp evening. I took two more and returned to my bed. After a while, I began to drift.

I like to focus on my picture of Jesus and then lie with my eyes closed, not to go to sleep but to be alone with Him. My head is on the pillow just in case, but normally, I stay awake. Sometimes I focus on the picture of the Virgin Mary, on the white dove with black legs, feet extended to land on the white shawl covering her shoulder.

My father had white homing pigeons that he kept in the same shed where Peter keeps his gardening equipment. No, no, not that shed. My Heavens, if my father were here he'd say, You're getting under my skin, Charlotte, the way you're mixing everything up. But, yes, passionate about pigeons: tumblers, fantails, and homers. He especially liked homing pigeons. When you release them, he'd say, they circle first to get their bearings. If there's a headwind, they fly high up above it. No one knows how they find their way. They navigate without the sun, flying so high they can see where everything is. They can go a hundred kilometres an hour, faster if they ride the thermals, and go as far as a thousand kilometres, farther when they ride the thermals.

Why am I telling you about pigeons? Because it's not right, Lord Jesus, giving me the arthritis that makes me take pills that make my mind wander from thinking about the Virgin's white dove into thinking about my father's white pigeons. But I know, if Bishop Humphries wasn't covering for me, the CFCS would have declared me unfit and taken away my children by now, taken away the pulse of my life, taken away my purpose. Although, if that meant giving up the only meds strong enough to control the pain, I could do that. I could endure the pain. But it's the panic in my brain that overtakes me when I'm reminded of Dr. Rebeneck's official diagnosis that I can't endure. When he took me off the oxys he said, This is not rheumatoid arthritis, Sister Charlotte. This is Huntington's disease. I'm referring you to a specialist.

But ahh, that's better. Feel it. Full speed ahead on the freeway spindle from the stomach to the bloodstream to the brain, and ahh, yes, Mr. Knight, I open my eyes to another lovely day. I love the smell of daybreak. I saw on television that dogs can be trained to smell diseases in your body, like cancer and diabetes. A Methodist pastor in Louisiana has trained his border collie to smell the Holy Spirit in certain Bibles, which he sells at a premium on the internet. I don't need a dog to tell me the Holy Spirit is in my Bible. In fact, just the other day, I opened a page quite at random, quite by accident, Mr. Knight, to Matthew chapter ten, and I read the words of Jesus: If anyone gives even a glass of water to one of these little ones, great will be their reward in Heaven. Well, Mr. Knight, I have given cups of water to Martha and to Owen when their mothers did not, so I'm now looking forward to my reward in Heaven. Imagine Martha's mother sending me the letter saying she wants to meet Martha and get to know her. And who did she get our address from? You, Mr. Knight?

It wasn't right giving Peter a brain and in this brain a memory that doesn't remember anything. That's like giving socks to someone with no legs, a bad idea because how would you feel, Mr. Knight, if you had to write Peter little Post-It memory-jogger notes with arthritic fingers: Peter, don't forget this. Peter, don't forget that. Double punishment, that's what — and not fair. Besides, all these notes thrown into the garbage are a waste of paste and paper and money. Plus, most of the time, he can't remember to read them.

I know, I know. Peter and the three monkeys. Of course, the children love him. He makes everything fun and leaves me to do the discipline, run the house, enforce the rules. That would have been okay, dear Jesus, if God had not given me Huntington's. I know, I know. God is not fickle. He saw that I needed to be stronger so that I can continue to look after these children, and He sent you, Mr. Knight. And if He sees that I need even stronger drugs, He will give me stronger drugs. It's not rocket science.

I love the smell of my leather-bound Bible. I saw on television that dogs — did I already mention that about the Methodist pastor in Louisiana? It was in the news. Or was it that Rebecca Brown woman who married Satan, who wore a white suit and a black tie and rented a Presbyterian church for the wedding. It was in the news. I don't know what that's called when you watch the news and identify with the person they're talking about. Not long ago in the news, a daughter smothered her mother lying in the nursing home, crying out in excruciating pain. They called the daughter an angel of mercy. What do they call a man angel of mercy?

The doorbell is ringing.

"Bishop Humphries. At least you ring the bell. When Mr. Knight arrives at my door, he walks right in. He has so many customers now that he carries a wire-bound book to keep track of his accounts. He doesn't ring the doorbell and he doesn't knock and there he is, his ledger book open, as though I owe him money."

The bishop seemed startled. "What do you mean owe him money? You're not paying him are you?"

"Of course not. Why would I? I'm just doing my job."

"Your job, Sister…" The bishop glanced around and shifted his feet. "Your job has become very complicated. The Catholic foster care scandals. Eagleman and the boys from Snowy River. I'm not the CEO of foster care but I might as well be. The church is trying to blame me for everything. But the church was the one that made the ruling that the wafer must be made from wheat."

"These things are sent to test us, Bishop Humphries."

The bishop glanced toward the kitchen. "Are Owen and Martha here or at school?"

"At school. They'll be home at four."

He stood closer and said softly, "One thing, Sister. You knew Joe Radley, I think?"

"He taught those boys handyman skills."

"Yes, I think so. Well, Sister, the Eagleman trial is coming up. I might need your help."

The Bishop left. I went back to my room and climbed into my bed. I remembered the Good Friday I attended Father Eagleman's Room for Private Religious Instruction. Father Eagleman was a black belt. He took each boy in separately. The boy I witnessed looked about seven. He wore glasses with a crack in one lens. Father Eagleman sat the boy down in a school desk and placed the open Bible before him. Read with me, boy, read this passage here. It's your turn. Easter Sunday, imagine the scene, at first, bright as summer noon, but then the clouds thicken, with no winter sun, and for nine hours our Saviour hangs in the frigid dark on the ice-covered cross, reaching out only one time for a single glass of melted ice.

I can't read, Father. It's too dark in here.

You can read. If the light is strong enough for Jesus to watch you from his cross to make sure you're not having pot-smoking thoughts, it's strong enough for you to read his words. But all right, you little snot, I'll put in a brighter bulb if you wish. There you are. Look at the page and read the words.

My word, it's raining again. The kids are back from school, clomping around in the kitchen, their wet clothes dripping water all over everything. Here comes Owen, clumping up the stairs.

I dreamed of him the other night, the sound of his boots became the footsteps of you, Mr. Knight, clumping down the stairs, out into the rain-filled cemetery to disappear into the crematorium, your white suit a grey shadow on the chimney that I was coming out of. I woke up in a sweat.

Oh, there's Peter now. He will have sent for a pizza, not remembering that he had pizza two days ago, pizza twice in one week with the pizza boxes still sitting on the floor where I'll trip over them. Forgive me, Father God, for thinking these thoughts, but Peter needs to learn that now, with this business with you, Mr. Knight, appearing any time you want, and Bishop Humphries arriving any time he wants, and the police looking for Bella any time they want, and now some sort of trial for The Eagle anytime they want, we should be keeping the doors locked against this anytime they want.

If you don't have a lock, Peter, you can't lock anyone out. But if you have a lock you need to look after your keys. You can't have an unlocked lock without having an effect, like CFCS taking away my children and oh, my Heavens, here they come, squish-squish their soggy feet on the steps, squish-squish their wet shoes along the hall to their rooms. Forgive me, God, for having selfish thoughts, but it doesn't seem fair that as well as everything else, does it always have to be raining?

Here you are, Sister Charlotte. Let me help you up. Doubled over on knees too bent to walk, here I am helping you up, helping you to the bathroom, helping you take another bud, and helping you take another glass of water.

The hand of Mr. Knight reaches out to me. The hand of Virgin Mary reaches out to me. The hand of Jesus reaches out to me. This trinity of hands turns on the tap and hand in hand together, Jesus and Mary and Mr. Knight bring the glass to my lips. It is a simple gesture, but conveying to my mouth a feeling far greater than the act, not unlike the simple gesture of God placing his palm on my forehead, and saying, There, there, Sister Charlotte, this is meant to be.

And then shoosh, feel it. Full speed ahead on the freeway spindle from the stomach to the bloodstream to the brain and ahh, yes, Mr. Knight, I open my eyes to another lovely day.

"Sister Charlotte. Why are you out here kneeling on the floor?"

Martha helped me up.

"Sister Charlotte, are you stoned again? What's the matter with you?"

"I'm fine, Martha. I was having a nap."

"On your hands and knees on the floor? Look at you."

"I was looking for my watch. What time is it?"

"Your watch is on your wrist. The other wrist. Careful you don't trip. Lie down. No, no, not there. Over here. Take off your watch and lie down and sleep it off."

"Do you know what, Martha? Uncle Merv had a brother who died when he accidentally cut off his left arm with the backhoe. At night, he liked to get up out of his coffin and wander around looking for his watch, which he wore on his left arm. But he couldn't find his arm because he had no eyes, just dark sockets where his eyes used to be. If you drove into the cemetery after midnight, he'd knock on your car window and ask, 'Have you seen my arm?' You see, he had things backward. First he should go looking for his eyes, and when he found his eyes, he could find his arm and then he would find his watch."

"Duh, Sister Charlotte. Without eyes how did he know when it was time to come out to knock on car windows?"

"He listened for the clock in the belfry, and when it struck twelve, he'd get up and start wandering the lanes, knocking on car windows, asking if—"

"Right, I know. Have you seen my left arm? I've never seen any arms in the cemetery. Maybe the rats ate it. There's lots of rats around there. The cemetery is full of them. Take off your shoes first."

"I think that story is not true, Martha. How could he be looking for his arm or his eyes or his watch if he was dead?"

"Stand up straight so I can unfasten your dress."

"Yes, he was dead. When he died, Uncle Merv got his toothbrush back."

"And what did Uncle Merv think of that?"

"Uhhh, well, he thought he'd seen the end of that toothbrush but after the funeral, he found it in his brother's stuff."

"Wow. That was lucky."

"I think there was something wrong with Uncle Merv. There was a gas leak in his stove, I think."

Chapter 16

MARTHA

What's wit Sister Soviet Union, Marta? Curtains hanging straight, towels folded proper, pots stacked just right, a mad Molly Maid who sleeps in her clothes so that in the morning all she has to do the moment her eyes blink open and her day's plan of chasing the dog hair in her head pops up — but you don't have a dog, Marta. You'll end up wearing her flat black shoes if you don't get out of there and come back wit me. Living here with me, Marta, was like living the dream, crumbs on the carpet, dirty dishes in the sink, the dining-room clock telling an incorrect time to not start whatever chore was not next. So the dog stinks. So what?

Shrug, sniffle, shuffle.

What's wit Sister Soviet Union, Marta? An hour to do your bedrooms, and without even being there, Sister KGB can watch and, at the end of the hour, appear in the doorway to inspect. Structure and discipline for the wards of the state, Marta, add to that laundry and vacuum and polish, followed by walkie walkie the guard dog, so what if it stinks.

Shrug, sniffle. Well, Gretta, that's why he sticks his head out the window while we're driving along in your filthy car.

What's wit this Brother Fruitcake, Marta? Has he got a gas leak in his stove? I tink you should keep blinds down and curtains closed, so people can't see in from the street.

Well, Gretta, there was a gas leak in the Open Hatch drop box. It was on the sidewalk next to the mailbox, so if you had a letter, you put it in the red box, and if you had a baby, you put it in the green Open

Hatch box, but see it was winter and the box was heated with gas — not the mailbox, the other box, see — the Open Hatch box had a gas leak.

Such nonsense, Marta. They wouldn't put the baby box next to the mailbox.

Shrug, sniffle, probably not.

For sure not, Marta. Those babies get adopted.

Duh. Shrug, sniffle, well maybe some woman as she dropped in a letter got a shiver of guilt because it's, like, winter so she started thinking about an imaginary life with a baby, what toys a baby will like, what cute little outfits she can buy, what relatives will come to say ooh and aah. So she opened the green box and took out a baby. I think she read somewhere that if you took a baby, the social worker from the Children's Aid would deliver a lot of good free stuff, like bottles, formula, soother, snuggles, blankie — all meant to plant in the babyless mother's brain the mommy thoughts she needs so as to not puke when she changes the diaper.

In my case, if you're interested, Gretta, which you aren't — that dog stinks by the way — Al and Fran's baby had died, see, and they couldn't have another. Well, what happened, one day Fran went out to mail a letter. But because a dog had lifted its leg against the letter box, she tried to put the letter into the baby box. But, like, the baby box was built like the mailbox but opposite. So when she lifted out me, the baby, to put in the letter, she couldn't put me, the baby, back.

What a story, Marta. Where would such a crazy story come from?

Shrug, sniffle, Owen probably. When I first met him, he had a whole library of invented stories to explain why he ended up a foster kid, all of them stupid: the name on his armband got mixed up and instead of being placed in the nursery with the regular babies with real parents, he got posted on Kijiji, Free to Good Home, to wait for let's-pretend parents with their starter kits to take baby Owen home to be a pretend son in the pretend family. Or he got put into the pet store with meowing kittens waiting to be adopted, hoping someone would take a baby instead. Or he got put in a baby store with babies lined up on shelves dressed in either blue or pink snugglies, the storekeeper saying, Pick whatever one you want and if you don't like it, bring it back.

Which most foster parents did when the baby they thought would be a nice decoration to show their friends became inconvenient and too much work.

One day I asked him, Do you know what really happened to your parents, Owen? And tell me the truth.

He said, My parents drowned.

Well, how did you know that? Who told you? You got left in Open Hatch.

My dead sister told me.

And how did your dead sister tell you — and don't say she told you when you were hanging out in Open Hatch.

He said, I have this tank, and when I look into the water clouded with algae, I imagine my parents' algae-covered bones at the bottom of the lake, strings of green slime swaying and floating in the underwater currents, fish nibbling their bones clean, like bugs in the cemetery nibbling clean the bones of my parents in their coffin.

The lies we tell ourselves about our mothers and fathers to make ourselves feel better about living in the foster system with dogs that smell and gas leaks in its stoves and bugs in our bedrooms.

Chapter 17

SISTER CHARLOTTE

Mr. Knight said, "I was raised a Catholic, the church central to my carefree days of childhood. I attended Sunday school. I became an altar boy. But when I got older, I started to read church history and learned about the Catholic atrocities. Pope Paul the Third, for example. He loved to watch the witches burn at the stake, the flames licking up to their knees, the naked bodies turning black, his hand to his heart while he sprinkled holy water on himself. When I read this, I thought, did he wonder which one might have been carrying a baby? Did the pope think of that, sending the baby to Hell with the mother when the baby hadn't done anything?"

"I know church history, Mr. Knight. Much not to be proud of."

"History is nothing more than the dominant lie told by the winners."

"If you'll just give me my buds. I have a taxi waiting." I didn't want to listen to Mr. Knight's ramblings. I pointed to the buds sitting on the kitchen counter. "I like the new ones. They give me energy when I need it and let me relax when I need to relax."

But Mr. Knight continued, "The Catholics had interesting ideas about protecting the faith. For example, the priest would give the wafer to the one suspected of being unfaithful and ask, 'Is this the body of Christ?' and if the answer was no, he would be referred to the pope for execution. Pope Paul the Fourth, 1555, complained that the infidels he executed didn't scream loud enough, so he experimented with different methods: drowning, hanging, beheading, drawing and quartering, pressing under stones. He found burning to be the most effective. He liked to close his eyes and, in the screams of the infidel and the roar of the fire, listen to the voice of the Holy Spirit."

Something about this fact caught my attention. I said to Mr. Knight, "Come to think of it, sitting on Peter's green bench watching the smoke coming out of the crematorium chimney, when I close my eyes, I too seem to hear most clearly the voice of the Holy Spirit."

"The buds will do that to you, Sister Charlotte. When I had my epiphany, and the rapture broke upon me, I heard the voice of the Holy Spirit, who gave me direct instructions explaining the reason for my earthly mission, and here I am and here you are and here we are, fulfilling our earthly mission."

"Those last ones were much better, Mr. Knight." I pointed to them, sitting there, waiting.

"Have a chair, Sister Charlotte. We need to have a talk about our earthly mission."

"I have a taxi waiting."

"You always have a taxi waiting. This time it's going to have to wait. Have a seat. You don't have to do anything but listen."

I sat where he pointed.

"I read about Tomas de Torquemada, born 1420, appointed grand inquisitor by Pope Sixtus the Fourth. As a member of the Knights of Malta, Tomas was responsible for burning two thousand witches. In other words, murder, an extreme form of protecting the faith, has been practised by the Catholic Church for centuries: the inquisitions, burning at the stake, mass slaughters of the Muslims. But Torquemada was extreme. He burned ten thousand two hundred heretics and added to that the two thousand witches he burned during the witch craze. The Witch's Hammer, they called him. He wrote a book explaining to the clergy how to locate, torture, and destroy the witches. He explained how the stake was to be erected, how alternating layers of straw and wood and leaves should be piled around it. The witch had to be stripped of her clothes and dressed in loose sackcloth. You needed a passage through the pile of wood for her to walk through, and space for her to stand while being fastened with chains to the stake. Then you filled the space with more straw and sticks.

"But those days, like my carefree days of childhood and your carefree days of the convent, are unfortunately over. Nowadays, no burning of the heretics and the infidels, no censoring of books, movies, or that smut on the internet. But the faith still needs protection, Sister Charlotte, not overtly as in the old days, but covertly, like the FBI. How many times has the FBI covered up the affairs of their presidents? The CIA as well. It's no mistake that the Central Intelligence Agency and the Catholic Investigative Agency both have the same initials, both kept busy in the recent past hiding the indiscretions of presidents and priests.

"Then I heard about Opus Dei, the Vatican group with close ties to the Knights of Malta, a secret society to protect the faith. As I said, the church's version of the CIA. Opus Dei had been trying for many years to take control of the Vatican. They were responsible for the death of the reformer, Pope John Paul the First, and the election of the Opus Dei supporter John Paul the Second."

I was feeling uncomfortable. I was growing suspicious.

"The job of Opus Dei was to promote and safeguard the doctrines and morals of the faith throughout the Catholic world. What the church taught, the church defended. To defend the Catholic world, Opus Dei defended the clergy. For that reason, everything which in any way touched matters of the clergy fell within the interests of a branch of Opus Dei called the Secret Society for the Protection of the Faith."

I got up and went to the living-room window to look down into the street.

"I am nameless and faceless, a middle-aged gentleman, medium height and medium weight, a little balding, a nobody, much like millions of other nobodies living in a million other high-rise buildings. You could say I look more like a collarless priest than the CIA-style operative that I seem to have become."

There were no police cars parked anywhere, no rough-looking, plainclothes officer pretending to fix a fire hydrant, waiting for the signal from the SWAT team commander.

I returned to my history lesson with Mr. Knight. He came over to stand before me. His piercing blue eyes looked directly into mine. He put on such a serious expression I thought he was going to say, I'm a CIA operative, Sister Charlotte.

My heart began to race, and I felt faint.

"Bishop Humphries has asked me to have this conversation with you. The boys from Snowy River will become another billion-dollar scandal. The church must be protected, which means Bishop Humphries must be protected."

At that moment, I knew what was coming. I put my arm across my chest so that Mr. Knight could not see the sudden pounding in my chest.

"The reason for my lesson in Church history was so that I wouldn't have to suffer through your displays of self-righteous indignation when, first of all, I remind you that Bishop Humphries is the father of both your children, both Martha and Owen, and if he's proven to be complicit in the Snowy River trial, you will lose the children. So, Sister Charlotte, he's asking you to save the children and himself and the Church by lying in court."

"For Heaven's sake, Mr. Knight. What are you asking me to do? Lie about what?"

"First, before I explain further, I don't give a rat's ass about the Catholic Church or about your children. But I do work for whoever pays me. My advice to the bishop was there's no point in trying to fix his situation by putting on Band-Aids, which is like using duct tape to hold the pope's airplane together. This situation with Eagleman and Bishop Humphries and those Snowy River boys can't be fixed with Band-Aids. So here is what you do. When the Father Eagleman trial gets to court, Bishop Humphries wants you to testify that Joe Radley, a.k.a. Joe the Hammer — not Father Eagleman — gave those boys the drugs."

I was more than startled. My Heavens were flattened. For a moment I felt dizzy. "I don't know anything about that."

"Well now you do. Bishop Humphries wants you to take the stand, put your hand on the Bible, and swear to God to tell the truth — and then lie your head off."

"And if I don't?"

"No more children, no more buds, and a bed in a rehab clinic."

The buds were sitting on the kitchen counter, close enough that I could snatch them and run.

"I understand your reluctance, Sister Charlotte. But I have just given you a lesson in Church history to point out to you that telling a few lies pales in comparison to the atrocities of an institution filled with infections that will continue to fester long after you're gone. Where is the bishop getting the money to pay me and to pay his legal fees, you might ask? From the Secret Society for the Protection of the Faith."

"I won't do it. Absolutely not."

"Fruit from the poisoned tree, Sister Charlotte. You'll just be one more sinner in an institution full of sin."

The buds were within my reach but I would not reach for them, because even if I did, there would be no more free buds for me. I said, "Some religions say you must pray five times a day. Do you want me to do the same for the bishop and Father Eagleman? Instead of propping myself up on my pillow, I'll fall on my aching knees and beseechingly repeat my prayers five times a day for the bishop and Father Eagleman. I'll do that, but I will not swear on my Bible to tell the truth and then lie."

"Well then, I'll give you pills strong enough to take the pain from your knees so that you can pray five times a day. If that solves the problem, you won't need to swear on the Bible and lie your head off. But, just in case history repeats itself, Sister Charlotte, and if your name must get added to that long list of sinners in an institution full of sin, then you will put your hand on the Bible and lie your head off."

Mr. Knight's piercing blue eyes demanded an immediate answer and I gave him one: "Ask Bella to do it. She was there. She knew what was going on."

"I've already talked to Bella. She's not in good shape. But if you can convince her to back off the booze and get herself in shape and take your place and lie her head off, that might work. Either way, keep in mind if Humphries goes down, the CFCS will take your children and put them back in the revolving door and put you in rehab to die a slow death from Huntington's."

He handed me the pills. "A month's supply. I think you'll like these. As you say, when you want to get moving, they'll give you a boost. When you want to relax, they'll make you relaxed."

I hurried away and climbed into the waiting cab. Protect Father Eagleman? He was a monster. He knew where to squeeze without leaving a mark. How many times had I seen him use his black-belt training with the children? A word here, read it, boy, a sentence there, read it, boy, a paragraph now, read it, boy, and this page here, read it later, boy, and if you don't, you little snot, did that burn your arm? Like a biting lightning jolt to sear each sacred word, sentence, and paragraph into the minds of each one of you little snots.

I won't do it Mr. Knight. I won't do it, Mr. Jesus. The thought of holding my Bible in a courtroom and lying about that man brings tears to my heart and turns my face red with shame.

From the back seat I asked the driver, "Do you have any water so I can take my pill?" When he turned to hand me the bottle of water, I thought, oh my goodness, Mr. Jesus has sent me the exact help I need. Not only is this man bearing the water for me to swallow the bud but he will tell me how to pray properly five times a day.

He said, "A nicely packaged can of Coca-Cola in the hourglass sand of the Arabian desert is no substitute for a plain bottle of cold water."

He smiled. Then he pulled over to the curb and wrote the instructions on a pad in the front seat.

I settled back with the water. I took the pill. I waited. After a few minutes, the July sun on the taxi window warming my bones, I felt my hourglass turn itself upright and felt the sand begin to run again. This was good water, and these were good buds. If I had taken one at Mr. Knight's, I might have been able to walk home on such a nice day. But then I would have missed meeting this nice Muslim driver.

Back in my bedroom I take another bud. I feel myself begin to drift into the sunlight flooding across my closed eyes. I feel the tightness leaving my face as the bootless and almost naked Mr. Knight comes down from the cross. He strokes my hair, his warm breath on my cheek, saying, Good idea, Sister Charlotte. Five times a day for the next few weeks is better that a lifetime in Hell.

Now Martha clumps down the stairs. Then Owen's footsteps go along the hallway and into the bathroom. His pee hisses into the water. What splashes on the floor will stay until Saturday chores day, when Martha scrubs the tiles with Mr. Clean and puts in the new toilet paper.

"Sister Charlotte. Owen is putting minnows in the toilet tank."

"Well, it is, after all, a waterproof container."

"Not too smart, Sister Charlotte. Everyone hides their drugs in the toilet tank, but no one uses it to grow minnows."

"I'll get going in a minute, Martha. Take the sausage from the freezer and unload the dishwasher."

"Owen was the last one in the washroom, and he won't flush. Look at him. Pee drops on his shoes. And look at what else he did. Soon he's going to start giving them names, like dropping his kids off at school. Are you in there, Sister Charlotte, or am I watching a silent movie? Who do you think looks after the mess he makes? The cleaning fairies? Oh, never mind. What's the use?"

Chapter 18

MARTHA

Every day, after I had done my Sister Charlotte-given chores, usually cleaning the kitchen, I liked to sit at the old-fashioned dining-room table doing jigsaw puzzles from Walmart. Peter had put in the extra leaf to give me more space to spread out the pieces. That's what I was doing the next time Bishop Humphries paid a visit. The sight of him made me want to hide under the table, like he was bending over, tap-tap, on the tabletop, peeking in at me. Hello in there, Martha.

He said, "Well, well, Martha, how is everything going? Fine at school, I hope. Making nice friends? I hear you're in grade ten now."

He stood by the table looking down at me. He was bigger than he looked, too big to fit into a small car, which is why he needed an SUV the size of an airplane to carry him around. Well okay, he was a bishop. From the corner of my eye, I could see his driver dressed in a black suit and black shirt, waiting at the door. Well okay, there was no driver. I thought a bishop should have a driver.

Then, with Sister Charlotte listening, he said, "The Martha in the Bible was a sister of Mary, as you are a sister of Owen."

I corrected him. "Foster sister."

"Yes. But like a real sister."

"Thank you," I said, not knowing why I said that. I hadn't meant to. He hadn't given me anything, hadn't helped me with my puzzle. Well. I do know why. Looking up at his jet-black hair, my eyes sight-lined down to his scowly black jowls to follow the button line of his jacket, down the crease line of his pants to stop at his wide black shoes that were so shiny I could see in them my reflection, and it looked like he was standing on me. So I must have thanked him for not really standing on me.

After Bishop Humphries left, Peter and me sat on the green bench next to the apple tree. Petunia came along, so I took her up on my knee. Usually, I told Peter about my stupid teachers and the stupid kids and the grade ten boys liking the grade nine girls that giggled.

This time, I think because the bishop mentioned Owen being my brother, I opened my cellphone to show him what this so-called brother made me deal with at school. "Owen is an embarrassment. Print on a piece of paper GREEK SALAD and take out the R and you'll describe Owen. Look at this one, Peter, standing at his locker. He's so skinny his clothes hang on him wilted, and his hair sticks up in clumps of carrot slivers that haven't rooted right, and his lopsided glasses hang off his nose like bent salad spoons. Even the cat that lives up the street thinks there's something wrong with him, and something wrong with me because I'm his sister. I tell the kids at school I'm a foster sister, which is not a real sister, but they don't know the difference. Sister is sister."

Peter sighed. He stretched his arms across the back of the bench. "I know. He lives in his own bubble, no different from all those other fifteen-year-old geniuses, which is what he is."

I think to make me feel better, for my fifteenth birthday, two weeks after Owen's, Peter printed pictures taken from his digital camera from when we were ten and eleven, mostly of Petunia and me, printed up nice and pasted in an album that Peter got at the Dollar Store.

Looking back at these photographs of me, I saw an eleven-year-old kid who was a little too sturdy — Owen's words were, "She's carrying a recessive gene for plumpness." Looking back, I saw Owen, who wore those big plastic-rimmed coke-bottle glasses that could sometimes see everything and sometimes see nothing, their plastic arms somehow fastened to satellite ears fastened into red hair that stuck up at the corners even though he combed it thirty-two times every day, his OCD thing. Why would Owen want to look back at pictures of himself? But to me, looking back, Petunia in photographs looked beautiful, and I loved her, something I had never before felt or never before given, until I met Peter.

I wish now, all these years later, sitting on Peter's bench next to the apple tree watching the smoke coming out of the chimney and flatlining into the spires of St. Mary's church, I wish I could have said that word "love" to Peter. Such an important word to never have said.

One time Sister Charlotte showed us some looking-back pictures of when, at eight years old, she sang on the Catholic Gospel Channel's *TV Hour*. She looked like she got to the studio by limousine. She told me about being at the studio. First the makeup lady would comb her blonde hair and do something to highlight her blue eyes. Then the lady would fuss with her little-girl white dress and blue knee socks. Then the taping would begin.

"'Ave Maria,'" said Sister Charlotte. "Even the men running the cameras and the microphones wiped their eyes when I finished. For the next song, the makeup lady fussed some more with my outfit and brushed more blush on my cheeks. The director told me to climb up on a stool and sit so everyone at home could see my knee socks. I held my head the way he said and sang the way he said, and when I finished everyone in the studio clapped and called me an angel."

Not until Sister Charlotte showed us pictures of herself dressed in her blue-and-white private-school uniform, skipping across the yard and dancing through the blue-and-white knee-high flowers of the garden with fresh-trimmed grass around the apple tree, did I realize how much her eyes, which were dying, came alive with her telling of these stories that, I was now beginning to realize, she thought happened in this actual house. I thought, if only she could OD and die right now, believing she was ten years old at home in the same knee-high flowers and in the same fresh-trimmed grass around the same apple tree, and miss all the bad stuff I was seeing in the grey smoke twisting up from the crematorium chimney.

I thought, sitting on Peter's bench looking forward to when I age out of the system — almost there in fact — I will not live anywhere that, when I look out the window, I'll see smoke coming out of the crematorium chimney. I will not marry anyone with stick-up red hair or anyone with snot and black bits all over his hands. I'll marry someone nice, like Peter, and have babies to push in a baby carriage, which is why, when I was a kid, I liked to dress Petunia in baby clothes, practising.

But I would never have silverware that needed laying out and polishing along with those stupid silver tea sets on those more stupid silver trays with those stupid silver round things for the cleaned and pressed napkins for the delicate fingers of guests. What was the point? There never were any guests.

Sister Charlotte would make me lay out the knives and the forks and the spoons on a towel, and while I did all the polishing, if I didn't put back the forks and knives exactly right, Sister Charlotte would say, "You silly goose, Martha. That's not how they go. This isn't how it should be done. I learned this from Sister Elizabeth, in the fullness of time departed now, with her Saviour, released from earthly polishing."

In the fullness of time, departed now, released from earthly polishing. It sounded like a prayer the way Sister Charlotte said it, looking forward to it.

Well, the guests arrived, appearing suddenly in the garden in the late-September afternoon the day after my fifteenth birthday. They showed Sister Charlotte their OPP badges. They stood by the stone fence, looking like suits at an outdoor wedding. The only thing missing was the gardenia in each buttonhole. They strolled into the living room. The one in the grey suit sat in the chair closest to the kitchen, polishing the lenses of his sunglasses the way I'd been polishing the silverware until, in the resulting shine, I could see my reflection. He held his glasses at arm's length to look, but I don't think he could see his reflection. He hadn't spent enough time polishing.

The big one with pockets under his eyes, I remembered his name was Paul, sat on the chesterfield by the front window. The third, an older man, stood by the door. In the middle of the room, looking like the ghost of dead Sister Elizabeth, stood Sister Charlotte.

She pulled herself together and offered coffee and rhubarb squares, served with the freshly polished silverware, which meant I would need to polish again. Sister Charlotte said, "Owen will take your orders for coffee or tea and a rhubarb square. Make your order as complicated as you like. He won't write anything down, but he will remember, and you will get what you requested."

Paul, the big one with the pockets, said, "As you may or may not remember from the last time, my name is Paul. I would like a cup of coffee, three lumps of sugar but no cream, and two rhubarb squares."

Sister Charlotte said, "From Peter's garden, baked by Martha."

She pointed at me. I felt like the kitchen help.

"And brought to you by Martha." Sister Charlotte pointed again. This time I gave a smile and a curtsy so polished I bet it looked like I'd been upstairs rehearsing their arrival. I don't know. Maybe I should have been.

Sister Charlotte said, "If you ask for half a rhubarb square, then that's what you will get. If you ask for two lumps, you will get two lumps. See if I'm not right."

Owen remembered, I cut and poured and delivered, cutesy curtsy, doing the rounds with the silver tray set.

Not using his fork to pick up his rhubarb square, Paul put the whole piece into his mouth. Then, remembering his manners, perhaps because I was watching him, Paul picked up his fork and cut off a bite of his second rhubarb square and put it into his mouth and said, still chewing, "Any visits from Bishop Humphries, Sister Charlotte?" Paul wiped his fingers with his napkin. "Any word from Bella, Sister Charlotte?"

The man standing at the door said, "Bella is around here someplace. I'm well trained in the area of knowing when someone is around here someplace."

Sister Charlotte stalled for a moment longer before coming back with, "What is this about exactly?"

Paul turned his napkin inside out and wiped his fingers. I took the pot and filled his cup. He took the little server creamer from the tray and took two lumps from the silver sugar bowl. When I asked if he would like another rhubarb square, he said, "No, thank you," so I took away his red-smeared plate.

Glancing from me to Sister Charlotte, Paul said, "Perhaps, Sister Charlotte, you and I could talk in private outside."

Sister Charlotte paused. She set down her napkin and her cup.

Paul said, "A nice fall day, Sister. How would you like to show us the back garden?"

Sister Charlotte said, "What is the best that you can give a child, Paul? What else but a strong moral and spiritual foundation to carry each one through life. Isn't that so, Martha?"

Shrug, sniffle. "I guess so."

"There you have it. A testimonial from our foster child, who as the result of being raised in a structure of strict discipline based on the scriptural teachings, has become a model child. Isn't that so, Martha?"

"I guess so."

When Paul glanced at me, I saw above those pockets, concern in his eyes. It was a glance that turned into a look of understanding that said, I know you want to meet your mother and I'll do my best to find her for you. You're a fine individual and a strong girl, and you deserve a decent mother.

Although he never said that, at that moment, that's how I felt. I felt proud to be Martha. I was not cute and girly. I was not a cheerleader at school. I didn't have my picture in the school yearbook. I didn't even have a boyfriend. But at fifteen I was capable, competent, strong, and polite and would have, in the old days — like the Bible Martha, who had lived with the sackcloth Brothers by the Dead Sea in that movie we saw, where those Bible stories came from in the first place — I would have been the one to go into the woods with a baby strapped to my back to gather sticks for the fire and make the meals and clean the kitchen and climb the face of the cliff to look after my mother as I was now looking after my foster mother. I saw recognition of all that in those eyes above the pockets.

But after the stroll through the garden and his talk with Sister Charlotte, Paul's do-my-best promise seemed to have changed. As they were leaving, Paul took me to one side and said, "I'm sorry, Martha. But we can't, at this point, give you more information about your mother."

This time his voice sounded different, like he was apologizing for running over my cat. He stepped close. I could see that the lines and creases in his face were filled with apologies for doing what he had to do. When he took my hand, I realized his hand was not big enough and his fingers not strong enough to change whatever had become my mother into anything that resembled a mother. So in his grip, my hand that a minute ago was strong enough to pour pots of coffee and carry plates a rhubarb squares and gather firewood and carry babies up the side of the cliff, this same hand collapsed and turned soggy as the wet rag I would use for wiping up their mess after they'd gone. With his soggy hand he pumped my soggy hand and together we pumped several useless pumps. Then his policeman eyes, in the centre of those lines and wrinkles, fixed a stare on me that I knew would grow fainter the farther he went down the front walk, looking back at me for one last apologetic glance for having given me hope that I would someday meet my mother. As I watched him climb into his unmarked car and slam the door, this last glance stayed fixed on me, still watching me in his rearview mirror looking back at me like a CFCS roadkill, waiting to see if I was going to stay down or stand up now that I had been told to forget about my mother.

Chapter 19

MARTHA

I sat next to Peter on the bench next to the apple tree. I said, "Tell me what you see."

Peter looked around.

I said, "Pretend you're the monkey on your dresser with his hands over his eyes and you're taking your hands away and tell me what you see."

"Well then. Looking to my left, I see my flower garden and the green grass and the stone fence and the cemetery. To my right, I see the back of the house and the driveway. Across the street, I see Tiny Tots Daycare with the parking lot where you and I practise baseball. Past the parking lot I see the swings and the slides for the boys and the girls. If I look off to one side, I see the apple tree."

"And if you look up, you'll see Sister Charlotte coming from the crematorium chimney. I'm going to OD her, Peter, if she doesn't tell me where my mother is so I can go and see her and find out what's going on."

Peter folded his legs up yoga style and dropped his hands into his lap. He stroked along the scar.

"I apologize, Peter. I didn't mean to say I was going to OD her. It's just, well, answer me a question. When you look straight ahead, not to one side or the other but straight ahead, what do you see?"

He gave me a puzzled, what-are-you-after look. I waited. Finally he said, "I see a woman who, in spite of the pain, has been able to provide a stable family setting with no looming revolving door for you and Owen to be sent through."

"You're not looking with your real eyes. You're looking with the monkey eyes. You're looking off to the right or to the left or any old direction but straight on. I can survive anywhere. But what's going to happen to Owen? He's still doing all the same things now as when he was nine years old. He's still experimenting with sperm using eggs from the frogs he caught in the pond at the back of the cemetery. The frogs still squirt out this grey gluey stuff that looks like snot with dead floating black bits that end up all over his hands, which he never washes. He still just wipes them on his pants, and then off he goes, wandering about the cemetery grass catching bugs to bring home to execute in sealed jars, revenge on the bugs that crawled over him in the Open Hatch while he was lying under his dead sister, the same as when he was nine years old. He's retarded, Peter. When he ages out of the system, what institution will they put him in?"

"The connection between genius and eccentricity is well documented. Look it up on your laptop. He's going to get a scholarship to U of T and will live in residence and become an eccentric university professor."

"Hear no evil. See no evil. Speak no evil. What about Sister Charlotte? What if you're looking straight ahead, are you seeing straight ahead what will happen to Sister Charlotte?"

"I don't know what will happen to Sister Charlotte."

"What if CFCS finds out she's an addict? They'll airlift us out of here by helicopter and take you away in handcuffs."

"Bishop Humphries is using his influence to make sure that doesn't happen. That's why he's here so often, to make sure that doesn't happen."

"But why, Peter? Why is he protecting me and Owen, and why is he keeping Sister Charlotte here? And don't say to look after me and Owen. We look after her."

"He's making certain neither of you, especially Owen for the reason you just gave me, get moved until you're both ready."

"Why doesn't Bishop Humphries make Sister Charlotte go into rehab and we stay here with you?"

"Rehab will report her addiction and, in your words, CFCS will airlift you two out of here by helicopter."

Peter was rubbing his scar, a sign this conversation was making him nervous.

"Look straight ahead at my next question. The police have been here asking Sister Charlotte about Eagleman and the boys from Snowy River. What's going on about that?"

"I don't know, Martha."

"Are your three monkeys preventing you from finding out?"

"I don't want to know. If I don't know, I'm not complicit. If you don't know, you're not complicit. When you get asked, you say you don't know."

"Right. Not my circus; not my monkeys."

I got up and walked off, leaving Peter sitting on his stupid bench.

***

If I was Owen's dead sister floating around above that chimney where I could see everything the way spirit people can, like they have tinfoil hats, if I could see everything starting from when I was a baby, like if I had a tinfoil hat, I could connect all that stuff into a completed puzzle, maybe more like a spirit umbilical cord going backward to the day my mother abandoned me. Then I would start my tabletop puzzle all over again without Bishop Humphries or Mr. Knight or Sister Charlotte or Owen. Or my mother.

Just Peter and me.

So hard to imagine how I ended up with Sister Charlotte now half the time passed out stone cold, in her dreams believing she's in the same knee-high flowers and in the same fresh-trimmed grass around the same apple tree as when she was nine years old. If only she could start all over again. The same for Owen, I guess.

Chapter 20

SISTER CHARLOTTE

I was sitting in Mr. Knight's big chair in his new apartment in a different high-rise. While we were waiting for my taxi, I told him the story of Uncle Merv's brother and his watch.

Mr. Knight said, "Rather than spending your time moaning about lying your head off in court, you should be genuflecting on the system of silicon and chips and wires and wheels that are taking you in tiny jerks around the circumference of what we call The Watch. I am a watch. You are a watch. We're all copies of The Watch. If there's a Watch, there must be a Watchmaker. A handful of odd parts dropped into that tiny compartment on a wrist would not create a watch. A contraption made from a mixture of metallic pieces would not create a watch. The intricate design of these parts suggests a Watchmaker who fits each wheel into the next, the teeth of one meshing with the teeth of the other, moving time forward, minute by minute, in your case sooner than you're admitting to. The life expectancy for Huntington's is fifteen years, Sister Charlotte."

Mr. Knight held up the container and rattled the buds. "Bishop Humphries is not the Watchmaker, but he's in charge of a lot of watches. The Father Eagleman investigation is picking up traction. There are time limits in these matters; they don't go on forever. A court date will soon be set. Your praying five times a day has not helped Bella. I'm not going to lie to you, Sister Charlotte. You're going to be called as witness to swear on the Bible and then lie your head off, unless of course, you can get Bella to lie for you."

***

Dear Jesus, I lie here alone in my room, listening to the sound of the water running through the pipes at the flush of the toilet, but I don't hear water running into the sink for a handwash, so I know it's Owen. I hear soft footsteps in the hallway, and I know it's Peter. I hear pad-pad down the stairs, and I know it's Martha. If I got up, I would see the three of them crossing the yard and going to Tiny Tots to practise baseball. Thanks to Martha's pitching, their team is unbeatable.

As you know, dear Jesus, for my birthday my first year with the Sisters, I was given a white plate with your praying hands. Your fingers were long. The caption read "In the hands of Jesus." The first time I became aware of my condition was when I picked up the plate. I lost my grip, and it smashed on the floor. That was the beginning, the praying hands a message from you, handed to me on a shiny porcelain platter. That I broke. This was a sign that one day I would break my covenant with you, which I now realize I have done by praying five times a day, like a Muslim. But I didn't face Mecca and I was not praying to Allah. But now, as punishment for breaking my covenant with you, I must do the exact thing that will send me to Hell: swear on the Bible and then lie my head off.

"Sister Charlotte, are you awake in there? Owen is walking all over the house with his dirty shoes on."

"Earth to Sister Charlotte. Owen is watching porn on his laptop."

"Knock, knock, Sister Charlotte. Owen is handling dead frogs and then going downstairs and making a meatloaf sandwich without washing his hands. Other people eat from that loaf, Sister Charlotte. And eat off those plates. Owen is an imbecile. I've had enough. Owen left his disgusting shorts on the bathroom floor for me to pick up. He belongs on Ward Five, Sister Charlotte. I've had enough."

"Use the kitchen tongs, Martha."

"Duhhh, Sister Charlotte. The kitchen tongs?"

Another dreary day, Mr. Jesus, one dreary day after another. Martha and Owen have spent all day in the cemetery finding earthworms for Owen's experiments. No doubt knee-deep in the mud, digging through the dirt along the fence line, no doubt right this minute sitting at the kitchen table spreading clods of mud underneath where I can't reach to clean. Well, no matter. Martha will clean it up. Oh, for goodness' sake, it's raining again, and there they are, clumping up the stairs. How time flies. Where did I leave my water glass, Mr. Knight? The buds wear off ten minutes after I take them.

Chapter 21

OWEN

Because Sister Charlotte was afraid of unannounced visits at what she called "any old time," she had become obsessed with locks to keep the unannounced out. She carried her house keys in her pocket. At lunchtime, she set them in front of her on the table next to her plate of warmed-up yesterday's meatloaf. One key opened the front and one the back door and one the office door. If Sister Charlotte found a door unlocked, she locked it, and since Peter never knew where his keys were — the car accident that had left a scar on his hand had left a scar on his memory —he'd have to borrow Sister Charlotte's.

"Did you lose your key again, Peter?"

"Afraid so."

"Where did you lose it?"

"I don't know. Somewhere in the yard, probably."

Even though I was almost sixteen, my job was still to look after the garbage. This took me forever because I read all the bills and flyers. On hands and knees, I stuck my head right into the garbage container under the sink, and from out of the garbage, which was not locked, I picked up bits and pieces of information, unfolding the folded and folding the unfolded, like unbuttoning the buttoned and buttoning the unbuttoned, recalling Joe the Hammer. I fit this and that together like Martha and her puzzle pieces. That is how I found the second ripped-up letter from Martha's mother, the same request: wanting to meet her daughter. This one seemed more urgent. I got the feeling from "must get together immediately" that Bella was being pressured into it.

I didn't feel like someone who would have a mother. Not one that lived for long, anyway. I tried to picture it, little Owen having a mother. What seemed more likely, I was made from leftover computer parts. Martha told me that. She said I looked like the picture of the guy on the back cover of the *Computer Tricks* book.

If Martha knew about the letter, she would have told me. So it must have been because Sister Charlotte was obsessing about locks that Martha began obsessing about information on her mother, like in files locked in the office, especially now that Sister Charlotte had eased back on drugs so she could keep track of all the doors she had locked so the police or Bishop Humphries or CFCS couldn't walk in any old time and find her passed out.

Sister Charlotte's arm, now back on rusted hinges, stretched out to the office door; her hand, now back to crooked and bent, closed on the round smoothness of the doorknob, and she turned her body to turn the knob. If the door was not locked, her stiff hand grew tight and her tight arm grew stiff, and her lips tightened, and her face scowled a tight scowl, and she locked the office door that Peter had forgotten to lock.

"The office must be kept locked, Peter. There's important information in that filing cabinet that inquisitive eyes might get into."

Martha heard Sister Charlotte say that, so Martha said to me, "They keep telling me there aren't any records, but there must be. We're Children's Aid kids; there must be files. You've got the key that Peter thinks he lost, don't lie to me, so now we go in there and find out about my mother, dead or alive, you not her, unless you want to die with those ridiculous girly red sneakers on. No guy wears red sneakers. OhmyGodprayforme…"

Chapter 22

MARTHA

From listening to Owen talk about his dead sister breaking the laws of the universe and floating around like radio waves above that chimney, my brain in the dark of night picked up voices from my long-dead grandpa buried in the cemetery I spent half my time in, his ghost drifting around among the tombstones while I slept, making me even more anxious to see my mother when I woke up.

Or maybe it was from that stupid Uncle Merv story. Or maybe from the spooky yowling of the cats at midnight that sounded like a dead baby sister. There's dead baby sisters all over the place, especially up there above that chimney. I don't know, it's like boots need walking to be boots, dogs need barking to be dogs, kids need grandpas to be kids.

I went up to Owen's room and stood in his doorway. He had a beaker cooking full blast. He had no idea what he was going to end up with. Maybe a donkey for Sister Charlotte to ride to Bethlehem.

"I want that key."

He gave me a serious look.

"Maybe, if you start treating me nicer."

"Yeah, right. By that time that key will have fallen from your pocket into the cemetery grass and rusted away to nothing, and I'll never see those files."

I went into the backyard and sat on the bench. I looked at the flowers. I imagined which ones I would pick and wrap in green paper to take to my mother for our first visit. I thought about Peter, my three-monkeys foster father. Peter reminded me of one of those Dead Sea sackcloth brothers in that movie: dress plain and keep life simple and tend the garden. With his bald head fringed with a horseshoe of hair, he looked like a real monk living next to a real Dead Sea full of walking corpses that looked like Owen, except for the red sneakers.

Peter had only two pairs of shoes, one for church and one for other times. "I don't need any more shoes. The ones I've got suit me just fine." When I teased him about his bald head and told him he better grow some hair else they'd make him into a three-monkeys monk, he said, "The hair I have suits me just fine."

Everything suited Peter just fine. Like, hello, Peter.

And one other thing, why did I end up in that plain brown bedroom like a servant girl? Sister Charlotte has that big king-size bed in her room with her own bathroom and a big closet. You, Peter, you sleep in that nice room at the end of the hall. And Owen has all that lab equipment that smells like he's cooking donkey shit in there. It isn't fair.

I went upstairs. I climbed onto Owen's bed and lay back with one leg balanced on one knee and hoped he would go to the bathroom so I could steal his key.

"I think you should go to the bathroom, Owen."

"I think you need to go the bathroom to relieve yourself, Owen."

"I think you need to take a leak, Owen."

"I think you should give me that key before you die with those red sneakers on, Owen."

Owen sat next to me on the bed, thinking about it. "I'll help you when you start being nice to me."

I said nicely, "Find my file and put me out of misery, Owen, and I'll change my mind about letting your frogs go on the subway tracks."

Chapter 23

OWEN

I closed the Venetian blinds covering the office window. I stood by the office desk the way I used to stand beside my old teacher's, next to her filing cabinet. Her name was Mrs. Colgan, but some kids called her Miss Colgan, or sometimes just Miss. I would stand there watching her filling out her attendance. After she had finished and put it into the top drawer of her filing cabinet, she'd ask something like, "What is 456 times 7,665?" I would tell her, and she would verify on her cellphone. "What is the square root of 55,555?" and I would tell her and she would verify on her cellphone.

Martha peeked in the door. "Remember, we're working in real time."

Now I was standing in front of the filing cabinet, which was almost identical to Mrs. Colgan's. But whereas I'm sure her files were in order, our files were a mess.

Martha peeked in.

I said, "These files are a mess."

"My last name is Brock. The first name is Martha. Under B. Probably the top drawer."

She came into the office to stand beside me. The top drawer had mostly Sister Charlotte's church announcements: upcoming anti-abortion rallies, food bank announcements, refugee programmes and a notice saying, "Don't use your cellphone at funerals."

"Why can't you use your cellphone at funerals?"

"Are you looking under B?"

"It says here Sister Charlotte wants to be cremated."

"I'm going to cremate you in a minute. Look under B."

"The Good News Crusade takes place every July fourth in Texas."

"Look under B."

The second drawer held bills and receipts related to the house, like roofing and car repairs, which should have been filed according to year and function but instead were mixed up with more of Sister Charlotte's stuff: bills for Bibles and religious books, the dates June then April then December.

Martha tiptoed down the hall for a listen at Sister Charlotte's door. I took a peek through the Venetian blinds. Leonardo da Vinci invented Venetian blinds. If I pulled the cord correctly, the slats went up and down in perfect mathematical order, one to forty dropping down, forty to one folding up. The backward counting reminded me of following Joe the Hammer's buttons pattern. The patterned whiteness of the slats reminded me of Sarah's smile, gleaming like the woman on the tooth-whitening kit Shelly bought. The thought of Shelly returned me to Big Joe's buttons. The thought of Big Joe's buttons reminded me that Timothy had called, wondering when we could kill Big Joe.

"Stop fooling with the blinds, Owen. Get on with it." She left to check on Sister Charlotte again.

Stop fooling with the blinds. Stop fooling with the garbage. Yes, Martha. No, Martha. While she cleaned the kitchen after dinner, a scrubbing and frowning dance with her Mr. Clean, making sure she got everything back to spic and span, I had to sort the day's garbage for recycling. I didn't think it needed sorting, the compost stuff, yes, but the rest of it — garbage was garbage. Sister Charlotte gave me that job when I was ten years old because it didn't matter if I broke something since it was already garbage. Now here I was, sixteen, my job in the kitchen still sorting garbage. While I sorted, I planned that as soon as I aged out of the system, I would eat my dinner in a nice restaurant, like Peter took me to in his taxi one time, and afterward, I would not sort garbage. I would get up and go home to my nice apartment.

No one wanted me to join any teams at school. No one asked me if I was going to the dance. All I could do was stay home and play with the blinds and sort the garbage and look after worms and tadpoles and frogs and algae and do sperm experiments and read books like *Discoveries in Cell Division* and go to the library to research DNA experiments.

"Owen, flood your eyes with a vision of my patience because this is the last time you will see any if you don't get on with it."

I went headfirst into the third drawer. I imagined myself as one of those Dead Sea brothers deciphering ancient parchment documents like bills going backward in time to 2018: an official requisition from CFCS in Sister Charlotte's handwriting for two desks, one for each of us. Going forward in time, a requisition from CFCS in 2019 for two laptops, one for each of us. I found a receipt for a new bedside light paid for by herself, Sister Charlotte. The requisitions for desks and laptops from CFCS needed a reason, but no reason was needed for the light for herself, Sister Charlotte. Attached was a refund, light for herself returned.

I examined Sister Charlotte's arthritic writing of 2019, which looked like ancient Egypt hieroglyphics. The reason she bought this light for herself was for deciphering the texts that would reveal to her, Sister Charlotte, the truths hidden in her nightstand leather-bound Bible. These obscure words, originally translated from bundles of Hebrew parchments by those Dead Sea sackcloth brothers, now spoke to Sister Charlotte in a celestial light direct from that angel she sang about, accompanied by the soundings of trumpets, praise be to Jesus! So she doesn't need an electric light, she's already got that light with the blue halo, which gives her a remote connection.

"Hello, Owen. It's me, Martha."

"I'm doing my best. Give me time."

I would like to have been there, sitting side by side with the brothers, heads bowed, by lamplight deciphering the scriptures inscribed on previously hidden tablets; now, on this day, buoyed upward by the Dead Sea salt from the dark at the bottom to the light at the top to reveal, by carbon dating testing, the secrets of Martha's mother.

"Owen, you moron. Peter just pulled up."

This was much cleaner work than sorting garbage and easier on the eyes than watching through keyholes and looking through microscopes.

"Owen, you moron. Peter's coming inside."

"No, he's not. He's raking the front lawn."

"He's not raking the front lawn, dipstick. It's nighttime."

Peter always used a one-long, two-short system and raked backward, starting near the building and moving to the street, his raking following a plan, even if his filing didn't.

Martha whispered, "I'll go downstairs and keep him busy while you finish."

"Nothing," I said when Martha came back.

"That's it? Nothing?"

"What do you expect? Here you are, Martha, I've got your mother on the phone. Hello, Martha. I've been phoning you all week wondering how you are and, oh my, with a little exercise and dieting and—"

"No address? No phone number? Nothing?" Martha was giving me her tell-me-the-truth-or-I'll-cut-your-throat look.

She said, "Jesus, Owen. Where's your belt? Your pants are falling off. Pull up your pants."

When I returned to the kitchen, I noticed the Venetian blind was not straight. I let it down and pulled it up correctly. Sister Charlotte had one of her notes stuck crookedly on the cupboard door: "Buy Martha her special toothpaste." I re-stuck it straight. These reminder notes reminded me of the reason I had gone into the office. Usually, for me, intention and result did not always follow predetermined order. The effect did not always follow the cause. My universe was not always parallel with everyone else's, no matter how often I tried to level it. The Venetian blinds of how things were done didn't always go up and down in logical sequence, unlike chess, which always played out in predictable patterns. Numbers always added up in predictable outcomes, and x's and o's always lined up or didn't. I didn't know how or into which of these categories the two birth certificates I found mixed in with Peter's house repairs receipts would fit into anything, so I left them where I found them. Martha's mother was Bella. We knew that. My mother was a lady called Rita VanWirrt. What kind of name was that? Big smile and give her hugs? Someone had to be my mother. I didn't care. A mother is just the egg's way of making another egg.

Chapter 24

OWEN

Sister Charlotte sent me to her bedroom to get a Tylenol for Martha's sore pitching arm. Inside, the air seemed damp and musty. The walls were bare, except above her headboard hung a crucifix and underneath it a picture of the pope. On the wall at the foot of her bed, which was covered by a grey blanket, hung her pictures of the Virgin Mary and crucified Jesus.

Sister Charlotte had her own bathroom, which smelled of disinfectant. I opened the door of the cabinet above the sink. On the first shelf was a small glass with a toothbrush and toothpaste. On the second shelf were jars and tubes of joint cream and, to my surprise, two bottles of hair shampoo. I didn't think she washed her hair, which looked like a wig, always the same, dry, brown, parted in the middle, and flattened straight down behind her ears with bobby pins. If you cut it off and balled it up, it would make a good fire. Martha's hair was always sparkly and clean, never dirty and stringy like Timothy's always was, used to be anyway, who I was supposed to meet in the library to talk about killing Big Joe.

I picked and poked through Sister Charlotte's drawers until I found, hidden under some sweaters, a photograph. Sister Charlotte was about twenty. I couldn't believe it. She looked almost pretty. Somewhere along, Jesus had done a fig job on Sister Charlotte, I guess for not bearing fruit. I continued to snoop. As I was closing one dresser drawer, I noticed a brown envelope stuck between the folds of a sweater, as though it had nestled itself in there by accident. Inside I discovered a sheet of ancient parchment in the form of a newspaper article with a picture of a priest identified as Father Eagleman visiting a battered-women's shelter in downtown North Bay. Beside him stood two young women, and beside them stood a younger man. I could find no date, but Bishop Humphries had a full head of black hair, and Bella looked young and healthy. The article was about the Sisters of Sorrows creating career training and job placements for Indigenous boys in North Bay. The name of woman standing next to Bella was Rita VanWirrt. Then I found a four-by-six photograph, same three people, looking down at a fresh grave, dirt mounded. In the green cemetery grass of the background were two tombstones I recognized, one black, one grey, both sunk at an off-level tilt. In the background, the crematorium. On the back of the photo was written "William John Humphries, 1950–2010." According to the math, he would be Bishop Humphries's father. In the same envelope I found duplicate copies of our birth certificates and a death certificate for Rita VanWirrt. I found a photograph of a nearly naked Rita on a nearly naked Bishop Humphries's knee. I put the envelopes into my shirt, crept along the hall to my room, and hid the information under my mattress. I decided not to tell Martha that the father the police were looking for was Bella's father-in-law. But that meant Bishop Humphries was Martha's father. Mine too, I guess. So there was no real father-in-law, not according to the definition anyway.

After supper, I did my homework, cleaned my frog tank, and picked through my dew worms. I put on my PJs. I could hear from across the cemetery Sister Charlotte's off-key organ moaning its seven o'clock Sinner Sanctum service. I went downstairs and out into the backyard to sit on Peter's bench. I watched the pigeons gather in the spires, not flying and flapping and cooing but, heads cocked, listening to Sister Charlotte's pigeon music.

That evening, lying in bed under my blankets, I brought out Shelly's picture. I ran my fingers along the shiny surface of her long black hair, back and forth across the soft skin of her face. With the tip of my finger, I traced the curve of her smile and the flow of the silk scarf she wore around her neck. I traced along the thin gold chain of her necklace. I traced the fall of her hair to her shoulders. I imagined it swinging over my face as she bent to kiss me goodnight. No matter which way I turned the picture, her eyes looked directly into mine. I ran the tip of my big finger down her cheek to her lips. I closed my eyes and reached up to put my arms around the warmth of Shelly's neck. I remember it was damp beneath the scarf, and her face was wet from her tears.

I returned the picture to its hiding place, under the box springs of the bed, close enough to the edge that, reaching from under the covers, I could touch her.

Around eight o'clock, still an hour before dark, I heard Martha next door changing into jeans and sneakers and a sweatshirt. She came along the hall, glove and hardball in hand. I listened to her footsteps on the stairs. When I heard the front door slam, I went to the window and watched her and Peter walk down the front walk and open the gate of the picket fence surrounding the yard. They crossed the black pavement to Tiny Tots on the opposite side of the street and, Peter instructing, she began her pitching warm-up, getting ready for the game next day.

Before each throw, Martha planted her feet wide, waiting for the sign from Peter, who was balanced half-crouched, feeding her signals. He was a slight, slow-moving person, but he had reflexes quick enough to catch Martha's blistering overhand blur, which would smack into his glove, leaving it smoking, sometimes knocking him backward.

Chapter 25

SISTER CHARLOTTE

I got out of the Diamond cab and struggled up the drive of Mr. Knight's new address, an inner-city semi in Parkdale, no BMWs parked on the bricked-over front yard but decent enough. He was tired of living in a box, he said.

As I climbed the front step, I checked my watch. Almost four. I knew he would be in his living room, one elbow on the chair arm, one leg slung over one knee, waiting for the clock on the wall to turn to four. An address can change but not the habits of the inhabitant. If I was five minutes late, Mr. Knight would be standing at the door, one elbow against the doorjamb, his penetrating blue eyes constantly flitting about, looking out the window, checking the time on his watch.

After I knocked, I leaned close and listened to make sure it was Mr. Knight's footsteps I was hearing crossing the hardwood flooring from his living room. Usually, after he invited me into the kitchen, he would go to his living-room window to peek out to make certain I had not been followed. Then he would offer me a cup of tea and a Dare's Digestive. Sitting at the table, I would make a note of places to hide if the police arrived: in a closet, behind a curtain, under his bed. By leaning forward in my chair, I could see into his bedroom, neat and tidy with matching spread and curtains and carpet, so inviting I wanted to lie down and curl up and have Mr. Knight dressed in his white suit bring me the bud with a glass of water and say, There, there, Sister Charlotte. It will soon be over.

"How do you like my new artwork, Sister Charlotte?"

"Very lovely, Mr. Knight."

The one above the chesterfield looked like Petunia did it. The one next to it looked like it was done by that artist in the seventies who put the canvas on the floor and used a soup spoon with a curved handle to throw the paint in the air. He said his mother raised him according to Dr. Spock.

Today Mr. Knight looked like what he was. I don't know why at that moment I truthfully saw him: a slight, unassuming man with sparse hair and a stoop, not much taller than me, dressed in his white suit, white shirt, and black tie. I do know why I took close notice: because I would not be seeing him many more times.

Mr. Knight took another peek out the front window before saying, "These are stronger, Sister Charlotte. But they come at a price. Take one now."

"I need a glass of water."

He opened a cupboard above the sink for a glass. He filled the glass and took a bud from the plastic container. "Relax and close your eyes and let the bud work its wonders."

With an unusual gesture for Mr. Knight, he pulled over a chair and sat opposite me. He placed the pill on my tongue. I drank the water.

"I can tell you, Sister Charlotte, situations change in an instant of time." He took my twisted hand in his and turned it palm up. "Bella, Martha's mother, had beautiful hands, and on the finger of the left, she wore a ring with a tiny white dove set in a blue stone."

I was liking the way he was holding and stroking my hand.

"Before you go, Sister Charlotte, answer this question. Do you agree with me, now that your end is near, that it's morally justified to take the life of a person whose pain has become unbearable?"

"I think what is making the unbearable bearable is the thought of the last ride on the roller coaster of those pills."

"You're a martyr, Sister Charlotte, perhaps even a saint. Are you prepared to be a martyr and saint?"

"Good Heavens, Mr. Knight. In no way am I…" I hesitated. "But of late, Mr. Knight, yes, I have a strange feeling like I'm being watched. I don't need to look to see if someone is watching me. I feel it prickly along the back of my neck. Being watched is different from being looked at. It feels like, I don't know, like sometimes there are scouts at Martha's baseball, watching her. That's what it feels like. It used to be I didn't need to turn around to know I was being looked at. People do that with nuns. On the subway with a hundred people, I can feel being looked at. But with being watched, being scouted, I feel my ears go red, and I know someone is watching me."

Mr. Knight sat back in his chair. "Like someone is following you? Like the police."

This time I reached out to take his hand. "It feels like that someone is you, Mr. Knight, and you're writing down everything I do in the pages of that ledger book you carry around. It feels like, even though your eyes are never in the room with me, I can feel those eyes turning the pages of my ledger book and I can feel those fingers writing down everything I do. I can't describe the feeling, other than it feels like I might be chosen."

"And I'm the chooser, Sister, like you cannot get to the Father except by me, you know from Matthew verse something or other."

"It's like trying to put shoes on feet I don't have anymore, which is very unsettling. Do you know what I'm talking about, Mr. Knight?"

"Your feet are being traded in for wings, Sister Charlotte."

"Yes, exactly, like I'm moving through air on wings I don't have. Do you see the parallel, Mr. Knight? And do you know, Mr. Knight, as I sat with my dying mother who was drifting in and out of consciousness, she would raise her hand, fanning the air, and say, 'Those pesky pigeons, why won't they let me be?'"

***

"What in the world is that?" The driver pointed to two girls with nuclear-green hair and chains hanging from their noses.

"What in the world is that?" A dog walker was standing there, looking around, pretending her dog was not pooping in the middle of the sidewalk.

"You're looking unwell, ma'am. Can I walk you to the door?"

"I've been needing new pain pills, praying for medication that would work, and they're definitely working."

"You got a better doctor than me," the driver said. "I ask him, and he doesn't give me nothing."

I climbed the stairs and, noticing the smell, closed Owen's bedroom door on the way by. I lay flat on my back on my bed.

Martha was at the door. "Sister Charlotte, are you in there, or am I talking to myself?"

"What is it, Martha?"

"Owen was born with bugs in his brain from lying beside his dead sister."

"And what do you want me to do about it?"

"Feed him bug killer."

"All right, Martha. Give me a minute." I pulled myself upright, opened the bedroom door, and took Martha's hand for support. We went down to the kitchen to feed Owen bug killer, a mixture of rhubarb jam and honey from a beekeeper friend of Peter's, spread on fresh bread from the Italian bakery next to the Bluejay.

I said, "Martha, what have you got to say to Owen?"

"I'm sorry I'm feeding you a jam-and-honey sandwich instead of bug killer."

Chapter 26

MARTHA

All Sister Charlotte wanted to do now was to spend time feeding the pigeons. I would sit with her on the church step and watch Owen throw and the pigeons peck in the spring sunshine until the bread was gone. Sometimes Owen would come over and sit next to her, and Sister Charlotte would tell us her Presto story: "One time, my father took me to see the magician Presto. He was dressed in black, like a priest, with a tall hat. I wondered if he could snap his fingers and say some words in Latin and there would be a white pigeon. I asked him, 'Can you pull a white pigeon out of your hat?' Presto put his hat on the table and pressed a remote switch, and the wind blew coloured streamers around, and he recited some gibberish. He lifted the hat, and there was a white rabbit, and then, when he put his hat over it and said some more words, the rabbit was gone. No rabbit.

"So I said, 'This time a white pigeon.' So he did it again, but it was the rabbit. He said, 'Let me ask the rabbit if he can turn into a pigeon.' Presto whispered in the rabbit's ear, and the rabbit whispered back, and then Presto pulled a card with a picture of a white pigeon out of my ear."

No sooner had she finished telling that story than she noticed a white pigeon hiding under the bush by the church step. Someone must have lost a white towel, which had blown in under the branches. The bird had hidden among the dirty white folds and was almost invisible. Sister Charlotte picked it up and cradled it. "I think it's got a crippled leg and wing."

She sat on the church step, stroking its head and rocking it. "The leg band means it's a homing pigeon. My father told me stories of homing pigeons that had been released hundreds of miles away from home and got lost in bad weather. But they always returned home, however long it took."

Talking about pigeons seemed to step Sister Charlotte out of the shadows to become a real person standing in the sunshine under the blue sky holding a white pigeon the same way her stories about being a little girl dancing and singing gospel songs made her a real person.

"But," she said, "wherever home is, this one can't fly all that way. So it can stay with us for a while."

When Sister Charlotte held the pigeon in her hand, I noticed that with Mr. Knight's new pills, whatever they were, she could cradle it into a comfortable nest. The pigeon closed its eyes and dozed peacefully in the cardboard box set up in the kitchen, not paying much attention to Sister Charlotte's rambling stories about doves in the Bible, which were its cousins. The pigeon looked as though it had heard the stories already.

A few days later, Sister Charlotte held the pigeon close to her cheek, whispered something in its ear, and took it outside. The pigeon surveyed the landscape and shifted its feet in Sister Charlotte's palms. When Sister Charlotte held up her arms and opened her hands, the pigeon sprang away, circled once over Sister Charlotte's head, tilted its wings into the wind, and disappeared across the cemetery, over the crematorium chimney, and into a cloudless sky.

Chapter 27

OWEN

Martha the strike-out queen struck out every batter except the ones she walked with wild pitches. Didn't matter. They won the championship and there was a lot of talk about why there were no women in pro baseball. I walked with her from the ball diamond and shortcutted through the cemetery, and we sat on the chapel steps. I noticed a tall man wearing sunglasses standing by those two tombstones that had sunk off-kilter. He had black hair in a ponytail and bare, tattooed arms. He was wearing jeans and work boots. When he noticed us, he left.

"He looks too much like a drug dealer to be a drug dealer. He's the OPP." I led the way along the lane to the two tombstones that had sunk off-kilter to see what he was looking for. I was going along sideways, kicking through the grass, when I intentionally tripped over my feet. My glasses intentionally slipped off my nose.

"Let me get them, imbecile. You'll step on them." Kneeling and poking about with her fingers, trying to find the lens that had separated from the frame, Martha touched something flat and black. I shone my BlackBerry on the spot, and together we cleaned the dirt and roots off the marker: WILLIAM JOHN HUMPHRIES.

I acted surprised. "This is not your mother's father the cops were looking for. The cops were looking for her father-in-law. This is your father's father, your grandfather."

"Moron. What are you talking about?"

"This is the grave the cops couldn't find because they had the wrong name. For sure that guy on the bench was undercover, waiting to see if your mom would come along for a visit with your gramps.

But if she had, she'd have cleaned off that marker, just like we did, to make sure it was the right gramps."

Martha was looking stunned, almost wordless. "What are you trying to say underneath what you're saying?"

"Bishop Humphries is your father."

She stared down at the name on the grave. Then her eyes snapped back to mine. She gave me the lens and the glasses and walked off.

***

The eye doctor said, "You've pretty much demolished these glasses, Owen. But while I'm examining your eyes, my assistant will put the glasses back together and give them a good cleaning." He put me in the chair and examined my eyes through his microscopes.

"How do we know if what we're seeing is true?" I asked him that, him being an eye-seeing doctor.

"There's one sunset in the sky," he answered, "but everyone watches a different sunset."

"If the pope removed his glass eye and put it on the other side of the door and looked through the keyhole at himself, what would he see, assuming his glass eye was able to see?"

A smile crept across the doctor's concentration as he continued with his lights and charts.

"Maybe, Owen, what you think you see depends on the size of the keyhole, like what I think I see depends on the size of my microscope." A twinkle came into the doctor's eye. "But not if your brain is distorting your vision because your glasses are cracked."

I wanted to ask him, since he was looking into my head and since I was feeling bad for not telling Martha sooner about those pictures I found, because now I seemed to be going around in circles in my head, wondering what Martha would do when she found out I was her half brother. I was hoping he would see in there, in some corner of that cranial vault called my head, a solution to my problem without me needing to figure one out.

The eye doctor said, "You're an interesting young fellow, Owen, but there's nothing wrong with your eyes and nothing wrong with your brain either. But I suspect you have difficulty with the four corners of reality. You confuse what is actually seen with what is thought to be seen; you confuse what ought to be seen with what ought not to be seen. In other words, you're the same as everyone else who sits in this chair."

Chapter 28

OWEN

I found Martha pitching fastball against the Tiny Tots brick wall. The impact on the one-foot square of flaked brick had chewed the skin off her ball — and the wall off the building, almost anyway. I said, "I got a call from Timothy. Now Big Joe is a handyman guy with a pickup truck. He goes around fixing stuff for old ladies."

"Forget about Big Joe. Tell Timothy to get lost."

"I wonder if Big Joe still wears a baseball hat and sunglasses. You know, those special aviator kind."

"Grow up, Owen. We'll soon be free to go."

Martha wound up her arm for another pitch. The torn-up wall looked like the grease spot on the paint above Big Joe's headboard in his bedroom magnified by ten. I remember the day the police took him away. It was summer and hot. I remember his aviator glasses slipped off his nose. No one bothered to pick them up. Big Joe's aviator glasses were plastic, so I wondered if they would melt. And I wondered, what about those little hinges lying in the wet grass? By the time Big Joe got out of jail, those hinges will have rusted away into nothing. Then I thought, for Timothy, Joe the Hammer's hammer wouldn't rust away into nothing. It wouldn't matter how many summers would come and go. Hammers rust, but not into nothing.

I found Timothy in the St. Clair library leafing through a human anatomy book, reading up on how to kill Big Joe. When Timothy lived at Big Joe's, he'd been a weaselly little squirt. Now he was over six feet tall, wearing army boots and leather pants and a badass t-shirt with tattoos to match the rings hanging from his nose. He said, "I'm trying to figure out the best place in the chest for stabbing Big Joe with a screwdriver. That's how I'm going to do it."

I said, "Why a screwdriver?"

"He had this big motherfuckin' screwdriver laying on his bench. Every time I got the hammer, I vowed someday I would do to him what he was doing to me, except I'd do it with a screwdriver."

We sat at a table to figure it out. I told him that driving a screwdriver through Big Joe's heart would require a combination of velocity and strength sufficient to penetrate the plaid shirt, the t-shirt, the skin, and then double that to go through fat and muscle. There would also be a velocity-strength ratio to take into account, in case the screwdriver hit the ribcage.

As Timothy returned the book to the shelf, he noticed a muscle-building magazine sitting in the rack one aisle over. Leafing through *Fitness Monthly*, he noticed a Pyramid Gym advertisement for developing bigger muscles. No one watching, he ripped out the ad.

I said, "Timothy, you're destroying library property. Go home and get the Scotch tape and bring it back and repair what you've done."

He said he stayed at the drop-in and they wouldn't lend anything. He went to the desk to borrow the tape to fix the damage, but they told him they don't lend anything. I said I would fix it later, but in the meantime, I helped him fill out the form. I drew rep charts and measurement and mass and energy graphs and said that when the real fitness stuff arrived, we could lift weights together. He said he was going to lie on the bedroom floor at the shelter and, instead of getting stoned, he would do push-ups and sit-ups. I drew him Before and After pictures to help get his training started and told him to stick a picture of himself on his wall beside a picture of a body builder, and every morning to say to himself, "This is your goal, Timothy. This is you now, and this is you two years from now."

I told him, "If every day you picked up a newborn calf, in two years you'd be able to pick up a twelve-hundred-pound cow, maybe more depending on how big the cow gets."

I said, "But we need to check out Big Joe's situation. Like, is Shelly living with him? Has he still got that screwdriver? And stuff like that. By that time, you'll weigh in at about two hundred pounds, and you'll look like you're on the Wrestling Federation Power List."

Timothy said, "When he smashed my toys, he held me right up against him, so I could hear his heart beating so loud in his hollow chest that it seemed like I had an extra ear on that side of my head. There was nothing else in there but the beating of that heart the size of one of them big clay pots he grew garlic in. For days after, I could hear Big Joe's hammer, like garlic pots banging, day after day, pounding in my brain. Then, maybe a week later, with a nice voice, Big Joe would say, 'To make you tough, I hammer you down, and then to make you tougher, I stand you up. Now that you're a tough guy, you can climb up on my knee for cuddles.' And I did because I knew I would start to cry. Then, after I finished and couldn't cry no more, all my hate was gone, and I got down from Big Joe's knee and climbed into bed, and for the rest of that day and night, the beat of that ten-pound heart tattooed on the inside of my skull would not pound on the walls of my head."

He said, "It used to be that when Big Joe did a hammer job in the winter, he didn't take off his plaid shirt and t-shirt that he wore night and day over his belly in the summer. But probably now, going around doing handyman work for old ladies, he has to dress a little better and not wear that plaid shirt."

I said, "I remember he had to do the hammer job a certain way, follow the steps. Number one: Wait in your bedroom until seven when the big hand of the clock on the wall ticks its way to the twelve and the little hand to the seven. As the gongs begin to sound — one, two, three — you have to creep, creep out of your bedroom and down the hall and across the yard. Number two: You have to sit on the little stool with your toy and wait for the tread of his boot, one step at a time, on the driveway. Number three: You have to wait for the heavier beat of those boots hollow on the floorboards. Number four: You have to place your toy on the workbench and say your prayers for the hand that's holding the toy. And then, number five: You have to use this same hand to clean up the smashed toy with the broom and the blue dustpan."

Timothy said, "I don't remember none of that shit. I just remember the hammer over my head and that motherfuckin' screwdriver laying on the bench waiting for me to pick it up and stab him. Sonofabitchcocksuckermotherfucker…"

I said, "Probably now, in his bedroom, if there's no Shelly to share the bed with, he sprawls out full length on his back for his afternoon nap wearing his dress shirt, one of those made-in-China ones that are so thin you can probably see his heart beating in his chest hair. This might mean your two-handed swing could plunge one of Peter's little screwdrivers through Big Joe's shirt, through his chest bones, up to the hilt, without needing use his big screw driver and without needing to figure all this stuff out and without needing do the full weight lifting program."

Timothy said, "He's got two hearts."

"Lungs are divided in two, but not hearts."

Timothy said, "No way, man. Big Joe has two hearts. When I sat on Big Joe's knee and I put my ear to Big Joe's chest, first on one side then on the other, I could hear those two hearts, each one as big as an underwater bilge pump. When I worked one summer for Black's Barge Company, they had these two bilge pumps. When they kicked on, man, I could hear in the heart of the two bilges the beat of Big Joe's two hearts. It was like, when the beating of those two hearts got louder and the breathing of Big Joe's two lungs got heavier, the hammer beat harder, thudding in my ear like an underwater pump in the underwater hold. Fuckin' true, man. I worked at the same dock where Big Joe went fishing. I remember the slime off the fish splattering all over my face when he hauled them out and made my same skinny arms that carried his fishing pole down to the water unhook the slimy fish. But look now at my arms. See this hammer tattoo? And this one? If I have to go to court, I'm wearing a t-shirt so I can show the motherfuckin' judge the hammer. Big Joe used to say, 'I hammer you down; then I stand you up again.' When I take him down, he won't stand up again. And it's got to be with that same motherfuckin' screwdriver."

Timothy promised every day to do push-ups and presses, getting his muscles big enough to drive his screwdriver through Big Joe's handyman shirt and through both Big Joe's handyman hearts and all the way through into the mattress. But I figured, after he'd done a few push-ups, he'd decide killing Big Joe was too much work and forget about it and go back to getting stoned.

Chapter 29

OWEN

Like Big Joe had two hearts, I had two brains. One was telling me that a trip by subway and streetcar to Big Joe's house was not a good idea. But the other brain was saying, stand well back from the house, hide behind a tree, cast glances up and down, don't get too close, and if you do see Shelly, well, you're the expert at figuring stuff out as it goes along.

I got off at Dundas, walked two blocks, and stood across the street behind a tree. Big Joe's pickup was parked in his driveway. The street was deserted. I decided to take a few peeks through his windows, hoping I might see Shelly. I would have liked to watch her making her morning breakfast of frog's eggs porridge. I remember she never got up and out of her night outfit until ten, after Big Joe had gone to work, so she wouldn't have to watch him slurp up his Frosted Flakes with a serving spoon.

As I stood at the kitchen window, I went backward in time to sitting with Shelly in her bedroom, hoping she would say, How be, Owen, I put on my makeup and then let's you and me go for a Tim Hortons, just you and me, while Big Joe is away in his big truck.

Shelly wasn't there. I returned to the street. From there, I had a clear view of Big Joe's workshop: green with a black roof, a black door at the front, and a window with divided squares of glass at the side. There was no sign of anyone, so I crept through the small backyard to the shed, intending to peek in the window. But then I heard Big Joe shuffling back and forth inside, but not like how I remembered. Now his footsteps were a tired plodding, like empty shoes crossing an empty attic. They sounded as far away as foster father Robert's footsteps in the basement room where he picked the flesh off cats, and as distant as the pope's glass eye that used to wink at me. I had outgrown them all. Even the hammer. It was still tattooed into my memory, like everything else, but I was sixteen and getting older every day.

When I risked a quick peek, the first thing I noticed was that Big Joe's chin seemed to be receding into his neck, and his hair was receding from his forehead. He walked to the door to stare into the yard. In the light coming through the doorway, I saw the folds of his work pants were shiny, unlike his unpolished shoes, which were scuffed at the toe and worn at the heel.

Perhaps sensing someone was watching, or perhaps waiting for someone, he glanced at the house, listening it seemed, for Shelly maybe, before returning to the workbench. He opened the right-hand drawer and brought out his hammer. He laid it on the bench and then brought out a small box, its lid on a tiny hinge that snapped it open and closed it shut. I remembered this box. He'd kept it on his workbench at his foster house up north. Inside was a spare key for the back door. Probably the same here. He closed the lid and glanced my way, but because he was squinting into the daylight, he couldn't see me.

I returned to the kitchen window. The refrigerator was in the corner, and the table was in the middle, almost the same as at Big Joe's other house. Maybe this was the same table. I remember I would sit across from Shelly at lunch, and she'd say, Pass the butter, Owen, and she'd use both hands to take the dish so I wouldn't drop it. It had a lid with a knob on top that she lifted off with her thumb and forefinger. Sometimes before lunch, if she wasn't looking, I'd scrape the butter from the dish into the garbage, so when she lifted the lid, she'd say, Damn him, referring to Big Joe for not putting in new butter.

I heard Big Joe leave in his pickup, so I climbed through the partly open kitchen window. I knew right away Shelly was never there. Inside was a mess, dirty dishes in the sink and horse-racing magazines all over the living room, which seemed to be furnished with junk from Goodwill. The house was old, with lots of creaking floorboards. As I crept up the stairs, I tested each step, leaning forward to listen, memorizing which board creaked and which didn't, writing it down in a diagram in my mind. The fourth and the eight and the ninth could not be stepped on. To skip these, Timothy would need to steady himself with one hand on the wall so that he wouldn't lose his balance. I memorized the pattern of each step along the upper hallway, counting the floorboards, testing each for creaks. All the doors were shut, the only light a thin glimmer glinting in a silver slice beneath the bathroom door, which was shut, light on, like at his other house. The closer I got to what looked like Big Joe's bedroom, the louder my heart thudded, echoing in my temples like the pump of Timothy's bilge, hammering inside my head in a muffled underground pounding from the bedroom shadows to bounce its beat off every wall of Big Joe's house.

I took a deep breath. I sat on the top step and thought about it. No question, if a stake from a garlic patch jammed through the heart of a vampire would kill it as it slept, then a screwdriver from Big Joe's toolbox would kill Big Joe as he slept.

I sank down at the kitchen table. Across from me Big Joe sat, eating his Frosted Flakes. Next to me Timothy sat, eating his Healthy Shelly Breakfast. From under the brim of Big Joe's baseball hat, through his ESP x-ray vision aviator sunglasses, Big Joe watched with eyes that wee Timothy could not see. No matter where wee Timothy was, he would look around and there Big Joe would be, watching. In his bedroom, wee Timothy drew pictures of himself wearing aviator sunglasses and a baseball hat, watching Big Joe. In wee Timothy's pictures, Big Joe wasn't big. He was little, and Timothy was big, like now.

Except, except, I knew that, even if I wanted Timothy to do it, which I didn't, and even if Big Joe seemed not so big, which he wasn't, I doubted Timothy, in the shadows of Big Joe's bedroom, would be strong enough to sink a screwdriver into the heart in his memories, beating so big and hammering so hard he would run like a seven-year-old out of the bedroom and down the stairs the way I had just done.

Now at some old lady's house, Big Joe will remove his aviator sunglasses so he looks like an honest person, not needing to hide anything, like at church. He'll be wearing nice cologne, so he smells nice, like he did at church. He'll be wearing his suit, so he looks nice, like he did at church. While the old lady explains the problem, Big Joe will nod, agreeing with each word. Big Joe, who usually talks in grunts, the same way he eats, in the nice old lady's living room will say in a soft and soothing voice, How do you do? Lovely weather.

Like he did at church. He might even come right out with it and carry a Bible clutched to his chest at the front door.

I returned to the shed to hide the screwdriver from Timothy. The light shining through the divided panes of glass fell in crisscross shadows on the wooden floor to form little squares like the games of x's and o's. Now these crosses looked like the ones above St. Mary's, framed against the grey sky when I looked out our basement window. I imagined a cross ten feet tall with a long spike on each end and one at the foot. I imagined wee Timothy so big and strong he could barehanded reach out and pull the spikes out of the wood and use them to nail Big Joe to a cross, and then, with a two-handed overhead Joe-the-Hammer swing, drive the screwdriver through the handyman shirt and through the t-shirt underneath and through the curly black chest hair and into each black heart as slick and as easy as a stake into angel food batter. Big Joe dressed as a handyman Jesus carpenter, hanging from his self-made crucifixion like one of those Salvador Dali pictures.

I didn't hide the screwdriver from Timothy.

Chapter 30

SISTER CHARLOTTE

Mr. Knight said, "Bishop Humphries must be protected. But, Sister Charlotte, more importantly, Owen and Martha must be protected. The lawyers for the Indigenous boys would be overjoyed at the Father Eagleman and Bishop Humphries scandal falling fast on the heels of the residential schools scandal. I suggested some time ago that you get Bella on board. But you haven't done that. Therefore, Sister, I'm telling you — *telling* not asking — your next job is to convince Bella that she witnessed Joe Radley selling the Indigenous boys the drugs. The two of you were there and saw it. But be forewarned, Bella is less than you imagine, not at all the woman you remember. Be prepared to meet someone entirely different from your expectations. A quotation comes to mind: From the twisted timber out of which man is made, nothing straight will ever come. Do you understand what I'm telling you, Sister Charlotte?"

Mr. Knight's new buds were powerful enough that I could walk with comfort to the garden, and using fingers that formerly couldn't clip coupons from the newspaper, snip a nice bouquet, which I placed on the dresser in my bedroom while I sat on my bed and clasped my formerly crooked hands, now almost as straight as the hands on that plate that slipped from my fingers and smashed long ago, and decided what to wear.

I slipped on my blue skirt and buttoned the long-sleeved white blouse, realizing that, not long ago, I would not have been able to fasten the little fasteners at the wrist. Because I was tall and thin — well, used to be thin — dressed up, I looked about ten years younger than fifty-two. I took seventy-five dollars from the petty-cash tin in the filing cabinet, thinking we might go to a nice restaurant for a late lunch. I needed to impress Martha's mother and show her that Martha was well looked after by a good Christian woman.

I wrapped the flowers in green paper with a red ribbon left over from Christmas. I was pleased to have chosen black-eyed Susans — oh no, I meant to take the carnations. What is the matter with you, Sister Charlotte? I had been remembering a few years earlier, when I had taken my trip to the Holy Land to walk the stony ground, the Sisters had stopped off at a retreat centre where black-eyed Susans filled the backyard. During the trip, the Sisters formed a singing group, calling themselves the Roamin' Catholics. But none could sing as well as I could.

So with the flowers and a few St. Mary's "Come to Worship" brochures that I had written my name and phone number on, I set off. I was sure Martha would not agree to the church stuff, but she would agree to my taking her mother a bunch of these nice black-eyed Susans. Of course I couldn't tell Martha I was meeting her mother, not yet anyway, so I had picked them while she was at baseball. Peter wouldn't notice missing flowers, the same as he didn't notice anything else.

Mr. Knight had written in neat printing "27 Elm Street, apartment A." I wished I could be saying that after all these years I was excited. I wished I could be saying, how wonderful, first to have found Bella and second to be visiting her. But the fact is I was having my doubts. I would almost rather be visiting Uncle Merv, who kept his beer in the oven. At least I would know what to expect.

And by the way, Mr. Knight, although I don't pay much attention to your meanderings, and I know you know I can't do more than what I'm already doing, I have my limits. I'm not like Job. As blameless and upright as he was, every day God the Father sent him another affliction. I hope, Mr. Knight, Martha's mother will not become another affliction. I agree that out of a twisted branch no straight limb will come. But perhaps now, with my help, Bella can be the twisted branch that lies her head off instead of me, and that's why I'm doing this.

I didn't need a taxi. I took the subway at Rosedale and went down Yonge Street to Dundas and from there walked one block to Elm, a short street with one big maple towering above a row of shabby houses, like where Mr. Knight now lived. Every trip a different address. The last time I saw Mr. Knight on that shabby street, I'd limped along the walk, dragging my leg like that white pigeon. Now I walked almost normally, one foot straight after the other, to the end of the street, stopping at a high mesh fence marking off the subway line, a silver train flashing past. I thought, whatever could be in these buds? They're like riding a roller coaster. I've walked right past the address. What exactly is in these buds, Mr. Knight? They aren't colour coded, they look the same, but they seem to affect me differently different days, depending on the situation.

The single maple stood in the centre of the brown patch of the front yard of number 27. The front door was open. Inside, to the right, was a staircase; to the left three doors: A, B, and C. I knocked on A several times, until finally the door for B opened and a woman buttoning her bathrobe, although it was one o'clock in the afternoon, stuck out her head.

"Who do you want?"

"I'm looking for Bella Brock."

"She's probably down at the Nugget Tavern." She nodded toward Yonge Street. "Just around the corner."

The back of my neck tingled and I took a step backward. I didn't want to go into a tavern filled with leering, intoxicated men, into a dark room too gloomy to see anyone's face clearly and too dark to recognize anyone, although Bella knew I was coming and would be watching for me. But if so, why was she not at home? Something fishy was going on.

Thankfully the tavern was only half full. I sat in an empty chair, one table over from a man staring into his glass. "Excuse me, could you tell me where I might find Bella Brock?"

He looked up sleepily, then glanced around the room. "Ask that broad over there, at the back."

I crossed between the tables to sit beside her. "I'm looking for Bella."

The woman looked at me. She sat back in her chair and stared. My eyes had adjusted to the dark, but because the gloom hung like a fog, I couldn't see the features of the woman's face. But I could tell by the heavy lipstick and eyeliner and the low-cut dress that I was looking at a broken soul.

"I'm Bella," she said finally.

Surely, I had found the wrong woman. I leaned close enough that I could smell the liquor on her breath but couldn't make out her features, only doughy-looking flesh. This could not be Bella. This could not be Martha's mother.

"Twenty-seven Elm," she whispered. "Lesbians are my specialty."

Lesbian? Is she one of those primal feminists?

When the woman waved one hand in a vague point, I noted the ring with the blue stone on the third finger of her right hand. I remembered that ring.

"Twenty-seven Elm," she said again. "Around the corner. Apartment A. Wait here five minutes and then come."

As she leaned over to pick up her purse, her red dress gaped open to expose her heavy bosoms. She slipped off the chair. She pulled down her hem to cover her thighs as her spike-heeled shoes wobbled her across the floor and out the door.

Because the stale beery air had started a pain behind my eyes, I wanted to get out right away. At the nearest table, a man slumped over his glass; while at the next, another stared into the gloom, mumbling to himself; while beyond him, in the corner, three women shouted at a fourth stumbling between the tables to the washroom. Several times while I waited, I pulled my wrist from the sleeve of my blouse, checking the time. At last five minutes passed. I wanted nothing to do with this situation. To make matters worse, the last bud was wearing down. I limped my slow way to Elm. I passed the row of shabby houses and crossed under the maple to number 27.

"It's open!" she hollered in response to my knock.

I stepped into what could have been either a bedroom or a living room, for it contained three odd dressers, a red chesterfield minus one of its cushions, and two end tables painted blue. Nothing seemed to be in its right place: a dresser beside a chesterfield, a footstool under a window. The only light came from a small lamp on a TV standing on a chrome-legged table between two doorways. She stood in the shadows of a third, the bathroom. "Find a place to sit." Her voice was loud and coarse. "Just move those magazines out of the way."

As I moved them aside, I put the flowers on one of the little blue tables. I didn't know what else to do with them.

"Flowers. Fuck. That's a new one."

She disappeared into the bathroom. I could hear water running into the sink. I sat down and rested my aching head on the back of the chesterfield and closed my eyes. Good God, Mr. Knight, I should be in my bed, not in this filthy apartment with this woman. My knees were beginning to throb, and I knew I must go.

If this was Martha's mother, and if we were sitting side by side on the bench next to the apple tree, and she was disclosing her sins, I could rejoice with Jesus at her repentance. If I'm here for that reason, sent by Jesus, then we must sit side by side here on this chesterfield, and I must listen to her story and help her scrub away her sins one by one, and then be on my way.

The toilet flushed. Another five minutes passed. At regular intervals, I felt coming through the floor the vibrations of the subway. Sometimes, sitting on Peter's bench, I could hear that same faraway rattle of the subway line in the ravine behind the cemetery. I worried about Owen climbing the fence to explore along the tracks, but the one time he did, Martha tattled. She dragged him into the kitchen and said, Tell Sister Charlotte what you tried to do. And not waiting for his confession, she said, He should be sent to the Treatment Centre, Sister Charlotte. Those rails are electric. Look at him. I think he's already stepped on one.

Thinking about the two of them, I began to feel a little better, even though the smell of the apartment, like stale French fry grease, had begun to bother me. It would stick to my clothes, and Martha would say, Where have you been, Sister Charlotte, coming home smelling of stale French fry grease?

I opened my eyes. She must have come out of the bathroom while the toilet was running, for she now stood a few feet away, eyeing me suspiciously.

"One reason I like doing women" — she picked up the flowers — "they're more thoughtful. Most men are pigs."

She went into the kitchen and returned with a small glass. She drank it in one loud gulp, then, with a shudder, set the empty on the nearest dresser.

"Flowers, what the fuck. All right, let's get started."

"Started?"

"Money first."

To avoid any disagreement, knowing the money was all she wanted, I gave it to her. She counted it, and then, leading the way toward the door nearest the TV, she began to remove her dress. She threw it over the TV. She flopped on her back on the bed, her sagging thighs and breasts and body white on the rumpled covers. I turned away. I had taken three steps toward the bedroom door when I spotted, propped up in a gold frame on the bedside table, a photograph of my Martha, taken at about the same age as when I first met her.

The woman waved her arm at me. "You've paid your money. Either do your thing or else beat it."

I stooped for a closer look at the photograph, just to make sure, before I said, "I'm Sister Charlotte. I'm here about your daughter."

Bella sat up, struggling to blink into focus. "You're Sister Charlotte?"

"Martha is under my care."

Bella pulled on her clothes.

"Is there any way I can help you?" I asked.

She looked at me, her eyes foggy but filled with suspicion.

"You don't have to live like this. I can help. Sit here with me so we can talk."

"Ring-a-ding, Sister Charlotte. Ring-a-ding."

"But what about your daughter?"

"Ring-a-ding, Sister Charlotte. What about my daughter?"

"You wrote a letter saying you wanted to see her."

"Humphries made me do that. He thought if I met her, I might have feelings for her and care about what happens to her."

"You don't care what happens to her?"

Bella lay back on the bed. She closed her eyes. "Lock the door on the way out."

"No, please, such a beautiful child, how did this happen? Maybe we can pray together, Bella. Maybe I can help."

But Bella didn't answer. She seemed to have dropped off to sleep, her left arm across her front and the right hanging over the edge of the bed.

I slipped away and retraced my steps to the subway. I went down the stairs to the platform, which was jammed with people. As I struggled with my swollen knees to the far end, which seemed less congested, the crowd pushed me suddenly backward, pinning my aching shoulders to the cold concrete wall. From deep inside the tunnel, the wheels of the train shrieked on the iron rails. It rushed out of the darkness and into the light of the station and stopped beside the platform. I pulled myself off the wall and through the crowd. When the doors slid open, I got on, and the train rattled into the tunnel and into the next station, where I got off. I limped through the underground light of the subway and onto the street. I had gone as far as my front door, almost reached my bed, when I remembered that Rebecca Brown woman on the news. I couldn't remember what she had done but in court she claimed it wasn't her fault because she had married Satan, who wore a white suit and rented a Presbyterian church for the wedding. It was in the news. I don't know what that's called, when you watch the news and identify with the one in handcuffs.

Vague thoughts lingered in my mind for the remainder of the day and all that night until early next morning, before daylight came, before anyone was awake, I got up and, taking my Bible and a double dose of buds, I went downstairs and into the backyard, walking almost normally now, concentrating on holding my feet straight, minimizing my limp across the grass to sit on Peter's bench next to the apple tree.

Sitting, my mind begins to drift as it often does, sometimes playing tricks on me, like having dreams wide awake. I open my Bible, looking for directions, like Peter in his taxi, his helping hand, his GPS. Now it feels like the finger of the helping hand on that broken plate is pointing in the right direction. There, there now, Sister Charlotte. Lie back on the bench and enjoy the early morning of another summer day.

I close my eyes and relax into the early morning of another day. I feel the hand of Mr. Knight stroking along my cheek. There, there, Sister Charlotte. Relax a while. You worry too much. I feel him lift my body from the bench and carry me across the garden. To my left the stone wall of the temple; to my right the water cisterns; and straight ahead the cross where I lie down with the other two women at the feet of Mr. Knight.

"Sister Charlotte, what are you doing out here all night sleeping in the grass?"

"I forgot. I forgot."

"How could you forget to go to bed?"

"Oh my. Yes. I must have."

Martha helped me to the bench. "Owen wants beans on toast for breakfast."

"All right, Martha."

"I'm going to kill him while he's eating his beans on toast."

"All right, Martha. We can do it together."

Martha sat with me. "How should we do it?"

"Something nice, make it a surprise."

"Killing someone usually is a surprise."

"In the convent, this was my favourite time of day, before evening mass."

"It's not evening; it's morning."

"Oh my word. So it is."

Martha settled herself on the bench, her hands in the lap of her jeans, her head a little tilted, staring at me. She said, "Now your angel food cake won't turn out."

"Why not?"

"For thinking about killing, Owen."

"You know, Martha, I volunteered at the drop-in centre when I was not much older than you. Almost everyone was stoned — except me, of course. At the first light of dawn, when it opened, I would go in and, Martha, can you guess what we served all those stoners for breakfast?"

"Beans and toast."

"How did you know?"

"Just guessed."

"Let's go in for our beans and toast."

"None for you, Sister Charlotte. I like you better when you're sort of stalled, no wind in your sails, like on a still day drifting. Sometimes those pills get you too wired. Owen's been researching the different buds. They don't show up on a drug test so they give them to racehorses, some to calm them down for loading, and some speed them up and get them out the gate quicker."

"Then let's not kill Owen today, Martha. Let's go into the kitchen and watch him enjoy his beans and toast. We'll do it on a day I'm wired to get out the gate quicker."

Chapter 31

MARTHA

I sat on the green bench next to the apple tree and watched Peter wrap a bush in its winter burlap, the same colour as Sister Charlotte's hair, sandy brown with sandy brown ends frayed out in strings. Soon it would be my grade twelve Christmas exams, which I had to study for, but Owen did not. I adjusted myself on the bench, trying to get comfortable, and huddled under my coat. When Peter stopped and rubbed his fingers to warm them up, I noticed the scar on the back of his hand. He pulled aside the apple tree's overhead branches. He came over and sat beside me.

He said, "I think now is a good time to talk about a few things. A nice wind, a clear blue sky. A good day to clear the air, watch our differences take wing and fly off, like Sister Charlotte's white pigeon."

Peter's finger was stroking the scar on his hand, which was holding the differences waiting to be released. When he caught me watching, he said, "I have another scar across the top of my head that you'll be able to see when you get tall enough to look down on me. I realize that, yes, I know what you'll see is the scar, and I know you'll be standing up looking down at me. And the scar that you'll see is Sister Charlotte. I knew before she came how she would end up."

Peter looked around, rubbed his hands together, not certain what to say next. "Do you understand, Martha? It's not arthritis. It's Huntington's disease. Bishop Humphries didn't know that. I didn't know that. I thought I could help her, and instead I left her for you to look after."

"You knew Bishop Humphries was our father."

"Suspected, yes."

"So my own mother abandoned me to foster care and then my father left me with a drug-addicted nun and a three-monkeys monk in a foster home turned into a nursing home."

Peter put his hands into his pockets. "I used to carry my gloves in these pockets; I lost them someplace. I used to carry my values in these pockets; I lost them someplace."

"No, Peter, don't change the topic. Don't try and put it in your pocket. I'm not one of your three monkeys. I don't believe in monkeys and I don't believe in Jesus. I'm a foster kid, which means I don't believe in much of anything. So what are you trying to say? You're sorry?"

"I started off with good intentions. Someone had a baby and didn't want one; someone wanted a baby and couldn't have one. That's how the system works. Bishop Humphries was doing his best."

"Look through my eyes for a minute, Peter: one foster place to the next, at each one feeling rejected, confused, abandoned, and scared. Most of all scared of being sent away to some other foster place when this one doesn't work out. I know. I was sent to seven different foster families. What happens on Mother's Day and Father's Day? My birthday? Do you know? You don't. You can't. I used to draw pictures of my mother and father. They had arms without birthday presents and heads without faces. I know why. But you don't. How can you know why? Were you abandoned? Were you given away? Were you adopted? Were you in foster care? So tell me, how was Bishop Humphries doing his best?"

"Bishop Humphries saved you from the revolving door you were in. He did his best."

"Stop saying that! I did my best too. I wasn't good at doing my best because of the strict rules. I was good at doing my best because I didn't want to be sent away again. But I was. I hated every foster family I was in. But what I hated most was having to start new again and find my way around again with different parents in different beds and different food and different kids. Foster kids are like plastic bags. We get filled up with all the stuff in one place. Then when we go to a new place, we have to empty that bag so the new foster parents can cram in all the new stuff. So then I got sent with my bag of stuff to Peter and Sister Charlotte, and I did my best. I was always good and did what I was told and followed the rules and did the chores and it made me tough and strong enough to do my best. But no, Peter, Bishop Humphries did not do his best."

I took a deep breath. I reminded myself that me and Peter were sitting on the green bench trying to solve a problem, not make it bigger. "Peter, remember how you taught me to throw my fastball? You said, 'You've got a good arm, Martha. Let's see what your fastball will do for us.' You put the ball into my hand and said, 'Hold your fingers like this and throw me one.' So I pitched the way you showed me."

"I remember."

"Then, for hardball, you said, 'Think Superman. Stretch forward both arms as though you're going to fly. Then lean back on your left and kick forward on your right and drive the right arm like a punch.'"

"And you changed our team from losers to winners."

"Even though I was a girl."

Peter nodded. "Even though you were a girl."

"So, Peter, if you had the power to help me find the strength to change our team from losing to winning, then I must have the strength in me already to change my situation from losing to winning."

"That's true, Martha."

"Then, Peter, if I have the strength inside me already, I want you to help me find it so I can leave this place when I choose without having to wait for permission from CFCS."

While I waited for his answer, an empty space seemed to open between us. I stayed there, sitting beside him, waiting. Finally, I said, "Okay, I admit it. All this time I've been complaining and blaming and moaning about going one place to another, and now that it's almost time to leave, I'm afraid to go, because I don't know what I'm going into. So I need your help."

I closed my eyes, breathed deeply, and tried to find inside me better words to explain how I was feeling. "Pretend you're the monkey on your dresser with your hands over your eyes. Take away your hands and tell me what you see. And don't say you see the garden and the green grass and the stone fence and the cemetery and Tiny Tots Daycare. Look up and away from all that, beyond the top branch of the apple tree, more to the right, what do you see?"

Peter sat quietly in the emptiness putting together his next line of three-monkey excuses. "Many years ago, I was driving my cab late at night. A return run from the airport. No passengers, thank God."

"And you got a cut in your head."

"A very bad cut. I asked if they could call a priest." Peter rubbed the tips of his fingers along the scar at the top of his head. "The priest didn't give me last rites. He laid his hands on me, and he prayed for me. It was the strangest thing. I had been lying in my hospital bed, shaking cold. When I glanced up and out my window, beyond the top of the tallest tree, I saw death. But then, when the priest laid his hands on me, I became warm. I didn't die. I got better. That priest saved my life. His name was Father Humphries. Your father."

"OhmyGod, Peter, like in some kind of war story, a buddy throws himself on the grenade."

Peter rubbed his hands together again and put them into his pocket. Finally he said, "Owen had this figured out a long time ago. That's because his mind travels at a higher altitude than the rest of us, allowing him to look down at us and see our scars and not get upset about it."

"Bullshit, Peter. As far as Owen is concerned, we're no different from bugs."

I left, almost running so Peter couldn't see I was crying.

Chapter 32

MARTHA

Abruptly the hall light snapped on. A sliver of white shone beneath the door and Sister Charlotte whispered, "Owen! Get away from there! Get back into your room and go to bed."

I heard the shuffling of feet as Owen crept along the hall. His door slammed, and the light snapped off. I opened my door a crack and peeked into the dim and empty hallway, the only light coming from one tiny bulb by the bathroom door. As I slipped back into my room to return to bed, Owen appeared.

"I've been to Big Joe's again. I got into his house to look around."

"You're lying, Owen."

"I knew you wouldn't believe me, so I hid in his downstairs closet and recorded him on my BlackBerry. Walking around."

He turned on his BlackBerry. It sounded like Big Joe was fixing his roof, walking around overhead, stopping for each turn, crossing to the other side. I listened to the shuffling back and forth until, unexpectedly, it stopped. Then, more heavily, as though Big Joe had changed from shoes to boots, the footsteps on the wooden boards began to beat harder, crossing the roof, turning back, crossing once more.

"See what I mean?'

"You broke into Big Joe's house and then hid in the closet to listen to Big Joe walking around on his roof."

A door opened. Owen hustled back to his room. Sister Charlotte looked out, her outline shadowed by the light from the hall, one pale hand resting on the knob, one thin shoulder leaning against the frame, and between hair and mouth, two eyes squinting from a face puffy from the drugs. She stayed there a moment, then pulled the door shut. I could hear her in her bedroom, getting back into her bed.

After half an hour, Owen returned for more of his nonsense. He led me along the hall and down two flights of stairs to the basement. To the right, between the two doors marked Storage Room and TV Room, was the sign marked FURNACE ROOM KEEP OUT. Owen undid the latch and opened the door. In the pale light coming from a small bulb overhead, the arms of the furnace reached out every which way across the ceiling. Curtains of dusty cobwebs clutched at my face as he guided me through the shadows to the far corner.

"See this crack in the wall?" I was waiting for him to tell me to peek in. God only knows what creature he found in there, probably a rat. "Put your hand in there."

"Are you nuts? Put your own hand in there."

He pulled out a Bible. "It came in the mail from that nutcase Pentecostal preacher who has a dog that can tell which Bibles contain the Holy Spirit. This one doesn't."

I was in pajamas; I had had enough. "La-la-la, Owen. I don't care. Find someone else to drive crazy. I was in my bed, almost asleep, which is where I should be — in my bed because I've got a ball practice tomorrow. Look me in the eye and repeat after me: I won't go back to Big Joe's. Holy Mother of Mary, Owen, you're all I've got."

There, I said it out loud. All I had was standing in front of me, looking stunned as the day they found him and his sister in the Open Hatch. Which one had I really ended up with? The one right side up or the one upside down. Or maybe, now that I was thinking about it, more than likely, when they took him out of the Open Hatch he got dropped on his head. Or maybe at one of his placements he'd been a headbanger— there were lots of those in foster care —they made them wear helmets that gave them an electric shock every time they hit the wall.

But there, I had said it out loud. He was all I had.

Chapter 33

OWEN

A winter storm came, covering everything with a foot of snow and closing everything down. Peter dressed up as Santa Claus to give out the presents Christmas morning, including one for Amelia, Sister Charlotte's pigeon, who had stopped off on her way somewhere to rest out the blizzard before continuing her journey. She sat in Sister Charlotte's lap while Sister Charlotte opened her Merry Christmas Amelia card, drawn by Martha, who was, I have to admit, a pretty good artist. It was a picture of baby Jesus dressed in a pink snuggly and bonnet, snuggled in the manger, sucking his soother. Except he was a pigeon. Sister Charlotte unwrapped Amelia's present: Snowy Mountain Bird Seed.

Martha got a new hardball and glove. I got more science stuff, beakers, and microscopes. So while Martha sat punching her fist into her glove, softening the leather, and I sat reading the scientific explanation for DNA testing, Sister Charlotte read the baby Jesus story to Amelia, sounding out the words like in a Simplified Reader, slow enough for Amelia to follow the plot.

Strange, sort of, but not really. We were seeing a human side of Sister Charlotte. Or maybe she had got it into her head that Amelia was one of us kids. It was such a nice Christmas that I thought I should have invited Timothy.

Christmas evening service on Jesus's birthday, candles but no cake, me in the pew next to Martha, my mind busy wondering how they could bury the dead lady they were praying for in the winter when the ground was frozen. Too bad we weren't living by the real Dead Sea instead of the one across the stone fence. Winter or summer, I could catch bugs all day long, and keep them in my cave along with the bugs that already lived there.

After the service we watched a repeat of the livestream Christmas program that Father Small had made for the children to watch at home on Christmas Eve. It was like a workshop in the frozen North, Santa's white-as-snow words like snowflakes from his white-as-snow beard sent along black cable wires from the North Pole to all the other poles up and down the street, bringing his Christmas message to the snowed-in boys and girls.

I thought about Timothy's Christmas Eve at the drop-in. I imagined on this evening of goodwill, Timothy receiving a million-dollar Christmas-gift court settlement. I imagined on this evening of goodwill, Sister Charlotte healed of her addiction. I imagined on this evening of goodwill, Bella healed of her addictions. I imagined on this evening of goodwill, Martha and Bishop Humphries having Christmas hugs. I imagined on this evening of goodwill, all this snow had fallen white to cover up our coming darkness.

I said to Timothy, "It's too cold to kill Big Joe. Let's forget about it."

Chapter 34

OWEN

Springtime came. I hoped the subzero weather would have in Timothy's mind permanently frosted over Big Joe's sunglasses and permanently frozen Big Joe's hammer and permanently turned Big Joe's body to ice. But no, even if it had, Timothy's springtime intention was to watch the poisonous insides of Big Joe melt out of his punctured chest like steaming Christmas pudding into a springtime snowbank. Timothy said, "So we'll do it closer to summer when it's not so motherfuckin' cold."

Springtime came. Tadpoles in the pond at the back of the cemetery, waiting for their arms and legs to grow them into frogs. Tulip buds in Peter's garden, waiting for their leaves to grow them into flowers. Pigeons in the three tall crosses, waiting for Mr. Knight's final pill to send Sister Charlotte up the chimney.

Springtime came. The thought of Shelly's hand in mine sent warm shivers up my arm and into my belly, like the hot-water bottle she brought me in the middle of the night for my bad dreams. The warm shivers I got from Shelly, I could understand. She could touch me all she wanted.

But never Sister Charlotte.

Waiting with Sister Charlotte for the subway, she took my hand. I didn't like being touched by Sister Charlotte, but on this warm spring day, when I felt her fingers locked with mine, I felt a connection. Maybe Sister Charlotte's fingers were less crooked this day, or maybe the skin of her hands was less limp and wrinkly, less like five shrivelled carrots dried up in a dark cellar. She had put on weight in odd places, mostly around her stomach. Her neck was as scrawny as the turkey she made with Martha at Christmas. And while Sister Charlotte was pale and flabby and fat and scrawny all at the same time, she was also turning yellow, like maybe her liver was being shut down. So what would be the reason for this sudden connection with Sister Charlotte other than it was a warm spring day?

Me and Sister Charlotte got off the subway at College and, hand in hand, walked along a short street opposite a tattoo parlour. The houses were shabby, and the people on the street were shabby, and the people sitting on their porches even shabbier.

I asked her, "Why did Mr. Knight move?"

"I don't know, Owen. Help me find this number."

"You should have a picture and ask the people we just passed, 'Do you know where this man lives?' He'd be easy to recognize."

"I think that's the problem, Owen."

She seemed frightened and lost, stopping at every house to peer at each number.

"I'll go into the houses for you," I said. "Maybe he lives in that house there. Maybe he lives over there in that house."

Sister Charlotte was getting anxious. I could see her mind printing the labels for the people we passed on the sidewalk: Drug dealers. Welfare bums. Lost souls, all of them. When a drunk approached, hand out for spare change, her grip tightened, and I realized she was thankful I had come along. She probably thought no one would bother a crippled woman holding the hand of a seventeen-year-old. Even better, she should have dressed up in her white head-cover thing, like normal nuns wear.

She gave another drunk a loonie, and he wandered off. Then she finally found it: a one-storey bungalow, not as shabby as the other houses. I watched Sister Charlotte labour up the front walk, glancing both ways, up and down. I waited on the sidewalk as she hoisted herself one step at a time, right leg first, up the steps onto the porch. Before knocking on the door, she touched her Sisters button for good luck. The curtain on the front window slid sideways, and a face peeked out. The door opened. She disappeared inside.

In ten minutes, she reappeared on the front porch. I couldn't believe it. Her transformation was something like Shelly in bathrobe, PJs, and slippers to short shorts and tank top with makeup and sunglasses. The transformation, as Sister Charlotte took my hand and we set off for the subway, was like Sarah and me heading off kind of bouncy to a Yonge Street restaurant for a nice lunch, her elbow resting on the table in the outdoor patio; between the two fingers of the hand, not crooked from arthritis, a cigarette. Maybe add to that net stockings and a miniskirt, and in her other uncrippled hand, a glass of wine.

Sister Charlotte looked the same, talked the same; her hair was the same, parted and flat, like pictures of ladies in 1950s' calendars. The same. The pain lines in the face were the same. But, like the transformation of a tadpole into a real frog happened only in the pond, Sister Charlotte's transformation into a real person happened only in my head.

Maybe because it was spring. I don't know. For whatever reason, I had begun to feel compassion for Sister Charlotte.

Chapter 35

OWEN

Usually at nine o'clock, Martha and I climbed out my window and onto the roof and crept past the office window to view the stars through my telescope. I had a new pair of College Star Reds. The blue laces were too long. Afraid I might step on them and trip and fall off the roof, I crawled on hands and knees. When I moved my legs from crouched to standing and looked between the office window frame and the curtain, I could see that Sister Charlotte was in the office with someone. We moved to one side to see better and sat down to listen.

The office window was always held open a little by a wooden block. Sister Charlotte liked to have fresh air in every room. Stale air carried bits and pieces of other people's bodies, she said, and should not be allowed to circulate through the house for everyone else to breathe.

I hadn't seen Paul the detective for about six years. He'd put on a lot of weight. Now he looked like the refrigerator repairman down the street who walked to work every morning, winter or summer. The repairman wore a work uniform with "Jerry" written on the shirt pocket. Big Joe's work uniform was a plaid shirt and work pants. Father Small's work uniform was his Sunday robes. I remembered that Paul's uniform was a suit and tie. But today Paul was wearing blue cargoes and a blue shirt.

Detective Paul and Sister Charlotte were sitting opposite one another, leaving the chair behind the desk empty. Paul seemed to be in pain, for he had slumped forward and was staring at the floor. My memory of him was a sit-straight, look-you-in-the-eye guy, so I knew he was having difficulty facing Sister Charlotte, who looked like she'd taken a steroid-injected racehorse bud and slipped into overdrive, so I knew out of her mouth would come a streams of windy nonsense meant to deflect the questions asked in some direction other than the one that would lead to an answer. Stoned or not, the words always came to her, like in her little-girl story: the words for the passion song "You Will Know the Angel When She Comes," just came to her. From an angel, I guess, up there above the chimney. Maybe my sister. In fact, that was the answer. It was my sister.

Paul shifted in his chair and straightened up a little, getting ready for whatever words were about to come back at him, and asked, "Are Owen and Martha safe with you and Peter, or should they be moved right away? Bishop Humphries insists they stay here."

"Of course, they stay here."

"But the Criminal Code is very clear when it comes to safeguarding the health of children. It seems, Sister Charlotte, you have found yourself in an impossible contradiction."

"And you have found yourself in an impossible contradiction. There's no place to move them to. And besides, they're soon eighteen and will soon be given the choice to either go on their own way or stay here with Peter."

"And you can honestly say during all this time you haven't been taking illegal pain pills, Sister Charlotte?"

"No pills. Absolutely not. I can swear on my Bible that I take no pills. Hand it to me, Paul. That Bible there. A brand new one. I'm a nun. I'll swear on this Bible I take no illegal painkillers. There. See? My hand is on the Bible. Ask me any question you want."

"Yes, I see your hand is on the Bible."

"But I'll admit, mornings are hard. So I get up early enough to rub Deep Relief into my knees so that I can hobble down those stairs to make a good breakfast before I send the children off to school. Then I go out into the sunshine, if there is any. And that's another thing: living in this dreary climate. By the time I limp across the yard and finally reach Peter's bench to sit a while, by the time I get myself comfortable, the clouds cover the sun while I'm sitting there, in the same manner they covered the cross while Jesus was hanging there."

"I know, Sister Charlotte. And no one carries your aching body back to your tomb and lays you down to rest. That is, until Martha gets home."

"What! Since when? Carries my aching body? What are you talking about?"

Paul sat back in his chair, his thumb and two fingers turning his pen. "I sometimes wonder. In fact, every time I come here, I leave shaking my head, wondering what we were talking about."

Paul got to his feet. "I understand you'll be testifying in court that Joe Radley — not Father Eagleman and Bishop Humphries — gave the drugs to those Indigenous boys."

"That is correct."

"And you know that perjury is a felony offence with jail time. You and Humphries and Eagleman will all be in jail together."

I couldn't hear Sister Charlotte's answer because she was ushering Paul to the door. From the veranda roof, I watched Paul leave in his black Chevy, a car suitable for him, like a limousine was suitable for Mr. Knight.

Chapter 36

OWEN

After baseball practice, Martha and I walked the four blocks along the street that ended at the far end of the cemetery. The houses we passed were shabby, like at Mr. Knight's, and the people on the street looked shabby, like where Mr. Knight now lived. All the shabby people sat on the front porches of their shabby houses and watched us walk to the chain-link fence where the street ended at the subway tracks at the back of the cemetery. I sat in the grass and leaned against the fence. Martha sat in the grass and leaned against the fence. We listened to the subway trains rattle by.

I wondered if living in one of these shabby houses on this shabby street would have been better than living with Sister Charlotte in Peter's neat tidy house. Probably in these shabby houses no one sorted garbage and no one went to church. No one had to tidy stuff away in special cupboards. Everyone would sit all day on their front porches and do nothing, their kids' toys scattered all over the front yards, which didn't have any flowers to not step on. Had Martha's foster placement been here, would she have ended up a different Martha? According to my DNA research, most people are like any other sentient being, born a certain way and stay the same their whole life.

***

Mr. Knight and Bishop Humphries arrived uninvited at eight o'clock next morning and joined us for a pancake breakfast cooked by Martha. Sister Charlotte took her place at the head of the dining-room table at 8:55 a.m. Luckily for Peter, he had volunteered to do a taxi run for a buddy. I listened to Bishop Humphries say the grace and then I listened to his chewing of the pancakes and to his slurp of the coffee, served to him by Martha.

Sister Charlotte had a small appetite and took small helpings with lots of quiet burps due to her drugs, sometimes double burps like double plunk on the organ. She was looking worried, so I guessed that Mr. Knight and Bishop Humphries were here to talk about the trial.

Gale force winds had been howling all night and had not subsided, so when Sister Charlotte invited them on a tour of the garden so that Martha and I couldn't hear their conversation, Bishop Humphries declined. He put his hand up to his black-as-shoe-polish hair, which I realized was a wig.

After Sister Charlotte and Mr. Knight left, Bishop Humphries said to Martha, who was doing the dishes, "Father Eagleman was an orphan. His parents were killed in a car wreck when he was a baby, both of them buried in a cemetery in Hamilton, which meant he didn't need to try to find them or didn't need to wonder about the whats and the whys of where he came from or how he happened to be in the first place or if his mother abandoned him because he cried too much."

Martha said, "Lucky him."

"I read somewhere birthdays are difficult for kids like you."

"Kids like me?"

"Birthdays remind kids like you that your birth mother gave you away."

Martha said, "Kids like me?"

"The CFCS saves kids like you from unfit mothers."

"Kids like me?"

Bishop Humphries was slouched on a kitchen chair, his black suit jacket open. Like Paul, he had put on a lot of weight, so now his belly hung over his belt, looking like it would take ten priests to carry his casket to the grave, which is where he would end up if he continued this conversation with Martha.

With no more expression on his wide pasty face than a pan of bread dough, he said, "Sister Charlotte has made a great sacrifice for you and for your foster brother, Owen. She has martyred herself all these years, refusing to take medication strong enough to ease her excruciating pain so that she could keep you and Owen until you reached eighteen."

"She hasn't been taking stronger pain medication?"

"We suspected she was. But she swore on her Bible she wasn't, and the CFCS will not question a nun as devout as Sister Charlotte, especially if she swears on her Bible."

"You mean a nun can't swear on her Bible to tell the truth and then lie?"

"No, she can't."

"How about a bishop?"

Bishop Humphries smiled like the man on that dentist commercial, except up close and real, the smile didn't look so smiley. It looked like yellow teeth in a red gumline of the devil when he said, "Of course not, Martha. A bishop is a bishop and cannot lie."

At this point Bishop Humphries should have got down on his hands and knees and begged for forgiveness; or he should have walked away, his shiny black wig and black suit disappearing into see ya later. Foster kids understand a see ya later from a father who would rather walk away than face the truth.

But I don't know. Many of the stories we tell ourselves are lies we make up to make ourselves feel better.

Bishop Humphries was just the same as everyone else, speaking the lies softly, hoping no one was listening closely.

Bishop Humphries flexed his fingers. "How do you like the mitt I got you for Christmas? Yes, that very expensive mitt was from me, in case you've forgotten. I nearly made the pros. Do you want to go behind Tiny Tots where it's sheltered and throw me a few?"

Martha stood poker straight, staring at him. She flexed back at him the fingers of her pitching hand.

Bishop Humphries said, "Yeah, I could have played pro. My pitch clocked in at about two hundred miles an hour."

"My hardball clocks in at about four hundred miles an hour."

"What team do you play with now, Martha? The Blue Jays?"

"What team did you play with, Bishop Humphries? The Yankees?"

"Well, this was the minors. But how would you like it if a taught you how to throw a curve ball?"

Martha stared at Bishop Humphries's black wig and pasty face and saggy stomach. I had never seen her not have a quick answer to a question she didn't like. She could always come back with something. This made the question so big that the waiting for the answer seemed to elbow its way into the room to stand in front of Bishop Humphries and say, Are you sure you want Martha to pitch you her fastball?

The previous Sunday, Father Small had preached a sermon about getting a new car or a new TV. "When a new car or a TV comes into your hand, it goes into your heart. When an uninvited stranger comes into your hand, he also should come into your heart. For surely an uninvited stranger in your heart is better than a new car or a TV in your hand."

So, of course, at this moment, standing before her was an uninvited stranger who had, first of all, got into her heart and was now giving himself into her hand, which, for Martha, looked at this moment better than a new car or a new TV.

Martha gave Bishop Humphries her old glove and, hardball in hand, she led the way to the parking lot behind Tiny Tots. She pointed for Bishop Humphries to stand by the wooden fence separating the properties. He fitted the glove and stood back, close to the fence. He slapped his right fist into the glove and crouched forward, waiting for the pitch that, if he didn't catch it, would smash through the fence and go clear across the neighbouring yard and through the next fence.

I had watched Martha deliver a pitch many times. She always stood dead still, arms hanging loose, hands at her side, centring herself, getting into the zone of a Zen-like trance as she drove strength into the muscles across her shoulders, making the batter wait, get fidgety, lose concentration — the technique Peter had taught her.

I watched Martha's body sag into relaxation as her pitching arm swelled and grew, sucking strength from the muscles of her calves and from the tendons in her thighs and from the long licorice-twist muscles along her back and from the cables across her shoulders, delivering power into her arm and into the fingers of her hand, compressing every molecule of strength into the ball, forcing so much strength through the skin of the ball that, at the exact second the ball would explode from all that compacted strength and Martha's arm would blur into the pitch, the ball would break from a grip aimed directly at the catcher's mitt. And simultaneously, between pitch and catch, no space or time but instantaneous lasers of transferred strength from the power lines of her heart into her arm to smack into Bishop Humphries's glove and sear like fire up his arm, leaving it smoking.

Bishop Humphries did not see the pitch. He did not see the ball leave the hand. If Martha had aimed at his glove, the heat of the fire in the ball in his hand would have split his arm in two and set to flames his shattered wrist. If Martha had aimed for his leg, he would have dropped to the ground with a shattered knee cap. If she had aimed for his head, it would have snapped off his neck like a pumpkin on a fence post.

Martha left him lying on the asphalt and, without a word, she went inside to do her Martha chores: to gather the firewood and carry the water and bake the rhubarb squares and make the pancakes and fix the supper and do her homework before she lay down and rested up for her next day of looking after her foster mother.

I phoned the ambulance. A police car came. While the medics loaded an unconscious Bishop Humphries into the ambulance, I asked the lady police officer if she'd like to see my experiments. As I led the way up the stairs to my room full of test tubes and beakers and frog tanks hatching eggs, I explained I had found a way to use flow cytometry to fertilize a mouse egg using genetic material from any other cell in the mouse. I showed her the mouse and explained that I had stopped experimenting on it because Martha had named it Albert and got Albert a wife, Minnie, and now they liked to cuddle up with Martha and Petunia on her bed.

Martha said, "My brother Owen is a genius. He studied the research on Kaguya, the first parthenogenetic mammal, and now he's been invited to give a lecture at the U of T. Owen just won the provincial Senior Scientist contest. His big presentation is tomorrow. His experiments are on the web."

Martha offered the policewoman a rhubarb square, but the officer said she could not stay. She had another call.

***

The next evening my old teacher, Mrs. Colgan, gave me a ride home because I couldn't carry all the charts on frog DNA. I hadn't seen her since grade eight, four years ago. She smelled like flowers. The clock on the dashboard of her car had fluorescent red numbers. Her fingernails were painted a different red, and a tiny stone in the centre of her earring was another red.

I would never forget all the fun things she did when she was my teacher, every morning bringing in boxes of stuff to use for lessons: tin cans, paper bags, Styrofoam balls. One spring, she brought in a box of day-old yellow chicks and hooked up a light to keep them warm and let the kids pick them up. She lived on a farm outside the city, and she had dogs and cats and probably pigeons. But now Mrs. Colgan worked at the school board office as some kind of go-between for CFCS.

"Tell me, Owen," she said, "what exactly have you discovered? In detail. I know you've explained it to me, but try again."

"Frog sperm has the same genetic material as humans. I think in the virgin birth, the male DNA has to come to the embryo from the mother's father. Peter said to submit it to the contest and take some pictures and include it as part of my resume for a University of Toronto scholarship."

"Virgin birth, Owen?"

I continued to explain about the frogs and about how I was linking my discoveries into T-cell research in cancer treatment, not paying much attention to what I was talking about, thinking that Mrs. Colgan smelled like rain, then thinking her car was warm and the seats were soft, not like Joe the Hammer's cold seats with all the windows always open, then thinking the police wouldn't charge Martha with attempted manslaughter because I was the only witness to an unfortunate accident: two people playing catch, one wild throw.

Chapter 37

OWEN

As we were coming through the front door, I saw Paul the detective, dressed in a blue suit and tie, go into the office. I figured something important was up, like maybe Timothy had murdered Big Joe without telling me, so I got Martha and we climbed through my bedroom window onto the veranda roof, where I had my telescopes set up, and crouched next to the open office window to listen.

"Bishop Humphries is improving," said Paul. "But I want a truthful answer, Sister Charlotte. Was Bishop Humphries playing catch with Martha? Or was someone else involved? Like Joe the Hammer Radley. The OR doctor says it must have been a blow from a hammer."

Sister Charlotte raised her right hand to rub her temple. She shifted in her chair. "Did you read in the social media that a foster child put Bishop Humphries in a coma?"

"Of course not. I talked with the doctor."

"Some people — not me, of course — but some people read nothing but Twitter. You know how they make up stories to make the news more interesting. Is that what you're doing?"

"Fake news, yes. Mainstream media does the same. But this incident with Martha was not reported in the media. Back to the question, Sister Charlotte. Did Joe Radley attack Bishop Humphries with a blow of a hammer to the forehead that might make him a permanent invalid?"

I waited for Sister Charlotte's brain to press its remote switch to set the wind to blow her streamers into words of nonsense. "A permanent invalid. Let me tell you something. I have seen men cured of alcoholism. I have seen cripples made whole. I have seen cancerous tumours healed and diabetics cured. I have seen lost souls come up on the stage and fall upon their knees, and I have watched the hand of God reach down and touch them, as the hand of God will come down and touch Bishop Humphries, and you too, Detective, if you're ready."

Paul sat back in his chair, his pad in his left hand, his thumb and two fingers turning his pen end to end like a windmill. I watched the pen's round-and-round turn. I saw in the detective's face a wish that the wind would blow this crazy person away. I saw that he knew, by creating coloured streamers and windy words and a blown-away look, Charlotte would go into court and climb onto the stand and dodge all the questions asked and probably create a mistrial.

He said, "I know what you mean. My grandmother, may she rest in peace, saw the light and was cured of gout by Benny Hinn."

"Well then, when God decides Bishop Humphries is ready to see the light, He will open the bishop's eyes and the bishop will see the light, and then you can ask him. But if you want my opinion, I'll give it to you: Joe the Hammer Radley had motive. Martha is a seventeen-year-old girl who has never in her life held a hammer, if that's what you were getting at. Write that in your little pad."

Paul's expression didn't change. He made a notation in his little pad. "What I've written down here, Sister Charlotte, is that you're refusing to answer the question."

"What question?"

Paul checked his watch and stood. He went to the door. "Oh. Almost forgot to mention. Obstruction of justice is a felony offence. Is there anything you'd like to change in the details you've given me?"

"Is your life empty of meaning, Detective? Is that it?"

Paul looked thoughtful. "Often it is. Yes. I understand what you're saying, Sister Charlotte. There's one bad apple in every basket, so to speak. One bad apple in an otherwise good basket. And my job is like that of the storekeeper. If the storekeeper has proof that the apple is bad, he takes it out of the basket. If there's no proof, there's no need to do anything. But even without proof, the storekeeper must sometimes take the apple out of the basket if it looks as though it might go bad. So yes, after a while, the job of finding bad apples before they get badder becomes, well, not empty of meaning, but discouraging."

Sister Charlotte tilted her head to look down her nose and fasten a frown on the detective, who said, "But the Criminal Code is very clear when it comes to perjury in the apple basket, especially when it pertains to safeguarding the health of children. So I think I'll pay a visit to Joe the Hammer and see what he's got to say for himself."

Chapter 38

OWEN

Through the shed window, I watched Big Joe flip the light switch and sit on his little stool at his workbench, today, for some reason, cleared of all tools, including his hammer, which I had intended to put under my shirt and place at Tiny Tots. I guess Paul beat me to it.

Big Joe slipped his aviator sunglasses into his shirt pocket, the one on his right where he carried his big handyman pencil. He took the aviator sunglasses out again and held them in the palm of his hand, staring at them. Then, with a sigh, he laid them on the workbench.

He looked up and stared off, his eyes blank. But not blank for me, for I saw in those unshielded eyes, diminished of sight by the glare from the window, his plea, imploring me, Please, Owen. You have to help me out.

His eyes were saying this in words not much more than a whisper, as though he didn't want anyone to hear. Yet I could hear them clearly: I took you in when your real father did not. I took you in as a child and gave you the love and attention your bishop father could not.

He was not saying that. But although I could imagine the feel of those words rolling off his tongue and into my ears, I knew that even if he could see me as I could see him, anything I said in return would not remove from his forehead those wrinkles of contrition or remove from his frowns those furrows of worry. Eyes that formerly could burn through the walls of poor wee Timothy's or William's or Luke's bedrooms and through the ceiling of poor wee Timothy's or William's or Luke's head and into each wee mind and into each wee heart the fear of that hammer — those eyes were now so watered and weakened they would fill even Timothy, if I could bring him here to look through the window, with nothing except pity.

He must have been reading my thoughts because he put on his aviator sunglasses and went to the door and looked into the yard. He had lost so much weight that his work pants hung in tired drapes and sagging folds around his thin frame. Hands clasped behind his back, he stared out the open doorway. He removed his aviator sunglasses, polished them with his handkerchief, and returned them to his nose. He straightened up and threw back his shoulders. The polish on the glasses seemed to have made him feel better. He took them off and, fishing the handkerchief from his pocket, gave each lens a few more wipes before returning them to his nose. He returned to his bench. Leaning over and placing his hands palm down, he examined the blue nail of one finger, which he must have hit with his hammer.

Then when he looked straight up, right at me, I saw with my combined twist of thought and memory and vision, peering in and leaning close, one eye shut, the other squinting, I saw that Big Joe's eyes, formerly staring at me from behind aviator sunglasses, were inside himself now, examining his own thoughts that were fluttering around without direction in his guilty conscience, like moths around a burned-out light. I was seeing Big Joe not with my eyes but with my heart.

I had found compassion for Big Joe.

But only for a moment. For with my squinting eye, staring through lopsided glasses into the clouded glass of a workshop window on this overcast day, that is how I saw Big Joe. But only for a moment. Because I knew that maybe Big Joe wasn't bothered about anything except that Shelly was gone. Maybe he wasn't feeling guilty about anything he'd done to Timothy or anyone else: foster children of no more importance than the rush he got smashing their toys. The only thing he was bothered about was being framed for doing a hammer job on the bishop.

Chapter 39

OWEN

Amelia didn't belong with the wild pigeons that hung out at St. Mary's. She was pure white, so we noticed her as soon as she arrived and knew as soon as she was gone. Every two or three weeks, she stopped to see Sister Charlotte, always staying two hours and then gone, making her way home. One day we noticed Amelia under the bush by the church, dragging one injured wing, hiding, thirsty and starving. She had managed to shelter herself in the folds of that same towel. Sister Charlotte carried her around for a few days and fed her and nursed her like the last time. But then, not like the last time, Amelia didn't want to leave.

"She knows a good deal when she sees one," said Peter. "But still, she a homer, she's bred to go home."

"She wants to go home," said Sister Charlotte, "but she's afraid to fly."

So Peter got a ladder and leaned it against the church roof, tucked Amelia into the crook of his arm, climbed to the top, and placed her on the edge. Sister Charlotte stood at the bottom, twenty feet out from the wall of the church, squinting into the sun, arms outstretched, palms up, crooked fingers coaxing.

Perched on the edge of the roof, looking down at Sister Charlotte far below, Amelia paced back and forth, wanting to fly to her friend but afraid to try. Finally, gathering courage, she came closer to the edge and leaned forward, stretching farther and farther, finally toppling over. She dropped headfirst like a tumbler until, partway through her fall, instincts took over, and she opened her wings. But the left one, still weak from the injury, stalled on the uptake, and she tilted to that side, until changing the wing-tip angle, she recovered and went into a glide. She circled Sister Charlotte's head twice; then, with two upstrokes, rose to the rooftop to land on one of the church steeples.

"You silly pigeon," said Sister Charlotte. "I knew you could fly."

Now every Sunday was, for Martha, the beginning of another week closer to eighteen. Instead of slamming into my room to call me names, she now tap-tapped on my door before coming in to sit quietly for a few minutes on my bed before saying, "Can I talk to you about something, Owen?"

And she would start about her mother. Martha was determined that when her job of looking after Sister Charlotte was over, she would start a new job saving her mother. Martha would put her into rehab and get her clean and sober and then, like the rehabbed mothers in the movies, do mother-daughter stuff to make up many years absent.

Sometimes she would get focused on one thought, like why her mother chose the name Martha. I didn't know why. Maybe her mother didn't choose that name. Maybe her mother left a tag on her big toe, Name Unknown, so the clerk who found her in the Walmart washroom named her after her favourite movie star. Maybe someone had a letter from her mother explaining the events leading up to her unwanted arrival, hoping when Martha got older, she would read that letter and understand her mother's situation and, by the way, Martha, you got named after your great Auntie Martha.

I said, "Lots of famous people have babies called Martha. Marthas all over the place, now grown up and elderly but still wondering why they got named Martha instead of Suzie or Jackie."

Now Martha had this mirror thing, wanting to look pretty for when she would meet her mother. After Martha finished putting on her makeup in the bathroom — well, she was never finished. To be finished, she would need a full-time makeup lady, like seven-year-old Sister Charlotte had, to comb her hair and do something to highlight her blue eyes. Fuss with her knee socks. Martha never wore knee socks and didn't have blue eyes. Well the makeup lady could fuss with something else, like her face, brush more blush on her cheeks. And she'd have Martha climb up on a stool and sit so Mum could take her picture. I could add lights and create halos over her head. I'd make sure the lights weren't noticeable, only the halos. There was probably an app on my BlackBerry for that.

The more we talked the more I realized Martha deserved to have halos for looking after Sister Charlotte and now planning to look after her other mother. For looking after me too, I guess. My face had started to grow pimples — from not washing it properly, said Martha, and not eating my vegetables. I'd wash my face and look into the mirror, and there would be splash marks on the glass, so then Martha would make me wipe off the face in the mirror and then wipe my face. Then she'd shove me out the door so she could put on her makeup and then she'd shove me out the door so she could wash it off at bedtime and then again in the morning, and so on, almost as bad as brushing my teeth thirty-two times a day.

I remember being little and standing in front of the mirror, and Shelly coming into the bathroom, and there she would be, behind me in the mirror. Maybe Martha imagined her mother coming in while she was putting on her face stuff, and there her mother would be, behind her in the mirror.

One problem. I couldn't remember what Shelly's face looked like in the mirror, because I was at the bottom of the glass looking up, and the top of my head was level with that biker-chick belt she liked to wear, which was black with a silver buckle. It held up her low-slung tight jean shorts, frayed at the bottom. At the top was a slice of the bare body, which my vision followed in a sightline up when her hand came down across the mirror to run through my hair and then slide along the back of my neck to a tickle-tickle that shivered down my back in ripples. Now when I looked into the mirror, my mind blurred into an image of Shelly and stuck there on the glassy surface. According to the theory, this was happening to me because I would be soon eighteen and should be having thoughts about asking some girl to go to the dance, not Martha of course, but … well, I didn't know any other girls, not ones that would go to the dance with me.

"Sister Charlotte, Owen is washing his face again. I can hear him, Sister Charlotte. Splash-splash, wipe-wipe-wipe, making a mess.

Yeah, right, Sister Charlotte, you know what he's like. You promised to have him put down."

"I did no such thing."

"You did. We'll put him out of misery, you said that."

"Oh, for Heaven's sake, Martha. Give a body nosebleeds."

"You promised. Today is the day."

"In a minute then, Martha."

"I've been trying to be nice to him, but this is too much."

"I know, Martha."

"Oh, never mind. What's the use? Dry your hands, Owen. I want to hear the drying of hands, not the splashing of water. That's splashing. It's not drying, Owen. I don't want to hear the splashing."

Martha was waiting for me outside the door so she could follow along behind saying "moron" as I walked down the hall to my room.

I shut the door and curled up on my bed. Now my pillow was wet from the water I'd splashed on myself. Little drops had dripped on the bedroom floor. I got down on my hands and knees to mop with my t-shirt. With a second t-shirt, I began to dry my hair, finally wiping my hands and face, and last, with a third t-shirt, drying my hair again.

Martha came in. She picked up my t-shirts. "These were clean, moron. I just washed them. I've had enough. Find someone else to do your laundry."

Oh, man, whiz bang, shatter my dreams just when I was thinking about asking her to a dance — well, not Martha, but to teach me how to dance, that's what sisters do, not thump-thump down the stairs to the laundry. I waited at my bedroom window for her to return. There had never been a time that she didn't return for a second round.

But now one thing didn't always lead to another with Martha. There seemed to be no logic in what was going on in her head. Maybe because Bishop Humphries, who was recovering in the hospital, told the police he and Martha were playing catch, no one's fault, Martha had to sort of forgive the bishop — we're even now — so she had no one to be mad at, other than me, and I don't count.

So now, for some reason — not some reason, because her hormones were growing cups full of eggs — she'd come into my room and lie on my bed while I was doing my work at my desk. She didn't disturb me, and I liked having her there. My computer desk was in front of a window, so if I didn't pull down the blinds I could watch Martha's reflection in the glass, usually dressed in jeans and a sweater, lying on her back, one leg hooked over one knee. Sometimes I would lie with her on the bed and pretend to be reading while I was trying to work up the courage to ask her to teach me how to dance. Late at night, I could peek out my bedroom door into the darkened hallway and send dance thoughts on gamma rays to Martha, and then, how could this be, Martha dressed in her PJs would appear, not walking but swaying and floating on the blue line of my thoughts that were leading her into my room to teach me to dance. Then I realized the only person my swaying-wave thoughts would bring would be Sister Charlotte, dressed in a white Shoppers Drug Mart coat that swish-swished as she walked her stony ground, so high on meds that she was going to float like smoke into the chimney before the day came for her to come out of the chimney.

Chapter 40

SISTER CHARLOTTE

I was having a cup of tea and a digestive biscuit in Mr. Knight's living room. He pointed at a crack in his coffee table from his last move. "I tried to fix it with Elmer's glue. Now it's back again. I had a crack in the lid of my favourite teapot. I tried to fix it with Elmer's glue. Same thing. It came back again. But you know what? I had a leak in my umbrella, and I fixed it with Elmer's glue, and it stayed fixed."

This bit of Mr. Knight nonsense reminded me that every time I visited my mother in the nursing home, I looked over at a crack in the wall next to her bed. It reminded me of lying on my bed in my little bedroom, the one Martha has now, with my dolls and teddy bears, wondering why my father, who always fixed everything, had not fixed the crack in the ceiling above my bed. I decided because he was always looking toward the horizon for the coming of that one special pigeon, like a stock broker looks toward the horizon for the returns on that one special stock.

"Are you listening, Sister Charlotte? We're talking about the nature of cracks. Some can be repaired with Elmer's glue and some can't."

"I don't know anything about cracks or about Elmer's glue."

"Yes, you do, Sister Charlotte. We have a crack we're counting on you to fix. The court date is in two weeks. Bishop Humphries is, shall we say, not fit to stand trial. But that doesn't change the charges against Father Eagleman. Are you ready?"

"I'm here for my buds, Mr. Knight. Not to talk about cracks."

"You hear a ring of the doorbell, Sister Charlotte, and you crack open your door and there will be an unexpected OPP in suit and tie, and a black unmarked vehicle parked outside, trying to find the cracks in your testimony."

Mr. Knight poured more tea and helped himself to another biscuit. He was a dunker — a disgusting habit. "You know the crack I'm talking about, Sister Charlotte. Your job now is to get yourself in shape for the trial. And don't give me that look. And don't play stupid. A court date has been set. A crack in a glass is an error along an unblemished plane, like a crack in my teacup could break wide open at any moment and make a mess in my lap, like the crack in Bishop Humphries's head could break wide open at any moment and make a mess for you and your children. Don't play 'Good Heavens above, Mr. Knight.' I need your promise to seal that crack. We talked about this while Bishop Humphries was playing baseball with Martha. You're the crack. I need you to be lucid and sober when you take the stand. The buds I give you on that day will make your mind sharp enough to swear to tell the truth and lie your head off."

"And lie my head off."

"An even bigger lie added to this lie. That both you and Bella, who was visiting Martha, saw Joe the Hammer drive up and smack Bishop Humphries on the forehead with the hammer and then leave the scene. But for this to work, you're going to take Martha to meet her mother and get Martha to stay with Bella to keep her sober until after the trial is finished. Don't give me that look. Thanks to me, Bella has sobered up and looks pretty good. But it's up to you and Martha to keep her pretty good."

***

The cab radio was playing rapper music. The driver said, "They give themselves funny names, like Icepick and Snoop Dogg and 50 Cent and Slick Rick."

I said, "Elmer's Glue would be a good name."

I drifted off. Then the driver said, "Can you make it to the door, ma'am?"

I placed the buds on the right corner of my desk where my pencils, standing stiff and straight as onward Christian soldiers, awaited orders from fingers that could not write. On the left, the children's grade twelve graduation photos, each with a blur of blue backdrop in a silver frame, Martha looking stiff and straight, Owen looking dizzy.

What do they see when they look at me? I'll tell you, Mr. Knight, hanging there in your white suit. A woman with a crack in her ceiling, that's what. But not when they look at Peter, who does have a crack in his ceiling. When they look at him, their eyes light up, wondering what fun thing he has in store for them. But when they turn and look at me, they wonder what chores I have in store for them. In their heads, after I'm gone, they'll carry a silver-framed photo of Peter, but the picture of me standing next to his will be of a cracked Sister Charlotte needing some Elmer's glue.

Soon Peter will be home with two pizzas. They'll eat it in the TV room in front of that wretched television. But I don't join them so I don't have to listen to Owen explain about the yeast living in pizza dough and then go on to explain about the yeast living in Martha's egg factory, which now at her prime works like a high-voltage restaurant-grade chicken laying new eggs every two minutes. But because Martha's brain is scrambled, most of her eggs are scrambled, except for the ones that are supposed to be scrambled. Oh, for Heaven's sake. And then to Martha's response, which could be almost anything short of murder.

I wish I had photos of my Martha as a baby. I wonder if Mother Bella could give me one. Such a thought, Sister Charlotte. Of course, she won't have any. Don't give feelings to that crazy woman by thinking about her as a mother looking after her baby. I am Martha's mother. All other children have brothers, sisters, uncles, aunts, grandparents, an army of ancestors. But Martha has no one other than that woman, who does not deserve to be considered a mother of Martha.

There's Owen again. First he'll stop at the washroom for another pee, then he won't flush his pee into the sewer, then he'll go into his room and lie on his bed without taking off his shoes, which will have drops of pee on them. All the same to Owen.

Why does my mind always end up in the sewer? While I was in the order with the Sisters, I thought continually about holy water, but I never associated water with sewer pipes and pee. And another thing, Mr. Knight, why is it that sometimes in the dark of night, the streetlights shining curtained shadows on the naked Jesus, he appears to be wearing a white suit?

Well, Sister, if you want my opinion, the situation you find yourself in does seem to be a mix of the holy with the sewer. But remember at the nursing home, Sister Charlotte, after years of looking after her, you watched your mother disappear down that barren hallway on a stretcher? You closed the door and lay with eyes closed on her empty bed. You stayed flat on your back on that bed in that room, feeling as barren as a winter's day. Then you opened your eyes a crack, and then the door opened a crack, and there was a chill, remember that? You could feel that chill distinctly because the peace you got from your mother's death after years of looking after her was still warm on your cheek. The peace Martha will get from your death after years of looking after you will still be warm on Martha's cheek as she watches you disappear down the barren hallway.

And now what am I hearing? Martha telling Owen to move his minnows out of the toilet tank. And now what am I hearing? Martha scolding Owen for dripping fish-smelling puddles everywhere as off to the cemetery they go to return the minnows to the pond. Next I'll hear Martha scolding Owen for bringing home some molecule from the cemetery dead that has migrated through the earth and into the pond and into a jar that Owen will keep in his bedroom to watch turn from amoeba to fish to mammal to person.

Will Martha stand at my bedside as I stood at my mother's bedside? I hope so. But I can do without Owen staring at me with that same wondering expression he gives to all lifeforms as they die. He'll bring a stethoscope and fasten it to his ears so that, as I feel the count of my dying heartbeats, he can make up a logarithm that calculates the number of maggots and the number of days it will take for me to go from my coffin to the pond so he can put me in a jar for Heaven's sakes. That is why I have a note in my file to be cremated, so that

Owen can't dig me up two days after I've been buried, like that old man with the wheelbarrow. It was on the news. He wandered around wearing latex gloves and carrying a flashlight and a jar of Vicks VapoRub. He said he was a grave robber, in business for himself. He'd check first at the funeral parlour for old ladies wearing diamond rings. The Vicks was for under his nose to cover the smell, if there was one, usually not, for he marked on his calendar the date and got there within a few days, before the earth began to compact and the body began to stink. When I saw him on the news walking along pushing his wheelbarrow, I thought, oh my goodness, for Heaven's sake, give a body nosebleeds.

But these thoughts I must resign myself to, at last. No more playing games with you, Mr. Knight, hanging there on your cross in that white suit looking forward to my crucifixion.

Well, I suggest, Sister Charlotte, if you want Martha at your bedside, like you were at your mother's bedside, I suggest you take her to meet the mother you saved her from. In fact, Sister, a visit from Martha might inspire Bella to clean herself up for good so she can do the mother-daughter thing. And don't give me that look, Sister. The fact is, you're no better than that Rebecca Brown woman who married Satan, who wore a white suit and rented a Presbyterian church for the wedding.

"Sister Charlotte, wake up. What were you looking for? Why are you lying on the floor with your head in the closet?"

"Mr. Knight's shoes. He's over there hanging on the wall in bare feet."

"Help me get her up, Frog Face."

"Tart mouth, Martha. Look at her, Sister Charlotte. Now that she's growing eggs, look how she's tarting herself up for those boys in grade twelve."

"Oh, for Heaven's sake, you two. I can't get a moment's peace with you two going at it. The pair of you give a body nosebleeds."

"This is how I am when I'm nice to him, Sister Charlotte."

"How did we get home from that Presbyterian church?"

"By spaceship."

"Where have you put Mr. Knight's shoes, Martha?"

"In the cupboard, where they belong. Help me, Owen. Get her into her bed so she can sleep it off."

"I want to join you for pizza."

"Stand up, then, Sister Charlotte. Let me help you up. We'll go down together."

I sat for my pizza. I asked, "Where is Martha?"

"She's standing beside you," said Owen.

Martha said, "The reason I've been trying to be nice to Owen is that I used to think there was no reason for him to have survived the Open Hatch, but I've finally come up with the purpose of his existence."

"I don't want to hear it, Martha."

"They're going to put him on television as an example of the need for Planned Parenthood, you know, like those Don't Smoke commercials. They show some wizened old lady talking through a Jiffy Lube funnel stuck in her neck."

"Why are you talking about Planned Parenthood and growing eggs? What have you two been up to, Martha, now that you've been tarting yourself up every day?"

"Show a picture of Owen and write underneath, 'Unplanned parenthood will arrive in an unplanned package on your doorstep with no return address.' Look at him. While he's sorting all the different pizza bits into separate piles, he's thinking up yeast jokes, and then he's going to eat the topping with his fingers one pile at a time and leave the pizza crust because it's got my eggs in it."

"Where is Peter?"

"He's the one on your right, Sister Charlotte. As soon as he finishes his pizza, to get a little sanity into his life, he's selling this house and moving to Halifax. Not my monkeys, not my circus."

"Oh, for Heaven's sake, Peter. What on earth will you do in the circus?"

"Look at Owen's hands, Sister Charlotte. If you don't make that zombified mental patient wash his hands before eating that pizza I'm going to puke."

"Oh, for Heaven's sake, Martha."

"You're not the only one with problems, Sister Charlotte. This is very sad, what's happening here."

Martha stomped away but in a minute was back. "Goodbye forever, Sister Charlotte. I'm going to live in a hotel. I've put a Servant Wanted sign on the front lawn. Find someone else to look after everything."

"Before you go off to live in a hotel, let's have our talk about parenthood. You're almost eighteen, so you'll be free to live wherever you want and I'm not going to be around to keep an eye on you so it's time we had a little talk, but for Heaven's sake, Martha, I want to enjoy my pizza. But all right. Tomorrow let's you and I and your mother have a talk. Why are you looking at me like that? You mean no one told you? Mr. Knight said it's time to meet your mother."

Chapter 41

SISTER CHARLOTTE

My first visit to that woman, I was confused. It seemed more like a dream, no doubt brought on by the buds playing tricks on my mind. But more than that, I remember my eyes were blurred by the clouded gloom of that bar. And the smell of stale smoke in that apartment gave me a headache.

Then I had seen that photograph of Martha. What a shock. I'd been thinking about wanting to meet her mother so badly and tell her what a wonderful child my Martha was. But what a shock. There on the bed lay this disgusting woman, and beside her, a photograph of my Martha. No wonder I got confused.

Yes, now I remember. I had double-dosed my buds that morning. As I rode the subway home, the wheels clanging and screeching, I felt like I was on a slippery-slope roller-coaster ride with Mr. Knight in the tunnel to Hell. What a thought. But I had managed to force myself to appear normal as I got off the train, and oops, sorry, almost knocked that old gentleman over. That's how confused I was.

All that evening and into the night, my mind had travelled in circles, imploring the crucified Jesus there in front of me, What must I do now? But he would give me no comfort as I counted the hours before I could begin my morning prayers. Whatever you want me to do, Jesus, I'll do it. Drying up my knees so that I can no longer kneel to pray — not even once, never mind five times a day — when I can barely limp my way back and forth and up and down. Blessed Mary, give me a sign, a gesture, anything that will prepare me for what I'm now being called to do.

Then I thought, of course, no answer is forthcoming because no answer is the answer. Of course. Of course. God does not give a test of faith to the faithful with the answers written on the bottom of the page. What would be the point in that?

So Martha and I set off, me wearing my heavy brown sweater and beige slacks under a heavy winter coat, not that it was cold, but to hide from those penetrating eyes in that bar that made me feel raw as a winter wind. Martha waited outside. From the doorway of the Nugget Tavern, I saw the woman, sitting on the same stool as last time, talking to a man in a black jacket. I wanted to turn around and leave, for the buds were already wearing off. I went directly to the Ladies and sat on the filthy toilet. I was feeling faint. I bent over, my head between my knees. That's what it felt like. Down on your knees, Sister Charlotte, before this filthy toilet, down on your knees for bringing Martha to this filthy place. How many times, Sister Charlotte, have you received sewer-sound warnings of where you will end up if you keep on this path with Mr. Knight? Ahh, yes, those sewer-sound warnings, now they make sense, portending my destiny, like the broken plate.

What have we here? I remembered to bring an extra along. Good for you, Sister Charlotte. Don't chase the buds. Beat them to the sewer line. Well that's where I am. At the sewer line.

I know, Mr. Knight. Every four hours.

No, no, no, Sister Charlotte. Three times a day, one every eight hours. That's the limit.

Well, Mr. Knight, Allah says five times a day to keep my knees working so I can say my prayers as I make my way between the tables occupied by the same people as the last time.

I took the stool beside the man with the black jacket. We were so close that when he lifted his glass, his sleeve touched my arm, and when he shifted on his stool, his knee touched mine. I ordered a club soda. I listened to what this woman Bella was saying as I waited for the warmth of the bud to seep into my stomach and up the spindle into my brain, ahh there you are, Mr. Knight, in your white suit, setting down my glass of soda.

"Let you in on a secret, Gary. I hate drunks. I hate the smell of them. Hate the sight of them. They stagger and stumble and knock things over and dirty up my place and pass out on my bed."

"I'm not a drunk," said Gary.

"I hate drunks," Bella repeated. "I never had anything to do with a drunk."

"If you don't like drunks, how come you're a drunk?"

"I'm not. I quit. I been sober two weeks now."

"You're a drunk, but you don't like drunks, so you quit and you've been sober two weeks and now you're drunk."

"That's right," she said. "Can't stand them."

"That's good because I'm not a drunk. I might be drunk right now, but I'm not a drunk. I gotta go to the can."

Gary staggered to the washroom. I glanced at Bella, briefly enough that she wouldn't notice. I didn't want to recognize her, because I didn't want this woman to be Martha's mother. I wanted to get a clear view of her face and be able to go back to Martha and say, That is not your mother.

I tried to get a better look at her but, because of the way she sat, her arms resting on the table, her shoulders hunched over, her head hanging down, I couldn't see her face.

Then she straightened up, opened her purse, and brought out a small compact mirror. She must have been very drunk, for in the glass I saw that her lips and cheeks sagged loosely, and her eyelids were nearly closed, almost resting on the bags beneath. As she stared, glazed and empty, at her image in the mirror, during that instant of her reflection, I saw that her features had been at one time the same as my Martha's and the same as the Martha in the photograph.

Gary returned from the washroom.

"Do you want to or not?" she asked.

He poured the rest of his beer into his glass, drank it, and turned to face her. "You got a deal."

She picked up her purse, heaved herself up, and, wobbling on the same high heels in the same tight dress as last time, followed him out of the bar.

A few minutes later, I left, Martha following. After the gloom of the tavern, the lights in the street seemed bright, even though darkness had fallen. As we hurried up Yonge Street and along Elm to number 27, I felt the second bud kicking in.

I followed the alley between 27 and the house next door to a narrow walkway, overgrown with weeds and long grass, leading to a back door. I stood in the shadows by the wall of the building to wait for Martha. When she didn't appear, I found her looking through the partly drawn curtains of one window. I could see Bella and Gary sitting on the chesterfield, drinking whisky. When the bottle was finished, Bella got up and lurched the few steps into the bedroom, removing her dress as she went. Martha crept along the side of the house to the bedroom window, open a little, neither the blinds nor the curtains closed. Over Martha's shoulder I saw Bella collapsed on the bed, her left arm thrown up over her head, the hair in her armpit a black snarl on white skin.

Gary sat smoking. When he'd finished, he got up and staggered at a tilt across the room and switched on the bedside lamp, removed his shoes, shirt, and trousers and flopped down beside Bella. With one arm around her neck, he attempted to pull her closer, at the same time trying to shake her awake. When this didn't work, on hands and knees he tried rolling her back and forth on the bed to remove the rest of her clothes.

Bella began to snore, softly at first, but very quickly rasping and whistling so harshly that, shaking his head in disgust, Gary gave up. He sat on the edge of the bed, rubbing his eyes and blinking, trying to clear his vision. Finally, he reached down to the floor for his shirt. He lit another cigarette, which he placed in an open Vaseline jar on the bedside table. He pulled on his pants and buttoned his shirt. Blue smoke rose in a long ribbon, and the cigarette blinked out. He took from her purse on the bedside table two tens and one five. Then he tried to relight his Vaseline-covered cigarette.

I crept away from the window to stand in the weeds between the two houses. Through the silence, I could hear the distant drumming of the Yonge Street subway's iron wheels. They seemed to stop, then come again. No sooner did one fade away than another came clanging close behind, pounding past.

Often I sat up late in the evening on Peter's green bench, listening to the subway. After one thundered by, the yard would be so quiet it seemed that if I looked across the cemetery to St. Mary's Church, its parking-lot lights shining down in yellow pools on the asphalt, I could hear the organ playing, and I could hear the hymns rising from St. Mary's pipes. I could hear those same words of praise now drifting across the cemetery and into my heart: Thanks be to Mr. Knight for giving me the strength to show Martha her mother.

I crept along the alley to the front corner of the house, looking for Martha. Then Gary came down the steps, staggered along the front walked, and lurched away, disappearing finally around the corner. I waited for Martha to emerge from the shadows so we could go home. I waited.

Maybe I wanted the front door to be locked because, when I discovered it wasn't, I didn't immediately go in. I stood in the doorway and held my head in my hands to gather strength before continuing inside. Martha was sitting on the bed, staring down at her sleeping mother. I sat on the bed beside her and picked up the photograph, which in my hands felt like it should be in my bedroom, not on the nightstand of this disgusting woman.

When I reached out to touch Martha's arm, she got up and began to snoop. She looked in the closets and wandered through the kitchen. She found the St. Mary's church bulletin on the kitchen table, but nothing else of interest until, returning to the bedroom and opening the top drawer of the bedside table, she found a photograph of Bella sitting on the knee of a younger Bishop Humphries — a younger Bella, slim and pretty, her long blonde hair hanging in waves to the shoulders of her blue sweater, her smile as bright as the glint from the flash glancing off the ring on one long finger of the hand she was holding up to the camera. Martha slipped the picture into her pocket.

Bella didn't stir when I got up. When I had entered the room, I thought I could hear the heaviness of her breathing. Now I could not. I leaned close and touched the arm. I nudged the shoulder. I picked up her wrist.

I know I could have tried harder, but I would have first needed to find in my heart enough strength in my fingers to find a pulse. I got up and walked across the living room, through the door, and outside,

Martha following. We continued to the corner and stood under the streetlights near a storefront. When I glanced at Martha's reflection in the window, I saw that she was holding the photograph of Bella and Bishop Humphries in her right hand. In her left hand she held a package of matches she must have picked up at Bella's apartment. When I looked again at Martha, I saw that her eyes, staring down at her cardboard mother and father, were empty.

Martha struck the match and lit one corner and watched the flames arc upward, consuming the blue sweater and the blue-stoned finger and that long blonde hair. When the fire burned away the bishop, just before scorching her fingers, she dropped the photograph to the ground where, smouldering, it curled into grey ash and blinked out.

Chapter 42

MARTHA

Timothy sat down, and Owen sat down, and I sat down. Timothy lit a cigarette.

"You shouldn't smoke, Timothy." I could tell by the way he sometimes did what I told him that he was interested in me. No, thanks. I wouldn't have anything to do with Timothy. The only reason I was talking to him was to stop him from dragging Owen into the killing of Big Joe. Timothy's words: BigfuckingJoe.

Timothy continued to smoke while I helped Owen collect caterpillars in cocoons to put in a box so he could use his BlackBerry to film them turning into butterflies. Owen wandered off to catch moths, which he said had just hatched and were waiting until dark when lights came on so they could go into people's houses and hide in their closets and eat holes in their clothes. He said he was going to take some to Big Joe's house.

Timothy said, "I remember the moths when I lived at Big Joe's. At first they'd flutter around, so I'd catch them and put them in his dresser drawer to eat holes in his t-shirts, for ventilation. Some days his BO didn't smell too good. I didn't know about Vicks VapoRub then. I don't want him smelling of BO when I, like, raise the screwdriver, deep breath, holy fuck, worse than letting off a ripe one."

Timothy brought out his cigarettes and matches.

"You can't smoke here," I said.

Timothy said, "No matter how windy, my real mother, I met her one time, she could light up one-handed, like a guy. She was a truck driver, cradling her hand in a cup around her lighter, flicking the wheel, striking the flint, lighting the cigarette."

"That's why you smoke. Let Owen examine your DNA. I bet it's got smoking in it."

I could understand why girls liked pushing baby carriages. Their baby-carriage-pushing DNA was telling them to get ready for it. And yeah, Owen was right. My mothering DNA was telling me, well never mind, Martha.

Timothy wandered off, up and down the lanes, to do what? Maybe rob a few graves. Owen and I lay in the grass, watching a fly buzzing overhead. It flew off, returned to the same spot, then flew off again, finally disappearing behind a tombstone. After a while, the fly came out from behind the tombstone and crawled along Owen's pant leg.

Owen and I and the fly remained for what felt like forever. I watched the shadowy shiftings of grey clouds move back and forth in the sky and listened to the tiny body buzz of the fly — kind of spooky, like midnight. I must have fallen asleep because, when I looked again, I saw the sun had begun to fade, and Owen and Timothy were gone.

***

I opened my bedroom door a crack. I opened it a little wider, listening for movements from Sister Charlotte's room at the end of the hall. I heard nothing, saw nothing, except the outline of the staircase railing at the end of the hallway. Assuming she was asleep, I stepped one step and then another. I came back to my room and waited. I heard a rattle as Sister Charlotte's crippled hand fumbled with her nightstand drawer. I listened for her footsteps, waited for the pad of soft-soled shoes along the hallway, waited for the raspy voice, "Can you help me, Martha?" But except for the rustle of the curtains moving with the soft breeze coming through my bedroom window, there were no more sounds. I crossed the hall to Owen's door and crept a few steps into his room, sliding my feet along the floor, tiptoeing close enough to the bed that I could see that Owen was asleep.

I woke him up. "Can I borrow some of your candles you use to boil donkey shit in beakers? I want to light candles for my mother."

"I thought you were finished whining and snivelling about your mother."

"Well I'm not. I like whining and snivelling."

I set the candles in a row on my dresser, one, two, three, just like at church. I lit the match and watched the line of flame run from the end of the match to the wick of each candle, one, two, three, just like at church. Immediately, I felt the warmth of the three tiny flames. Sitting down on my bed, I felt the warmth of each creep from my hand and along my arm and into my chest and into my heart.

Peter tap-tapped on my door. He came in and sat beside me. "Can you guess which of the three monkeys is complaining about getting smoke in his eyes?"

I said, "I fell asleep in the cemetery and Owen and Timothy left me there, by myself, asleep."

We watched the last candle burn down, and then we were left with nothing to watch, sitting side by side on my bed. I began to shiver.

I said, "Now when I put on my makeup, I think about how almost every other girl has a mother beside her to show her how to put on makeup. But Sister Charlotte doesn't put on makeup."

I said, "The other night I had a dream that, when the limousine comes with Mr. Knight dressed in his white suit in the back seat, I'll see that the driver is dressed in an undertaker black suit in the front seat. Then I'll see that Sister Charlotte is sitting in the back seat of that limousine with Mr. Knight, on her way to the funeral parlour to get fitted for a long black dress. I could see on the tag, you know where it says dry clean only, that it was designed by Mr. Knight. That's how vivid the dream was. As the limousine backs out of the drive, I'll wonder how the driver can steer such an enormous vehicle through city traffic, especially since in my dream the night is stormy, the wind is slanting a curtain of rain sideways as the limousine glides down the street and disappears into the mist. But the mist is so clear I can see in the headlights glints moving in sparkles along the black asphalt."

I said, "These dreams, Peter, as I count my days to my eighteenth birthday, come to me in chills of truth. I blink awake, and there's Mr. Knight sitting on my bedside. Well, hello, Martha. Happy birthday."

"Sister Charlotte is going to a better place, Martha."

"Not if she swears on God's Bible. She thinks because she has a Bible with no Holy Spirit, she won't go to Hell. But I googled it. The court doesn't require swearing on a Christian Bible. It doesn't matter what you swear on. It's taking the oath that matters. I can't let her die thinking she's going to Hell. I'm going to help Timothy kill Big Joe."

Chapter 43

OWEN

I followed Peter into the backyard to help tidy the garden before he put the house on the market. It was now mid-September, but the yard was still an oasis of lush grass and green shrubs and late-blooming flowers.

Peter stood, wiping his hands with his lawnmower rag. "Strange weather we're having. Like spring, except it's almost winter."

In his taxi days, Peter would set his watch beside him in a little cupholder thing so he wouldn't lose track of time on his way to a pickup. Peter didn't care about time or about how long anything took, but I knew he was trying to keep himself going in the right direction with Martha and me, to keep us safe until we reached eighteen, even though our streets were becoming, one by one, bent as pretzels.

I said, "Yesterday Sister Charlotte had pictures of me and Martha spread out on the table. She was all rambley, her train of thought all over the place talking about the three of us in the backyard with pigeons and the apple tree and the flowers. She thinks we're all nine years old."

I said, "I think by now someone should have figured out that if Big Joe arrives for his trial looking like Mr. Radley wearing his Sunday suit so he doesn't look bad and wearing his Sunday cologne so he doesn't smell bad, and if he removes his aviator sunglasses so he looks like he isn't hiding anything — in other words not looking like Big Joe — as he takes his place behind the stand and puts his hand on the Bible to swear to tell the truth, he'll look like one of the lawyers, and everyone will believe Mr. Radley is going to be more truthful than Sister Charlotte, who looks crazy."

Peter nodded. "Truth is whoever is the best liar."

"So, while Mr. Radley's lawyer explains about Mr. Radley being an upstanding citizen doing his civic duty, Mr. Radley will be nodding in agreement. And when he speaks he won't talk in handyman grunts but like the lawyers in words of solemn jurisprudence, so that the jury will set aside Sister Charlotte's testimony that Mr. Radley demolished Bishop Humphries's brain with the hammer and Mr. Radley didn't supply those boys with drugs, and Mr. Radley will go free. And Sister Charlotte will go to jail for perjury."

Peter leaned back and stretched his arms across the back of the bench. Finally, he said, "The three monkeys on my dresser, Owen. See no evil. Hear no evil. Say no evil. During my night shift driving a taxi, I've seen a lot of evil, which to those involved I said, 'I did not hear and did not see.' A lot of people owe me favours for being the first two monkeys and especially for being the third monkey."

Peter held my hand. "Big Joe will be gone in a day or so. When Sister Charlotte presses the buzzer to open the gate to Heaven, Sister Charlotte's God is going to say, 'Depending on how you look at it, Sister, having added it all up, having consulted with the three monkeys, I think we can say, welcome home.'"

Back in the house, I climbed the polished-by-Martha stairs with the polished-by-Martha banister. I continued along the wooden floors of the upper hallway to my bedroom. I sat on the floor next to the head of my bed and leaned back against the pale brown wall. I brought from its hiding place under the mattress the picture of Shelly. Her white dress, open at the neck, revealed a tiny cross on a thin gold chain I had never noticed before. Upon her long hair, which hung in waves and curls to her shoulders, a white light shone. I had never noticed this before.

"Like a sunbeam through a stained-glass window," I said to Martha, who'd come from checking her makeup to sit on the floor beside me.

Martha said, "She looks like a hooker."

I said, "Like a sunbeam on pond water scum. That's how the makeup transforms Martha into a tart."

"Like an ungrounded AC current from an electric blender. That's how Owen's brain got transformed into scrambled snot." Martha dialed on her cellphone. "Hello, 911. There's a new strain of brain dead moron in my house. Send the police."

I said, "I kind of like you, Martha, almost like a sister, that is, not like to go to a dance … although—"

"I kind of like you, Owen, like a brother, that is, not like to go to a dance … although … yeah, if you want, I can teach you a few steps, in case at the prom you find someone desperate."

I went along the hall to the washroom. Turning around and tightening my belt and doing up my zipper, I glanced at myself in the mirror. I was so preoccupied with thoughts of going to the prom with Martha that I wasn't looking at me. My look at me was more like I might look at a chair or a table, not reading anything into what I saw, other than what it was. What I saw now was not the little geeky Owen from the past. I saw an Owen almost six feet tall and getting bigger, with broad shoulders. It was as though I'd spent so much time in front of the mirror, rubbing and cleaning my face, trying to erase the geek in the mirror, that I hadn't looked at the me that Martha might teach how to dance.

Chapter 44

MARTHA

Mr. Knight, in his white-and-black Ralph Lauren knock-off outfit, arrived unexpectedly, right on time for a free breakfast. "How about Martha's pancakes, served in the dining room."

He smiled at me.

Sister Charlotte and Peter ushered Mr. Knight into the dining room. With me in the kitchen, Owen did his best at serving, no cutesy curtsies, that's for sure. Owen, six feet tall, skinny as a scarecrow, serving the coffee on the silver trays with the silver sugar bowls and the silver creamers. OhmyGodprayforme. Sister Charlotte, high as a kite, smiles as broad as two ten-pound bags of pancake mix placed end to end, her words pumping imitation syrup into her recited breakfast grace beamed from her raspy crow voice, like almost on worldwide satellite transmission from a World War II movie: "In the face of these children we see the face of Jesus and the hand of the Blessed Virgin and, of course, our Heavenly Father and, of course, Mr. Knight…" On and on she went, spare me, until Peter put his hand on her shoulder to shut her down.

As Owen scraped the chunks of half-finished pancakes that looked like donkey poop into the garbage, I imagined Sister Charlotte on a donkey riding into Bethlehem, and Owen, the donkey keeper, following along, picking up a few take-homes.

Sister Charlotte, Peter, and Mr. Knight took their coffee into the living room to talk. I pointed to the pancake Owen had dropped on the floor and stepped on with his new blue sneakers with red laces. He must have been dropped on the tile floor of few times in Neonatal because — "Mother of Mercy, Owen, you're stepping in it again."

"I'm eighteen now, Martha. My frontal cortex is beginning to register hurtful insults."

Damn. I was so busy thinking about other stuff, I forgot to give him his birthday personal care kit.

On my hands and knees, I cleaned up the mess. I could hear Mr. Knight telling Sister Charlotte and Peter a story about a pig-farm scam where the farmer sold about two thousand piglets over the internet, and when you went to see your piglet, the farmer showed you one with your number on its ear and said, "This is your piglet."

Except he only had about fifty piglets and was showing the same fifty piglets to about ten million people.

Mr. Knight said, "Guess what happened when the piglets got big enough to get hung up by the hind legs and turned into a McDonald's BLT?"

Sister Charlotte said, "Is this like a pig walked into a bar...?"

Then, although there were no special lights in the living room, no sun through the window, the room seemed to fill with crematorium shadows. They continued to talk, and when Owen glanced at me, I knew he'd already picked up that they were talking about giving Sister Charlotte her terminal bud on my coming birthday. Sister Charlotte, who was attempting to keep a sharp watch on us, tried to level a glare that would back us out of earshot. When she motioned for me and Owen to go off somewhere, like she was throwing water at us, Mr. Knight got up. He came over to look down at me, still on hands and knees on the floor with a rag and a bottle of Mr. Clean and a bucket of tap water.

He bent close. "Sister Charlotte wants you to be with her for her final hour."

I thought, staring up at Mr. Knight from this angle, he looked like a bottle of Mr. Clean on a top bathroom shelf. I thought that if I could look at his reflection in the mirror of this bathroom, I would see that the Mr. Clean on the shelf could still be mixed with tap water but the Mr. Clean in the mirror had already been mixed with sewer water. I don't know why I had those thoughts, but I think they came from listening to Sister Charlotte's ramblings about sewer water. And holy water. And marrying Satan in the Presbyterian church.

Chapter 45

OWEN

I sprayed the bathroom mirror with Windex. I wiped the mirror clean, wiping away the old me and creating a new better me for Martha's birthday. Or for Sister Charlotte's death day. I wasn't sure. This was like Martha putting on makeup, tarting herself up until she looked ready for the birthday and then taking it off, untarting herself for the death day. It was like sitting in your living-room chair, listening for the knock on the door, waiting for the occasion to arrive but not knowing which one it would be: the birthday or the death day.

I wanted to take one more look around at Big Joe's for Shelly. I think that's a foster care thing. The closer you get to being sent out on your own, the more you want to hang on to where you've been.

I took the subway and stood behind the tree and peeked left and right. I walked past Big Joe's pickup and I stood at his workshop window. Through the glass I saw Big Joe dressed in his plaid shirt and baseball hat, wearing his aviator sunglasses, the ring of keys hanging from his belt loop rattling and jangling as he sorted his tools, all but the hammer. I heard his footsteps creaking on the floorboards, crossing the shed and coming back as he tidied and arranged, stopping finally to stand at the inside corner of the window at almost the exact spot I stood on the outside. He was looking toward the street, I don't know, maybe knowing someone was coming.

It had begun to rain. The base of the shed was high enough off the ground that I could slide underneath. I removed a piece of lattice and, through the resulting hole, I wriggled under the joists. On my back, I squirmed my way across the dirt. I looked up through cracks in the floorboards, but all I could see was the rafters directly overhead, one wide beam spanning the length of the shed and a second shorter beam supporting the ridge.

Looking out from the darkness through the wooden web of lattice to see if anyone had arrived, I noticed that the sky, crisscrossed like the lines for x's and o's that Martha and I played, had become overcast and heavy. Thunder rumbled and lightning flashed. I heard the tap-tap of rain. I saw the leaves of nearby bushes begin to shiver, and the branches of nearby trees begin to tremble. From above, I heard shuffling and scuffling and the harshness of grunts.

More scuffling as I slid out, pulling myself free, scrambling around to the front of the shed. But by then, Big Joe was dangling from the overhead rafter, one end of a slip knot around his neck. As I watched, he jumped and jerked six inches above the floor, his feet trying to find the stool now lying on its side. My first thought was to hoist him up from hanging at the end of the noose and place his feet on the stool. I stepped forward. Big Joe was smaller now and me bigger, strong enough that I could have easily lifted him off the end of the rope. But as it seared into the skin of his neck, he thrashed about so violently that his work pants and boxers slipped from his waist to his knees to land in a pile on the floor, exposing his hairy belly button like that cyclops eye of the pope. I backed away to the door of the shed and watched as he reached one hand over the rafter. Unable to support his weight, he clutched at the rope, yanking and pulling, drawing the slip knot tighter, gradually strangling his sputtering struggles into weak groanings, which grew faint and thin and ended, finally, at last, somewhere inside his black barge heart.

I ventured into the shed and approached him from behind, thinking if I couldn't see that eye, I'd be able to put my arms around him and, careful not to touch his naked parts, hoist him up and unfasten the rope and lay him on the floor. But when his legs began again to jerk in spasms, I shrank away.

I picked up his aviator sunglasses and his ring of keys, which had been kicked into one corner. I hurried outside and looked around in case there was a neighbour nearby or someone passing in the street who could have seen who did this. No one around, I returned to the shed.

Now Big Joe was hanging quietly, his feet pointing down, twitching a little, his chin twisted down on his chest, one arm dangling at his side while the other reached out, maybe for a glass of water.

I would have liked to dial 911. I would have liked to listen to the police sirens in the distance. I would have liked to watch the paramedics cut down the body and the ambulance beep-beeping backward, positioning itself to collect the bagged body when the police were finished.

I put my hand into my pocket and brought out Big Joe's keys. From my shirt pocket, I took Big Joe's aviator sunglasses. That time he hammered my Air Hogs Remote Control Thunder Trax, Big Joe made me hold his keys because they got in the way of his swing. When the hammer slammed down on the bench, he jumped a little hop, and his aviator sunglasses slipped off his nose, and his keys fell to the floor.

As I navigated the street to the corner to the opposite sidewalk listening to the keys that dangled jangling from my index finger, the question ran through my mind: Is there a special prayer I should have recited as he died? I think yes. So I said, "Oh, for Heaven's sake. Give a body nosebleeds, hanging from the rafters like that."

Chapter 46

MARTHA

It used to be, as me and Owen and Timothy walked the cemetery laneways, the pigeons pecking and cooing in the gravel flew off, afraid of us. But sometimes they would immediately flutter back to peck in the dirt close by, stretching their necks, watching us warily, first with one bright eye then the other. As they got to know us better, they just hopped to one side. Sometimes they were so busy pecking and cooing, and we were so busy walking and talking, neither paid the other much attention. Finally, the pigeons learned to ignore us completely as they pecked for weed seeds, breadcrumbs, whatever.

If Sister Charlotte were with us, she would have sat on Peter's bench. She liked to sit and look at the pigeons perched high up on the three crosses, and they liked to look down at her. They seemed able to see Sister Charlotte everywhere she went, and wherever she stopped, they flew down and gathered at her feet. Every time, she asked in a little-girl voice, the same question of the pigeons: "How come God never says anything about you in his Bible? There are sparrows and doves and goats and sheep and lambs but no pigeons. Didn't Noah take any of you with him in his boat that time? I bet Father Small wouldn't tell me to stop feeding the pigeons if they were in his Bible. And how come Noah only took two of everything? What if one fell overboard? The other one would be lonely."

We noticed the white homer, Amelia, standing off to one side, eyeing the others. When we approached, she flew off to the chapel roof. From there, she flew off again and pulled sharply upward, lifting herself with a single wing flap to glide on a wind current, circling like a tiny white cloud against the blue of the sky before landing on one tall spire. She was looking for Sister Charlotte.

Timothy, who could run the fastest, went for Sister Charlotte to see if she was awake and functioning. When they returned, Amelia flew down and landed on Sister Charlotte's shoulder.

"She's been flying for a long time. I can tell by her weight," Sister Charlotte said. "Probably delayed by bad weather. Her owner will be worried, wondering what happened to her."

We sat in the grass. Sister Charlotte stood in the lane holding the pigeon and stroking her head and letting her rest. "If it's a short flight, she doesn't stop but flies straight home. If it's a long flight, like five or six hundred miles, she'll stop for a rest. The crosses above St. Mary's are her landmark. She uses them if she can, but she doesn't need to. She's got a built-in compass pointing the direction, sixty miles an hour all the way home. She's trained to fly straight into the coop. The first thing her owner does is hold her and stroke her head, like I'm doing now, and talk to her and say, 'Welcome home.' They live in coops, like little houses, with their mothers and fathers and sisters and brothers. Other birds don't like to fly in the rain, but homing pigeons close their feathers and fly above the clouds. That's how bad they want to get home. They want to get back to their families."

Sister Charlotte didn't seem to know much of anything except religion, but she knew about pigeons, and being with them transformed her. And she seemed to have a special connection with Amelia.

"Amelia's been coming here a long time," Owen commented. "How long do they live?"

"This isn't Amelia. This is Emma, her daughter. For a while, they came together. But the last time, Emma came by herself. She's got a leg band with a phone number, so I phoned. I wanted to know what happened to Amelia. The lady who answered told me that she and her husband travel all over the country with their flyers. I should come for a weekend and get to know the other flyers and go with them flying."

Tears were streaming down Sister Charlotte's cheeks and falling in drips on the cupped fingers that held the flyer. Finally, after drying her eyes with the back of her hand, she continued, "'So where's

Amelia?' I asked. I knew something was wrong because the lady kept talking about the other flyers and about flying and about raising the babies and not answering my question. 'Amelia is dead,' she said finally. 'Someone found her on the side of the road. We don't know what happened.'"

I don't know what happened to make me do it but I put my arm around Sister Charlotte's shoulder. I felt her side against mine and I felt the warmth of her leg against mine. I felt my bones unthaw and felt my feelings for Sister Charlotte grow warm. But not for long, for when I felt through the cotton of my thin t-shirt the hands of the grief she had brought into my life creep up from somewhere —below it felt like, but maybe from above, I don't know — to crawl along my spine like those nighttime shivers, I moved away. But at least for a minute I had felt genuine and honest warmth for Sister Charlotte, and I felt good about that.

Sister Charlotte reached over and placed Emma in my lap. "Hold her, Martha. She's still a baby. Let her get to know you, for when I'm not here, you can look after her and then she can look after you."

The pigeon flew off and Sister Charlotte left. Timothy lit a cigarette. I watched his jet of smoke curl into white fluffy clouds that seemed to hang over us for a minute before rising up and floating off to join the heavy black smoke from the crematorium chimney. Timothy said, "I hope Big Joe won't be cremated."

"They're calling it suicide," Owen said. "It's on the internet: do-it-yourself death, a manual of instructions for leaving planet Earth. Pretty cool."

I gave him a look. He shouldn't have said it that way.

Timothy asked, "How'd he do it, man? Rig up some kind of a pulley thing, like a clothesline? Big Joe was a handyman so he'd know how to lubricate the pulleys and stuff, fasten the ropes, tie a weight to one end, then stand on a chair and jump."

I gave Timothy a put-a-sock-in-it look, but he wasn't finished.

"It feels like Big Joe took me out to his workshop and smashed my screwdriver with his hammer."

Chapter 47

OWEN

The clerk stood at the counter at the back of the hardware store, filling out some sort of form. Behind him, cans were lined up in a row. To his left was a contraption with cylinders for mixing the paint. While I waited, I scanned the chips, all the colours in the spectrum arranged in order from light to dark.

"A long-handled Phillips number three," the clerk said in answer to Timothy's question. "Aisle four."

Friday afternoon at two o'clock, the Joe Radley funeral was held at St. Joe's Catholic Church in Little Italy, where he'd grown up. This I learned from the photographs of Little Joe on a table near the entrance. It informed me of all sorts of things: Little Joe riding his bicycle; Little Joe going on camping trips with a buddy; and so on.

I didn't think Big Joe could have a Catholic burial if he committed suicide, but there he was, laid out not in a pine box but in an expensive cabin cruiser, top open revealing interior off-white satin upholstery, exterior shiny brown with black trim and gold handles, floating in solemn and silent splendour at the front of the church. Pretty cool. To the left of the pulpit, next to the organ at which a woman in a red gown played a hymn, sat the flowers. Pretty nice.

To my disappointment, Shelly was not there.

The pews to the left and right were empty, except for an older woman who got up to lead the way down the aisle for three others, followed by three more, relatives maybe, all wearing the same dresses and hats. They didn't immediately sit but went straight to the coffin to pay their respects, so I knew I should do the same.

To hide the burns and the bruises around his neck and to cover the discolouration of the pasty skin, the undertaker had applied a layer of powder and rubbed a smear of red on each cheek. He had dressed Big Joe in his church suit. Okay. But he had arranged what hair was left in a combover part on the side, laid down flat so now he didn't look like Big Joe or Joe the Hammer or Mr. Radley. The hair should have been different, and a plaid shirt and t-shirt might have been better. He should have had his aviator sunglasses in one hand and his ring of keys in the other, which I didn't think to bring. Big Joe was a Jekyll and Hyde, but neither was in the cabin cruiser.

Didn't matter. It was whose heart was in there.

I took a seat in the front pew next to Timothy and Martha. A priest dressed in long robes came from a door behind the altar and stepped up to the pulpit. The music stopped. Staring at some invisible point at the back of the church, the priest began: "God's finger touched him, and he slept. God's hand touched him, and he slipped away to Heaven. Let us pray."

As I knelt, wondering about God's hand, I saw Timothy's hand slip under his t-shirt. While everyone was seated and bowed, heads lowered, eyes closed, reciting Our Father, Timothy stood and, at the precise moment the priest raised his finger in what looked like some kind ceremonial gesture meant to send off Big Joe from his cabin cruiser, Timothy walked calmly to the coffin and raised his hand. But the priest's garments, fanned out by the raised arm, blocked my vision, so I couldn't tell if Timothy had plunged the eight-inch, green-handled Phillips into both of Big Joe's hearts or into only one. And if only into one, would Timothy have plunged the screw driver into the left or the right side?

"Amen," I said, hoping I would not have to help Timothy dig Big Joe up to do the deed again.

Chapter 48

OWEN

I went downstairs and opened the deadbolt twist lock of the front door. The iron bar sprang out with a thwunk. I turned the iron bar into the door and pushed it shut. I turned the dead bolt again. The iron bar thwunked into the door frame, and the door was locked. I unlocked it and went outside and shut the door. I turned until the iron bar thwunked out and the door was locked.

"Sister Charlotte, he's playing with the doorknobs again. Guess what I'm doing? I'm washing windows, wiping counters, cleaning floors, polishing silverware, vacuuming carpets, dusting furniture, washing the car, hosing down the front steps, and shovelling the sidewalk. What is Owen doing?"

"After you finish shovelling the snow, do the bathroom mirrors and the sinks, and check the toilet paper. Don't forget, it has to roll down from the front, not the back."

Martha said, "Duh. Guess what, Sister Charlotte? It's September. There's no snow."

Like when I was little and I found the brushing of teeth soothing, at eighteen I found the repetition of mechanical things soothing. It was the over and over of the exact same predictable pattern, like loaves of supermarket bread that came off a mechanical slicer, always twenty-four.

I moved past the doorways and up the stairs with my broom, counting my quick firm strokes along the bare boards of the hall, working my way from door to door to the office. I slipped in my key and the iron bar thwunked out, and the door was unlocked. I reversed the key, and the door was locked.

Five minutes later, when Mr. Locke, a social worker from CFCS arrived, I set my broom aside and sat on the floor. That wasn't his real name. That's what his wide jaw and straight thin lips looked like to me because I'd been playing with locks. Sister Charlotte limped Mr. Locke upstairs to the office. When they were settled inside, I went out my window and hunched low on the roof to peek through the slice of air under the office window. Mr. Locke was sitting opposite Sister Charlotte at the desk. He folded a little pocket pad to a clean sheet, took out his pen, and wrote something on the top. It seemed everyone who came to see Sister Charlotte had a little pocket pad jotting down what she said. To compare notes, I guess.

"The reason I'm here…" He jotted down a few sentences. "Any psychological or emotional issues?"

Sister Charlotte shifted on the edge of her chair, trying to get comfortable. "With whom?"

"With the children."

While he waited for the answer, he continued to write. The pad in his hand was the same whitish-grey as Sister Charlotte's hands, which were resting in her lap. The whirls and the crinkles in Sister Charlotte's skin were like the wrinkles and crinkles Mr. Locke was making with his pen on the white paper.

Mr. Locke searched through his suit jacket pocket for another pen. "How many children do you have here?"

Sister Charlotte sat ramrod straight in her chair. "You know how many children I have here."

"And you have severe arthritis."

"I have Huntington's disease."

Mr. Locke looked through his papers. "Arthritis it says. Why were we never notified?"

"I don't know."

"What sort of medication are you taking?"

"My motto is I'll See You Tomorrow, the four most important words in a foster child's vocabulary. The security of knowing that the person who is looking after them today will be there to look after them tomorrow. I have Huntington's, yes. But I'm always here for them in the morning when they wake up, and I'm always here for them when they get home from school, and I'm always here for them last thing before bed. When I say I'll see you tomorrow, they know they will see me tomorrow. But while they're in school, I'm in my bed. To control the pain, I take pills. But these are mild painkillers, prescribed by my doctor."

"Your doctor's name?" He tried his pen again. "Could I borrow a pen?"

Sister Charlotte hesitated. "Why are you here? What is this about?"

"Your doctor's name."

"I haven't seen him for a while. I've been managing without them."

"A pen, Sister Charlotte."

She gave him one.

He tried to write, but his fingers seemed too big, and the pad, which seemed to have become too small, appeared clumsy in his hand. "Could you write down the doctor's name and address, Sister Charlotte?"

She stared at her twisted fingers. "Yes — these hands — I admit I could not have managed without Martha."

"The name of your doctor, Sister Charlotte. I want to watch you write it down."

"I walk in the footsteps of my Lord Jesus Christ. What I need to know he writes in my heart."

He tucked his pad away in an inside pocket. "You're a nun. Why did you go into foster care?"

"The Sisters of Sorrows Foster Care were my family. Now this is my family. These kids are like my own. Thanks to the Sixsteps family-values philosophy, they have been trained to look after everything. They do all the housework, all the cleaning. Their rooms are always neat and tidy. I don't look after them; they look after me. It's a marvel how responsible and helpful well-trained children can be."

"Well trained, yes. Independent, yes. But the problem is the equation has, for some time now, been upside down. The foster children should not be looking after the foster parents. Why was Bishop Humphries covering that fact up? He was visiting regularly and hiding the truth of this situation. For what reason?"

"You'll have to ask him. I don't know."

"That's not possible. The bishop is not very lucid as the result of a baseball accident while playing catch with Martha."

"So I heard."

"And did you hear Joe Radley passed away?"

"So I heard."

"And the charges against Father Eagleman have been dropped."

"So I heard."

"Bella Brock has passed away. The police found her in her apartment. She'd been dead for several days."

"Oh. I didn't know that."

"One other thing, Sister Charlotte. If these children are your life, what will you do when they finally leave?"

"Jesus Christ called me to this mission, and I responded. When this mission is over, He will lead me to the next path."

"You have no fear of a future in a nursing home, Sister Charlotte?"

"Will that be your recommendation? That I get put in a nursing home?"

"That I put you in addiction rehab."

Sister Charlotte reached for her Bible. "Rehab? I'm a nun. I take my vows seriously. So ask me the exact questions you want to ask, and I'll place my hand on my Bible and give you the answer."

"Are you an addict, Sister Charlotte?"

"No, I'm not. There. You see? My hand was on my Bible."

***

I answered the postman's knock. "I have a registered letter for Martha Brock and Owen VanWirrt."

"I can give it to each of them," I said.

Not wanting to crease or crumple the letters, I slipped them into my shirt rather than stuffing them it into my pants pocket. I wanted to keep the pages as clean and crisp as priceless parchment sealed for centuries in a Dead Sea cave so Martha couldn't say, Pew, gross! You didn't wash your hands. Jesus, Owen, pull up your pants, blah, blah…

The letter rustled against my shirt, and the corners tickled against my belly as I short-cutted through the tombstones, past the statue of Jesus hanging on his big stone cross, to the chapel. It was sitting perfectly parallel with the wire mesh fence at the back of the cemetery. And the subway tracks, hidden in a shallow gully, were running parallel to the line of poplars beyond the subway tracks. And there, in the grass off to one side, not parallel to anything, sat Martha.

She read the letter. She gave me back the letter, as though she didn't want it. She said, "So we're free to go with CFCS support until we turn twenty-one. Where do you want to go?"

"I haven't had time to think about it."

She said flatly, "You've had eighteen years to think about it, moron."

Chapter 49

OWEN

Martha couldn't sleep at night, so she liked to lie in the cemetery grass, her head resting on her arm, and fall asleep in the afternoon sun. Sometimes Petunia would wander by and lie beside her. Sometimes I would look at Martha and think about my dead sister lying there, face down in the Open Hatch with me face up. I imagined my dead sister would have looked like Martha, and I imagined the two of them dressed in white would look like angels, one with real wings floating around up there with the pigeons, and the other with fake wings down here pecking at me every ten minutes.

When Martha's eyes blinked open and she rolled over, I saw that she was looking up, so I looked up. I saw a trail of vapour that looked like it was coming from the chapel belfry but, in fact, was coming from the crematorium. I looked at Martha, now standing, watching the smoke lean across the chapel roof and slant over St. Mary's roof. I looked at Martha and I saw where she was going, and I saw that Petunia was following her. We followed Martha single file through the gravestones and through the open chapel window and up the stairs to watch from the belfry the tail twisting from the chimney, waving at us for a moment in the wind before flatlining across the horizon and disappearing into the mists somewhere beyond St. Mary's steeples.

I didn't see any star in the east nor any eclipse of the sun overhead. I felt no telepathic messages spiralling downward from my sister up there above those skyway crosses. But in those few minutes of unexpected realization, what I saw suddenly before my eyes was a transformation of Martha's face. It had been changing from the day she visited her mother. But this was the first time I noticed the change, not in the shape of the nose or the slant of the eyes but in the pattern of her features, like a sudden change in the sequence of same-design squares on a blanket or like the sudden change of the same person into two different shadows. And like the transformation of a tadpole into a frog happened only in the pond, Martha's transformation into a real sister happened only in my cranial vault.

I had begun to feel compassion for Sister Martha.

I knew through my research that from time to time the activity of the laws of nature suspend themselves in order to bring about an atypical state of affairs. If you're willing to admit that a Supreme Designer made the atoms and molecules and the galaxy into a cosmos, then the making of a foster sister into your half sister into your real sister is not a big deal.

Martha was crying. Maybe she had started to cry ten minutes ago. Maybe she had been crying since the day I met her and had been crying all along, ever since, and I hadn't noticed. I don't know. I don't know what came over me. I put my arms around her and hugged her.

I knew from doing my research that your brain has a mind of its own. Often it seems to take you in directions you hadn't intended, like instead of you thinking your thoughts and instead of your thoughts thinking you, you realize it's Thought that does your thinking. Nothing could have transformed my thought into Thought quicker and with more clarity than watching Martha watching her mother coming out of that chimney.

Chapter 50

MARTHA

High as a kite, Sister Charlotte led the way from the kitchen and along the hall, me following, up the staircase, wide and long with one turn, didn't matter. One, two, three — today no grunting and sighing at every step — four, five, six, seven, eight, nine to the office.

"New buds, Martha. Much better, although one day my left knee is a bit creaky, next day my right, but overall, what a relief." She opened the office door for me to enter. "We need to have a little talk. I've already talked with Owen. Now you."

I sat in the chair by the wall lined with Peter's gardening and baseball books from shiny hardwood floor to slanted ceiling. On the wall opposite the desk, below a wide mirror, stood the filing cabinet. I waited for Sister Charlotte to reach out and open one drawer of the filing cabinet and give me the brown envelope containing my emancipation papers. I waited for one drawer to slide itself open, and a brown envelope containing my papers to appear. I waited for me to get up and open the filing cabinet drawer and give myself the brown envelope containing my emancipation papers.

"As you know, Martha, I have sacrificed my life to foster care, for many years in the North, for my final years with you. But now my mission here on earth, salvation for you and Owen, is almost finished."

Sister Charlotte reached for a ring of old-fashioned skeleton keys hanging next to the portrait of the pope, the shoulders of his cloak filling the frame, his shadow leaning forward into the room, his eyes studying me from above with a long steady stare. Maybe because that artificial eye seemed brighter than the other, I didn't know which one to focus on. I tried to fix on both at once but could not. I tried to shift from the one with a glare to the one more vacant but could not. I knew what this glare was about: Martha, now is the time she needs you the most. Shame on you for leaving her. Bow your head in guilt, Martha, feel the sting of contrition in your heart for all the bad thoughts you've had about Sister Charlotte. Lower your gaze in penance, Martha, and get down on your knees and say, Please forgive me, Sister Charlotte. I promise I will not abandon you now, and I promise to stay with you forever.

I felt the sting of contrition coming up from my throat. My lips began to quiver. Here it comes, shame on you, Martha, shuffle, shuffle, sniffle, sniffle.

"These big skeleton keys" — Sister Charlotte lifted them from their hook — "they aren't for entering any worldly door, neither for going in nor for keeping out. They're called the Resurrection Keys, seven on each ring to open the door to the Kingdom of Jesus, each of the seven days of each week."

I took the keys. "But when do I have to leave?"

Sister Charlotte blinked herself into a focused sternness.

I said, "I get these keys now because I have to leave now?"

"The same as Owen. You each get a ring of keys as a gift from me when you leave and I leave."

I put the keys back on the hook. "I don't want to leave. I want to stay here with you."

"You must leave. Mr. Knight is here."

Mr. Knight appeared at the door. "Sister Charlotte wants you at her side, Martha. And then you're free to go."

"Now? Not now."

"Look at it this way, Martha. Dying is like floating into cyberspace. We come from water in its purity. Into the light we come. Then back into the dark we go, disappearing mysteriously into the currents from which we came."

"I want to stay here and look after Sister Charlotte. For as long as she needs me, I'll stay with her. Please. Don't take her from me now."

He took my arm and Sister Charlotte's arm and led the way down the hall to Sister Charlotte's bedroom.

She went immediately to her window, which looked down at the garden. "Like the Garden of Eden, Martha. It was from a drawing of Eden that I planned this garden, every last detail, except the apple tree, which was here when I bought the property. I planted seeds I brought back from the Holy Land, all the way from Bethlehem. Can you imagine that, Martha? And the seeds for those narcissus came from Bethlehem. And those over there, Martha, those are carnations from Damascus."

Mr. Knight led Sister Charlotte to her bed, and Sister Charlotte climbed in.

"Sit up a little, Sister Charlotte, so I can place the pill on your tongue. There you are. Now in a few minutes you'll feel yourself float into eternity. But not alone, for Martha will be with you to show you the way and to light your path. There you go, Sister Charlotte. Now, caught in the moment between the temporal and the eternal, you're entering a different zone. Your entire life is flashing before you, not from beginning to end but backward, from end to beginning. Yet it seems to take the same amount of time to go back as it did to go forward."

Mr. Knight bowed his head. "Sister Charlotte, who is here with us today, is ready to go, and Martha, who is here with us today, is ready to let her go. So, Sister Charlotte, open your eyes one last time, for today at — let me see — at precisely three fourteen on September twenty-fifth, with Martha at your side, you will take your place in Heaven. And, Martha, stop your sniffling and snivelling and wailing and let her go. You're slobbering all over Charlotte's Sisters of Sorrows button."

Chapter 51

OWEN

The following Sunday, Father Small's announcement was prefaced with regrets. In a voice that sounded like an official declaration from a Vatican bulletin, he announced that a new organist would be playing every Sunday from now on and would be practising every evening from eight to nine o'clock for anyone who wanted to come to St. Mary's to listen, worship, and pray.

That evening, lying with Martha on my bed, I felt a cold draft along my spine, like the feeling I often had in the chapel — like the swish of a breeze through the curtains of an open window. Then suddenly from somewhere outside sounded one long chord on an organ followed abruptly by several short bars in a series. They sprang through this open window to dance all around me. They stopped. Then springing up again, they continued. I listened to this hymn — not one of Sister Charlotte's and not played by Sister Charlotte, for the notes weren't wrong, the tune not off-key. I got up and went to the window. The music was coming from St. Mary's, played by the new player, but played on the same organ and carried on the same breeze through the same tombstones and across the same cemetery.

That week, every evening in my room, Martha propped up beside me on my bed, we waited. A few seconds before the music started, Martha would set aside what she was doing and close her eyes. And then, as though the music was waiting for her to give consent to the silent pipes, I saw her eyes open, and at that same instant the first strains of the organ sounded chord upon chord from pipe to spire, crossing through concrete tombstones, climbing clapboard walls to enter this bedroom window, delivering by healed fingers the hymn that Sister Charlotte had seconds ago sent.

At Sinner Sanctum two Sundays later, Father Small stood behind the altar preparing the Communion. I couldn't tell if he was listening to the hymn or to the pigeons gathered outside, flapping and squawking, wondering what had happened to their pigeon music.

At the end of the service, before his benediction, in a voice that sounded like the second official declaration from the Vatican bulletin, he announced that the memorial service for Sister Charlotte would be held the following Thursday.

Chapter 52

OWEN

It was now the first week of October, so the yard was not an oasis of lush grass and green shrubs and late-blooming flowers. That was all dead.

Peter and I finished in the garden and started on the shed. We hung up the tools on a series of hooks, starting in the corner next to Petunia's baby carriage and running lengthwise, left and right, parallel to the overhead rafters. Peter would have stuck them in any old place, but Martha wanted them neat and tidy and hung up straight. Martha wanted everything neat and tidy and straight so the house would go on the market neat and tidy and straight. Peter needed the money for his move to Halifax.

Martha, watching from the bench, was looking like Sister Charlotte when her pills hadn't been working, her hands resting lifeless in her lap, looking so useless she wouldn't have been able to butter toast or even clip the grocery coupons out of the paper or even fix my glasses or even measure out the angel food cake ingredients.

That Thursday, seated in the front row, ten feet from the closed casket surrounded by flowers, sat a group of former Sisters of Sorrows, and behind them about fifty dog-collared priests. And behind them, standing room only, maybe a hundred Indigenous men and women from the North, come by the busload to pay their respects.

Sunlight through the stained-glass windows fell in red and blue bars on the yellow flames of three tall candles placed on the white-clothed altar before which, dressed in black-and-gold robes, stood Father Small.

After a hymn and some prayers, he motioned for one of the Sisters to come to the front to talk about Sister Charlotte.

She read from her notes: "We are grief stricken by the death of Sister Charlotte, who worked day and night for others, organizing and mobilizing thousands of workers into our foster-care mission. Sister Charlotte had a remarkable presence. When you sat with her, it was as though you were in the presence of God. Some people are chosen by God to offer their life for the well-being of others. Sister Charlotte was such a person. Her work with the Indigenous boys in the North is legendary. So, when the question was asked by those far-north social workers and by the far-north police department and by the far-north politicians who had come up to shut down the mission of the Sisters of Sorrows, 'Who is this woman?' I'm reminded of the question asked of our Lord Jesus, 'Who do men say that I am?' Well I have just told you. Sister Charlotte lived a life of heroic virtue, following the teachings of Jesus."

When she finished, Father Small said a long prayer that ended with some waving of his hands and some muttering of his words that ended in a low slow voice: "May the Spirit of the Lord come upon you, Sister Charlotte."

On the street outside, I waited. The pigeons waited. The sun, which had burned off some early morning mist, was peeking over the church roof to shine directly into the lens of my BlackBerry. Frightened by the buses outside the church, the pigeons stayed on the roof, out of harm's way.

At the exact moment the Sisters of Sorrows emerged as a group from the church, the white homer, Emma, returning from somewhere, circling high above the three tall steeples, preparing to join the flock, spotted the Sisters all wearing the same blue dress and flat black shoes as Sister Charlotte had always worn. Emma folded her wings and dropped, but wary of all the people gathered round, she switched to a glide, circled back once, and stalled directly above the Sisters, where she remained suspended, her white feathers glinting silver in the morning sunlight. She wanted to land but, unable to spot Sister Charlotte, confused by the activity, she tilted her wings, made one more perfect circle above the gathered Sisters, and rose again.

In the resulting video replay I gave to the six o'clock news, the sunlight through the mist reflected in silver glints off the white blur of the pigeon's wings to create in the eye of the camera a ghostly halo silhouetting the pigeon as it descended and then stalled for a moment above the Sisters before it disappeared into a sapphire sky framed between two of the three giant crosses of St. Mary's. I emailed the news clipping called "The Descent of the Dove" to Peter, who had already left for Halifax.

Chapter 53

MARTHA

Sometime during the night, fog had settled in and was now so thick I could barely see from my bedroom window across the street to Tiny Tots. Yellow-fingered headlights and red-blurred tail lights of one early morning car drove past. Maybe Peter in his taxi, I thought. I had never seen him driving anything other than his yellow taxi.

Come back, I wanted to say to Peter. I've never really seen you.

A man passed by, the red point of his cigarette swinging as he walked in the darkness between the white streetlights. Maybe that was Peter, I thought. But I had never seen him smoking a cigarette.

Come back, I wanted to say to Peter. I have so many questions I still need to ask you.

I went downstairs and sat at the kitchen table. Come back, I wanted to say to Peter. There's still so much I need from you.

I glanced out the back door at the dead flowers and the dead grass and the dead apple tree. Come back, I wanted to say to Peter. I need so badly to meet you again and get to know you better.

Come back, I wanted to say to Peter. I need you to help find my way.

I stood at the back door watching the autumn rain form brinks of icy water on the bench where Peter and I often sat, trying to figure stuff out.

Come back, Peter, I wanted to say. I should have got to know you while you were here.

Come back, Peter, I wanted to say. I should have taken one last look at you before you left.

Come back, Peter. In all those years, I never told you I loved you.

Chapter 54

MARTHA

"I'm calling about the apartment for rent."

"The address is two fifty-four—" The woman's wheezing voice broke into a fit of coughing so loud and harsh I took my cell away from my ear. She recovered, cleared her throat, and took a drink of something. "Cork Street," she concluded.

Cork Street was another row of shabby houses with garbage cans in front yards along with leftover Christmas trees, derelict bicycles, kids' toys, and assorted junk. Owen was waiting right there in the middle of it, in one hand his BlackBerry, in the other a birdcage big enough for a chicken.

OhmyGodputmeoutofmisery. "What is that for?"

Owen looked a little sheepish. "I found it over there."

"Leave it on the porch," I said. "You can't walk in with a chicken cage."

Both front windows were covered with yellowed blinds, although it was two o'clock in the afternoon. A living-room chair with ripped cushions was on the front porch. Disgusting. But with Owen on student assistance and with my minimum wage on the housekeeping staff at the Holiday Inn, we needed someplace cheap.

Besides, the house, though small, looked cozy in an oddball Owen way. After pressing the bell several times with no answer, Owen standing off to one side, his head lost in time, I rapped on the peeling paint of the door. It was opened immediately by a woman with 1972 pink slacks and blonde candy-floss hair piled up and held in place by a purple comb.

OhmyGodputmeoutofmisery. "I'm Martha. I phoned about the apartment."

In her right hand, she carried a glass of what looked like ginger ale. "It's upstairs," she said hoarsely.

She glanced at the cage on the front step. "How'd that cage get up here?"

"Owen, my brother."

"The apartment is for Owen?"

"For both of us."

When Owen reached out to shake her hand, she hesitated. Owen had combed his hair, but it had a mind of its own and persisted in going off at odd angles in space, like his brain. Now that I was working long hours at the hotel, I had no time to look after his glasses, now balanced lopsided on his nose.

"He's a student." I needed to ease her into it. "He's very smart. He's won a scholarship to the University of Toronto, and this location is close to the subway."

She shook his hand and motioned us into a front entrance that smelled musty and stale, not like at Sister Charlotte's, which always smelled of disinfectant. She laboured up the stairs, the ice cubes in her glass clinking at each step. Because her pink slacks were too short, the wide cuffs waved two inches above her ankles as she climbed. Halfway up, she broke into a fit of coughing, so severe she had to sit on the step. We waited. Chicken cages, a landlady with TB, and Owen. Have mercy.

Recovered somewhat but still panting, she continued along the upper hall to a door that opened into one large dingy living room-kitchen arrangement with two bedrooms, each with a grease spot on the wall where the headboard would be. Through a third door was a small bathroom with a shower.

I opened the closets and looked inside. I tested the bath and kitchen sink. The living area ceiling was low and sloping, like an attic, so, depending on where I stood, I had to huddle so as not to bang my head. Owen was taller, but he wouldn't notice his head being banged, except maybe against the overhead hanging light, which had sharp corners. There was no room for his experiments, but that didn't matter. He was using the lab at the university.

The woman was staring at Owen, now seated on the floor, looking like he didn't know if he was going to lie down or stand up.

"The apartment is nine hundred twenty-five a month. Me and Stan — that's my man. I'm Goldy by the way — we live downstairs. There's just you up here."

After a slurp from her ginger ale, Goldy set it down on the sill of the window, which looked down on the street at the front of the house. "You can decorate the room if you want," she said, taking from the wall a calendar with a picture of three kittens in a basket. "But Stan don't want you hammering nails in the plaster. And no pets, if that's what you got in mind with that cage. Stan don't like pets."

"In your ad, it said we'd be part of the family."

Goldy did another once over of Owen. "Yeah, well." She seemed not too sure. "I put that in because this isn't like an apartment building. There's just the one unit, know what I mean? You can come on down and watch television with Stan. Sit in the living room. Anything you want."

After counting the money, she paused and scowled at Owen. "Where do you live now? Stan's gonna want references."

I said, "We used to live on Erskine Ave. I know he looks, you know, but he's, you know, one of those genius types. He's got a science scholarship at the university in the genetics department."

A black beetle crept out from behind the window frame and scurried across the wall. Goldy's left hand snaked out and smacked the bug. It dropped to the floor and lay on its back by her foot, legs like tiny identically bent sticks waving spastically, all but one, which seemed not to work, bent now at a different angle, like Sister Charlotte's fingers. But a beetle had lots of other legs to do the work of getting around. One more or less didn't matter. It managed to get back on its feet and carry on, until Goldy stepped on it.

Goldy was staring at Owen, who was bent over, staring at the crushed bug.

"Stan don't like bugs. He don't like pets. He don't like kids, and he don't like fish. He said make sure I tell everyone that."

"Owen doesn't have any pets," I said.

"That cage, what's he gonna do with that."

"I'll make certain he throws it away."

As we followed Goldy down the stairs, I noticed on the windowsills all sorts of porcelain knickknacks with gold trim: a red toad on a gold leaf, a white rabbit wearing gold trousers, a blue windmill with gold blades, and there, hanging on the wall, ohmyGodputmeoutofmisery, an old photo of someone's sad parents, a mother sitting, the father standing at her side. Add to that, in the odd junk living room across from the staircase, a thin derelict Stan watching football on a giant flatscreen, one long finger poking into one ear, excavating stuff too gross for me to look at.

But the apartment worked out okay. Goldy invited us for Sunday supper the next week. Goldy said by the look of Owen he'd probably lived on Froot Loops.

Chapter 55

OWEN

I went upstairs to wash my hands for Sunday supper. I stood at the sink and looked at myself in the mirror: no pimples — just plain Owen. I dried my hands and combed my hair, but I didn't look at my face again before turning off the light. I didn't want to see this six-foot-tall person caught in its frame, like not wanting to look at a picture of someone you would rather forget.

Bend low to the keyhole, Owen, and you'll see Sister Charlotte sitting up in her bed, her empty bud bottles piled next to her flat-heeled shoes waiting for her crippled feet. Bend low to the keyhole, Owen, and you'll see from the bottoms of her bud bottles, from beneath even more bud bottles, crouching like mice at her feet, comes not only her pain but also her sacrifice. Bend low to the keyhole, Owen, and watch these sacrifices creep across the floor to kneel at the toe of your red running shoe. Bend low to the keyhole, Owen, and have a good look. Can you see yourself sitting at the dinner table eating nothing but stale bread? Do you see, while you eat your stale bread, Sister Charlotte scratching scabbed-over tracks? Bend low to the keyhole, Owen, and see that Sister Charlotte is sitting up in her bed, crooked hands clasped, looking your way, wondering why it took you so long to see her.

Chapter 56

OWEN

From my bedroom window I watched Stan and Goldy leave, probably going for groceries for Sunday supper. An hour later, I heard Martha come up the sidewalk, the hard rubber heels of her flat black shoes tapping on the concrete, walking quickly, for it had begun to rain.

At the front door, the tapping stopped, the lock rattled, and her shoes crossed the hall and came up the stairs. I wanted to ask, as she passed by my door on the way to her bedroom, Would you like to go to a movie sometime?

But, of course, she'd say no, so I didn't step into the hallway as she reached the top of the staircase, didn't call out hello as she stepped into our living room, didn't strike up a conversation as she walked past my bedroom door.

Martha reached her door, opened it, and went inside. I could hear the hard rubber soles of her flat black shoes clap across the hardwood floor. She must have immediately removed them, for next I heard her bare feet pad to the window. The Venetian blind rattled down.

Because it was raining, she'd been wearing a large floppy hat, so I had not seen much of her face when she arrived, so I could not know what kind of mood she was in. Half an hour later, when she came from the shower, she was drying her hair with a large towel. When she came from her bedroom, she was dressed as usual in a plain blue skirt and blouse and low-heeled black shoes.

"Owen, you have to set targets for yourself. You have to start eating better. Not that crap Goldy serves you. You need chamomile tea and herbs and yogurt and stuff. And you need to eat your vegetables. I'll go with you to the health food store."

Martha held her back straight and had six freshly sharpened pencils standing straight up like soldiers in their pencil holder. Charlotte 1 and Charlotte 2.

I removed my running shoes and tried on the new pair of cargoes with a blue shirt that Martha had got for me. I tried on a pair of designer jeans. After that I began to weed through my clothes, throwing most of them out, as I had done with my microscopes and my tanks. I had better equipment in the lab at the university.

Martha said, "Don't forget. Goldy invited us to eat with them."

We went downstairs and sat with Stan. From the kitchen Goldy shouted, "What do you want for supper?"

"Soup," Stan mumbled.

"What else?"

"Just soup."

"Owen and Martha are here to eat with us. How about a couple of pork chops?"

"How can I eat pork chops when I got no teeth?" Stan flipped from football to CBC Breaking News.

Goldy said, "There's that bishop."

"I got eyes. I can see."

"He's got a funny haircut."

"I got eyes. I can see that."

"How about rice pudding, with raisins like my granny made."

Stan considered this. "A hamburger sandwich. With gravy."

"There's the picture of the nun."

"Don't forget the raisins."

"There's a clip from her funeral. The picture of the dove. That's fake."

"All news is. Shut the fuck up. I can see it's fake."

***

I looked out my window, still raining. A man riding an old CCM Balloon Tire went by, glancing up at me as he rode past. A girl in sandals stepped on something as she walked by, dog dirt probably.

She sat on the wet curb and, with a stick, began to scrape it off. The way she got up and the way she threw the stick into the street reminded me of the feisty Martha who used to play hardball.

I began to change the newspaper on the floor of Emma's cage. Now she was well rested and ready. I was waiting for the weather to clear. After three days of hard rain, I was hoping for sun tomorrow. Released, Emma would fly nonstop, straight to St. Mary's steeple and from there home; that's how bad she wanted to return to her family. When she reached home, her sisters would coo and flap and say, "Welcome home."

Using Martha's coffee grinder, I had turned Sister Charlotte's ashes into a fine powder. I didn't want to touch it at first, but then my scientist self took over, and I set to work. Before I released Emma, I would pull aside the feathers along her back and wings and sprinkle some of the powder, as much as I could, into the down close to her skin. In flight she would hold her feathers tight to her body to reduce wind resistance. She would clamp her long wing feathers snug to catch wind currents, which would take her to the thermals where she could relax into a glide.

I was folding an old copy of Stan's *Toronto Sun*, taken from the floor of the cage, when I noticed on page five an interview with the crown attorney who outlined the details and ended by saying, "Much of the credit for breaking the case against Bishop Humphries and Father Eagleman goes to Detective Paul Kosinski for uncovering the church cover-up of the Boys from Snowy River in the Diocese of Moosonee, an investigation that spanned almost a decade."

I took off my cargoes and hung them neatly on a wooden hanger. No clothes left lying around, nothing out of place, towels hung precisely straight. Charlotte 1 and Charlotte 2. I stood before the mirror, examining my face with my new contact lenses, which didn't allow me to see and understand any better than my lopsided glasses. But I looked less geeky.

I don't think Sister Charlotte ever wore high heels. Maybe because she never went anywhere. Martha wore flat black shoes to our high school graduation, which she insisted I attend. I sat in the front row wearing my suit. I watched different shoes go across the stage, like at the funeral parlour on their way to Big Joe's viewing. The boys wore brown or black, and the girls mostly black high heels. Some wore short dresses. Timothy, sitting next to me, leaned forward and tangentially looked up. But he didn't know any better. When the turn for our row came, first Martha then me, I walked across the stage and took my high school diploma. When I glanced down, I saw, sitting three rows back, I'm sure of it, my dead sister. I saw that she was smiling, proud of me.

A knock sounded on my door. Goldy stepped in and stood with one hand on the doorknob. "Stan says you can't have pets. He says that pigeon's got to go."

"I'm releasing it in a day or two. I'm waiting for the rain to stop."

"I told you when you moved in, Stan says no pets, and especially he don't like pigeons."

"I'm letting it go as soon as the rain stops."

"He don't go for that kind of stuff, hamsters, canaries, so you got to find another place to live. And goldfish. He hates goldfish."

"I'm letting it go tomorrow, maybe."

"Don't get me wrong. I got nothing against pigeons. But Stan don't like pets, white rats, gerbils, dogs, cats, goldfish, kids. God knows what else he don't like."

"It's not supposed to rain tomorrow. By tomorrow it'll be gone."

"You're paid up till Friday. I'll give you a refund." She held out the money. "Don't get me wrong. It's Stan."

"I promise by tomorrow it'll be gone. No more pigeon."

She went away, and in a few minutes returned. "Stan says get rid of it by tomorrow or he's gonna bring over his buddy. His buddy don't like pigeons either."

Chapter 57

OWEN

Martha and I hurry along the edge of the cemetery to the first lane, which stretches before us like a long corridor through the shadows of the silver poplars swaying overhead in the sunlight of a beautiful October afternoon. We go into the backyard of Peter's house, still not sold. We sit on Peter's bench by the apple tree. Petunia arrives. I hear the crackle and rustle as she wags and sniffs and pokes through leaves from the apple tree blown up against the stone fence. I thought that after two days of rain they should be soggy, but I guess not. I notice that all Peter's flowers have died, and the withered flower stalks are lying flat, and the lawn has turned brown. Martha shifts position to give Petunia a pat and then pick her up and settle her down with her blankie and bonnet in the baby carriage. We walk over to the flower shop on Yonge Street.

The sun is locked behind the clouds, and the wind is gusty, and the feeling of rain is heavy as we enter the flower shop.

"Two white carnations?" The clerk looks puzzled. "We sell them by the dozen.'

I say, "Just two. It's a special occasion."

The clerk stares at me. I don't know why. My hair isn't sticking up; I'm not wearing crooked glasses; my shirt is tucked into my cargoes.

"Whatever you say. Four white carnations."

Martha corrects him. "Two white carnations."

I pay the clerk and we leave the store, the carnations wrapped in green paper, open at the top. The wind gusts and swirls, blowing Martha's long hair to one side as we walk along Yonge Street back toward the cemetery. Entering the gate, Martha points to the clouds building above the row of swaying poplars, unfurling silver leaves not yet fallen. I was hoping for sun, but it's too late to turn back.

As we continue along the lane, we hear a car behind us. We step aside into the grass. But it doesn't pass, so we continue, walking in a single-file procession, first Martha pushing Petunia in her carriage, then me, and then the car, past the stone statue of Jesus and up the hill. In deliberate motion through the long, monotonous procession of tombstones we move, so slowly that the car, when I glance back, seems to be suspended behind us, not moving at all, like one of the tombstones. At a fork in the lane, we turn to the left, it to the right. Near the top of the hill at the back corner of the cemetery, the car stops. A man wearing a black suit and a woman dressed in red carrying a bouquet of white and yellow step out and cross the grass to a grave on this side of the stone crucifix. She stands by it statue-like, head tilted a little to one side. She seems to be listening to the wind cutting through the trees and the monuments.

We continue toward our first stop, not far from the maple tree, which will shade it for many years from the summer sun. No sun today, though. Situated in this corner near the end of the lane, with such a small marker, the grave is so hidden that, day after day, people will walk over it without knowing that Grandpa is there.

Martha picks up a stick from the roadside and kneels at the almost invisible marker to clean off the grass, but with only a stick, she can't do much. As she finishes, the car we saw earlier appears. The driver points at us as though he knows who we are and can't figure out why Martha would be laying flowers on this grave. Neither can I, but Martha will have her reasons. By the time the car has completed its gradual journey through the tombstones and out the gate, Martha has finished. She stands back to examine her work. We watch some sparrows fly down, first one, then a second, followed by a third, chopping down in a swirl of brown to hop and peck in the vegetation that Martha has tidied. She lays her white carnation.

To my right are new tombstones in rows marked with fresh wreaths and flowers, while to my left, a funeral procession brings in one more body, weaving through the trees to stop beside a freshly dug grave, ready and waiting. The pallbearers carry the coffin to the graveside. The friends and relatives gather around while the priest, carrying his Bible, adjusting his black cassock, waits for the mingling mourners to finish their handshakes and hugs.

He opens his prayer book. Gesturing toward the deceased, he reads in a solemn voice, "As it has pleased the Almighty Father to receive unto himself the soul of this brother here departed..."

A gust of wind rips away the priest's words as he bends and stands to cast the handful of earth upon the coffin. He holds up his hands and makes a sign with his finger telling the soul it is time to go or not go. Being a priest, he knows that the good souls go immediately over the Silent Bridge into Heaven, but the bad ones must hang above the head of the coffin, waiting a few days before beginning their trip to purgatory.

Petunia was snug in her baby carriage, but now she gets up and wants out. At first she wants to play with the fresh ghost, waiting there, hovering above the grave. Then she wanders off to investigate other deceased floating around. But when Martha calls, Petunia sets off, leading the way, plodding in slow resignation, face full of sadness and frowns, on stumpy legs trudging a path ahead of us toward the chapel to say goodbye to Sister Charlotte, soon to be carried by the waiting wind, barely stirring now, from time to time shifting its feet in silent ripples in the cemetery grass, anxious to begin its journey through the silver-leafed poplars to that somewhere beyond St. Mary's crosses.

Aware that someone has joined us, I turn. Mr. Knight seems thinner and smaller. But he is still wearing the white suit and white shirt and black tie.

"I haven't seen you for a while, Owen. I guess you've been too busy trying to figure things out."

A stout woman appears on the crest of the hill. She wears high heels. She leans a little forward as she wobbles a few feet along the lane before turning to labour across the grass toward a graveside.

"Can I ask you a personal question?" inquires Mr. Knight. "What are you going to do with that white pigeon?"

I tell him, and he likes the idea. He gives me the keys to the cemetery, so we don't have to climb through the window.

The day becomes dark. The wind picks up. In the distance, thunder rumbles. Along the cemetery lane, we continue, following Petunia's slow stumpy steps, one right turn, then right again to the iron fence to the front step. Framed by the windy poplars behind and the heavy grey clouds overhead, the chapel waits. We unlock the door and walk past the pews, past the altar, to open the stained-glass window at the back. Clean air rushes in. I stand by the window as Martha opens the green paper. A special occasion, I told the clerk in the flower shop, hoping that when I leave today I'll never look back, that it will all be over. Not forgotten but set aside.

We lay the carnation on the altar. Then we follow Petunia single file up the steps and into the belfry. The wind stops, and the day becomes still and dark. I hold Emma at the belfry railing. As I raise her high over my head, I feel her warmth in my hands and feel the beat of her tiny heart in my pulse, steady and strong, anxious to answer the call that will lift her to the clouds and from there to the thermals.

The tears of the angels crying at the same time. I see them coming, starting at the back of the motionless yard, skipping across the roof of Peter's shed, dancing through the blue-and-white knee-high flowers of Peter's garden. The fresh-trimmed grass begins to sway, while in the leaves of the apple tree, the rain begins to hum and sing. I feel it fall upon my hair and wash over my upturned face. When I open my hands she springs from my palm, circles once to get her bearings, and then, the curve of her white wings flashing silver against the sapphire sky, she opens into flight.

"Amen," we say together.

END